BAD CITIZEN CORPORATION

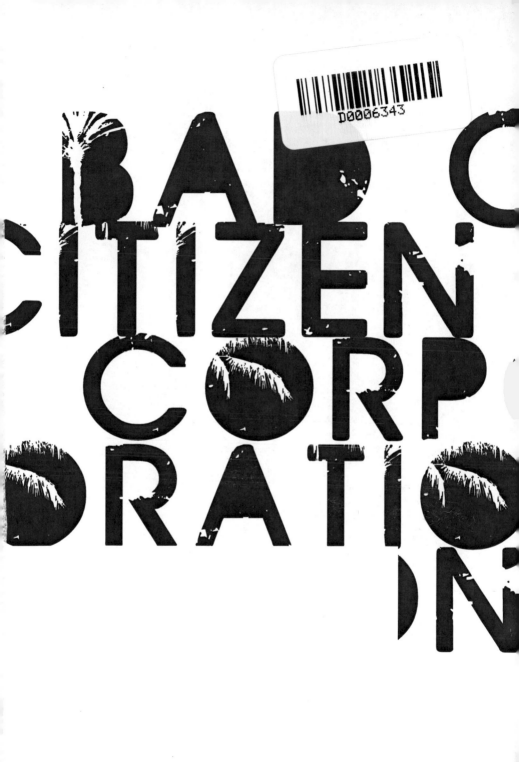

a genuine rare bird book & los angeles, calif.

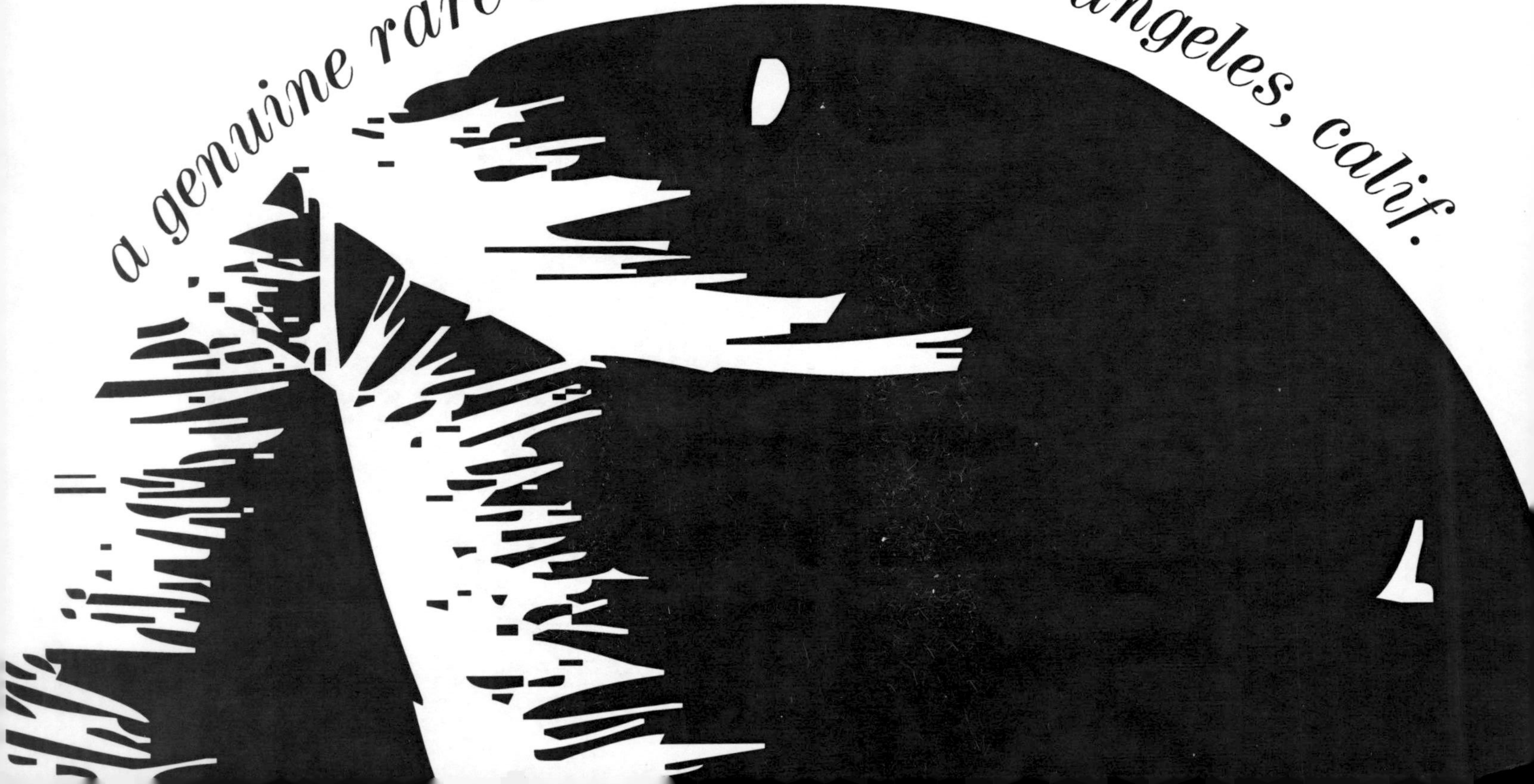

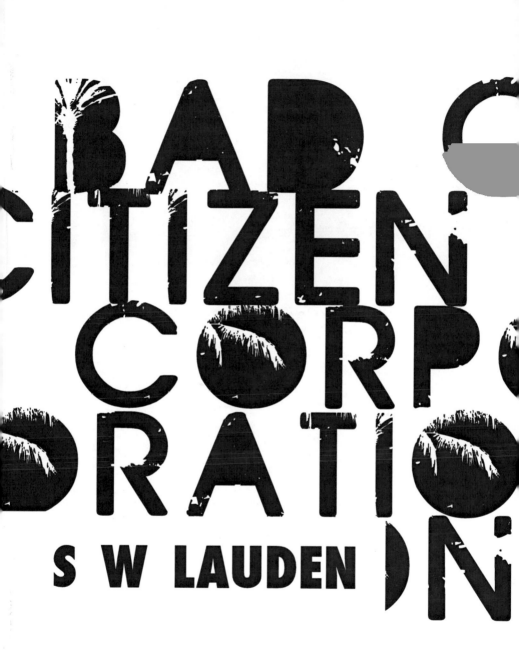

BAD CITIZEN CORPORATION

S W LAUDEN

THIS IS A GENUINE RARE BIRD BOOK
453 South Spring Street, Suite 302
Los Angeles, Calif. 90013

Distributed by Publishers Group West,
a division of the Perseus Books Group
Printed in the United States of America

First Edition, 2015

Library of Congress Cataloging-in-Publication Data
available upon request.

Book Design by Robert Schlofferman

rarebirdbooks.com

To would have beens
could have beens
and should have beens.
—Keith Brown

CHAPTER ONE

Old people slip and fall in the shower all the time.

The front door and windows of the small beachfront bungalow were all locked, but the kitchen door was propped open for the cat. The refrigerator was more of an icebox, and the stove had the sturdy feel of post-war American industrialism. It was charming, in a way, despite the paint chipping from the cabinets and the stained counters. The built-in shelves and breakfast nook would be a big selling point once they were updated. A lot of work had to be done and time was running out.

The boxy tube TV was the centerpiece of the living room, which also included an avocado green sofa, spindly wooden coffee table, and matching end table. A colorful throw blanket that was laid carefully across the rocking chair looked like it had been crocheted by hand. There was a curio in one corner bursting with decorative plates and figurines. A pendulum swung silently behind glass in the mounted wall clock. Some of this stuff might actually be worth a few dollars to one of the local antique shops once the place was cleared out. *But somebody else could worry about that.*

The hallway was lined with framed pictures from the sixties, seventies, and eighties. Faded little league teams and family vacations, mostly, mixed in with more recent weddings, graduations, grandchildren, and great grandchildren. It was hard not linger and ponder how such a long life could be summed up in a few feet of paneled wall. A couple of unremarkable bedrooms on the right and left were the last stop before the single bathroom. The door creaked as it swung open, releasing a puff of steam from the shower.

It was disappointing to see that the bathroom needed updating as well, but no real surprise. People learn to put up with a lot of small imperfections when they've lived in the same house for decades. The location is the important thing.

One last check of the rubber gloves and a yank on the rattling shower curtain. Some of them dropped dead from the shock alone. Others required a little more coaxing out of this world.

It was all so familiar now. The wrinkled body. The shower rail screwed into the old tile. A look of resignation and horror.

Don't overthink it.

Just grab the wet, grey hair and bring the skull against the tiles in a single fluid motion. You only get one chance.

Nobody slips and falls twice.

Then let the water keep running while the moans slowly fade. The plausibility of the accident was worth a little water damage, hard as it was to watch.

CHAPTER TWO

Greg Salem was a long way from the beach. Thin streams of sweat raced from his short blond curls and down his neck. The tips of the tattoos that covered his back and chest were poking up just above his collar, like the tentacles of a giant squid. His hands shook as he forced a clip into the Glock. It was almost impossible to concentrate over the sound of the woman shrieking, but the sickening silence that followed was worse. Greg tensed and waited for the shooting to start.

His partner was a rookie, so new to the force that they'd only met that day. The third partner he'd had in as many months. The last one left the force to become a private security guard for some Hollywood starlet. Greg didn't keep in touch with any of them.

The rookie was pressed against the hallway wall making ridiculous hand signals that he must have memorized at the academy. Greg winced. Some part of him still hated taking orders from cops, even though he'd been one himself for a decade.

The sleeve of his partner's nylon jacket made a soft scratching sound as he motioned. The high-pitched ringing in Greg's left ear was drowning it out. Tinnitus was a dubious badge of honor from years touring the punk rock circuit. It only got worse when his heart raced.

Greg swung into the hall, lifted his foot and kicked hard with the sole of his boot. The door split away from the jamb, spraying splinters. His partner slipped into the apartment ahead of him, waving his gun from side to side. A bedroom door slammed shut on the far side of the living room. The woman began shrieking again, louder this time, like a caged animal. Greg followed his partner deeper inside.

They split up, Greg securing the kitchen while his partner checked the closets. The coast was clear leaving only the bedroom. The two officers edged toward the door slowly. Tense moments ticked by. The shrieking was replaced by muffled sobbing. His partner checked the doorknob. Unlocked.

Greg turned the knob and let the door creak open. The officers waited for any signs of movement. There was only stillness and a faint humming sound. They traded looks, silently daring each other to go first.

Greg always thought of his brother Tim in situations like this, when everything was on the line and there was only one person in the world to rely on. Whatever was waiting for them inside that room, he knew it wasn't going to be his brother. He closed his eyes and tried to clear his thoughts before entering.

A middle-aged woman sat tied to a chair, tears streaming down her round cheeks. Balled up socks were lodged in her mouth and held in place with a pair of nylons tied around the back of her head. She watched the two men with terror in her eyes. Her panties were down around her ankles and she was shifting in her seat in a vain attempt to edge the hem of her skirt forward. An oscillating fan was behind her, mindlessly scanning the room and ruffling the curtains around the open window.

His partner untied her while Greg made sure the room was clear. The woman collapsed into his partner's arms, never taking her eyes off Greg's Glock.

"No more guns, *please...*"

Greg was turning back to check on her when he saw something move outside of the window. He spun around with his gun leveled. The suspect dropped to the street from a drainpipe that ran vertically along the corner of the building. Greg ran out the apartment door, taking the stairs two at a time. He looked up at the bedroom window to get his bearings and then started off down the street at a sprint.

He was almost forty years old, but still pretty fast thanks to all those early morning runs on the beach. The sidewalks were mostly empty except for the occasional warehouse worker wheeling dollies full of boxes between buildings. He bounded at full speed from block to block looking for the blue baseball cap and white T-shirt. The plastic sheath that held his badge swung from the string around his neck and banged into his chest.

The blocks passed by in a blur. His lungs were burning from the suffocating industrial air, so he stopped to catch his breath. He was bent over with his hands on his knees when a blue and white streak flashed between two slow moving busses across the street. He ran out into the light weekend traffic, narrowly dodging trucks as he crossed. He kept his eyes focused on the blue cap bouncing in the distance a few blocks ahead of him, and watched as it vanished between two buildings. Greg used his last burst of energy and rounded the corner into the small service alley several agonizing moments later.

The kid in the blue hat was standing on top of a dumpster trying to climb into a second story window that was just out of reach. Greg pointed his service revolver and shouted, "Stop! Police!" The kid half looked over his shoulder in disbelief while his fingers groped for the sill. Greg repeated his warning, motioning with the

Glock toward the ground with a series of exaggerated gestures. The kid's hands slowly left the wall as he raised them up above his head in a practiced motion.

Greg acknowledged his surrender. He gestured for him to climb down off the dumpster. The kid reached the ground and spun to face his captor. Greg watched the fear flickering in his eyes as they darted from side to side, desperately searching for an escape route. Greg planted his feet and leveled his weapon at the kid's chest to discourage him from making another run for it.

Moments passed. Greg inched forward, closing the distance between them. The kid looked young, not much older than his friend Junior's son. He was half way there when the kid reached into his waistband, bringing his hands up in front of him.

Greg had practiced for this. He instinctively squeezed off two shots, the first he ever fired in the line of duty. A deafening sound echoed off of the tall brick walls surrounding them. The black object flew from the kid's hand and spiraled up into the air before clattering across the pavement and out of sight.

He seemed to fall in slow motion. His body twisted and his arms flailed around him as he spun from the force of the bullets. Greg couldn't see any blood on the white T-shirt yet. He prayed he had missed, but had spent too many hours at the firing range to have that kind of luck.

The kid's legs crumpled under the weight of his own limp body. His eyes rolled back in his head as he first fell to his knees and then slumped to the pavement headfirst. The blood quickly pooled under him the moment he stopped moving. Greg's feet felt like they were bolted to the ground.

Footsteps came thundering down the alley. Horrified gasps followed as the first witnesses ran past him and found the kid lying there in a heap. They were shouting for him to lower his gun, pleading with him. It became the soundtrack to Greg's unfolding nightmare. It took everything in him to finally obey. He only did it so that the growing crowd would stop yelling at him. Where had all these people come from?

First they were yelling at him in the alley and now they had him seated on a curb. Endless questions. The people around him now seemed more familiar, or at least their uniforms did. They were wearing rubber gloves and shining bright lights in his face. Their voices sounded like a chorus of nonsense. Like endlessly reverberating drums during sound check in an empty club.

The kid. Where was the kid? The people around Greg wouldn't let him stand. His knees felt weak, like they couldn't possibly hold his weight anyway. He never got the chance to test them. Somebody was standing behind him now with both hands planted on his shoulders. He threw his head back to see his Police Chief's concerned eyes peering down.

Greg blurted out the only thing on his mind.

"Where's the kid?"

The Police Chief motioned with his head. A siren came to life a few feet away from where he was sitting. Greg craned his neck to watch the ambulance speeding away.

"Did they find the gun?"

"Not yet. They're still searching the alley."

"He pulled a gun, Chief."

"We'll find it, if it's still there. A lot of civilians have already been through here tonight."

"He had a gun, Chief. He had a gun…"

Greg's low-top sneakers squeaked along the linoleum floor. The cardboard box was half empty but still felt heavy in his thick arms. It had been a week since the shooting and he was still in a haze.

There were only two other officers in the station at the moment and they both made eye contact with him to give silent support. The Police Chief strained to hold the heavy glass door open for him at the end of the hallway. Outside the bright Los Angeles sun beat down on factories and processing plants surrounding Virgil Heights Police Station.

"It's only a couple of weeks, Greg. We'll get all of this straightened out and you'll be back on the job before you know it."

"Then why take my badge and gun?"

Greg could see his baby blue 1970 Chevy El Camino. It was flickering in and out of view between the crisscrossing semi trucks. The car looked like it was floating on the heat that was rising off the pavement. He could picture the back up Glock in the glove compartment, but there was no back up badge to go with it.

Two more officers arrived, pushing a handcuffed suspect between them. Greg sized up the scrawny teenaged kid wearing a white T-shirt and blue baseball cap. The suspect fixed him with a cold glare in return. Greg's fingers dug into the side of the box until his fingernails started to hurt. All teenage boys were starting to look the same to him.

"Greg. Hey! Are you all right?"

He felt the Police Chief's hand on his arm before he even heard the words. His gaze traveled up to meet the older man's stare. Greg studied the familiar face. He noticed the creases and bags that framed his tired eyes, split by a nose that shot toward his mouth like a lightning bolt. Small red veins fanned out from his nostrils and gave his papery cheeks a rusty patina.

Greg knew that the mangled nose was courtesy of a car chase gone wrong, and that his red face was a daily reminder of his recovery from alcoholism. What lasting effects would a lifetime in law enforcement have on his own face? He might never get the chance to find out.

"Listen to me, Greg. This isn't going to be easy. You'll think you see that kid everywhere you look. But he's not dead. And you didn't do anything wrong. Do you hear me?"

The Police Chief gave Greg's arm a squeeze before letting go. Greg turned his head and squinted as he took a tentative step out into the summer heat. The sun beat down on his head and he was overcome with an urge to go surfing. To bob along on the rolling waves and forget all about the world back on shore. Everything that had gone wrong in Virgil Heights. Especially the kid in the blue hat.

"Might be a good idea to take a vacation. You know, lay low for a while until this investigation blows over. Didn't your dad have a cabin in the mountains?"

Greg wanted to remind the Chief that the cabin was his now, but couldn't see the point in bringing it up. Maybe he was just trying to avoid saying goodbye to the man who had gotten him admitted to the police academy despite a lengthy juvenile record. Or maybe he just didn't want to talk about his dead father.

"Sounds pretty good right about now."

"Well, whatever you do, stay out of Virgil Heights."

Greg didn't think that would be hard. His eyes traveled around the concrete skyline and imagined the thousands of teenagers who followed their dreams to Los Angeles every year from whatever town they grew up in. None of them had even heard of Virgil Heights when they first arrived. And he doubted they were any wiser when they went back home with their tails between their legs a few years later. For every one of those forgotten dreams, a thousand other people had to work dead end jobs in towns like this one just to keep the lights on Hollywood Boulevard glowing for the tourists.

He wasn't exactly sure how he'd ended up in Virgil Heights himself.

"I'll give you a call in a couple of days. Hoping we'll have some more news by then."

Greg nodded and stepped out into the four-lane street. It was easy enough to wind through the slow moving industrial traffic. Unlike most of the other small cities that ganged up to create the greater Los Angeles sprawl, Virgil Heights was primarily a factory town with only a couple square blocks of rundown apartments for migrant workers and their families. The streets teemed with refrigerator trucks and flat beds from sunrise to sunset, quickly becoming a ghost town after dark and on Sundays.

With a population of two hundred and fifty full time residents and a crime rate that was almost non-existent, the VHPD was known as little more than a glorified security company.

But that all changed one Saturday afternoon when they got a frantic call.

Greg opened the unlocked car door and glanced back at the station. The Police Chief was still standing in the open doorway, watching him. Greg nodded and bent low to get his tall frame into the cab. He twisted the key and the engine growled to life.

Greg turned up the volume knob on the stereo and rolled the window down, all in a single fluid motion. The Pennywise anthem "Fuck Authority" was already mid-chorus as he merged into afternoon traffic toward the freeway and home.

CHAPTER THREE

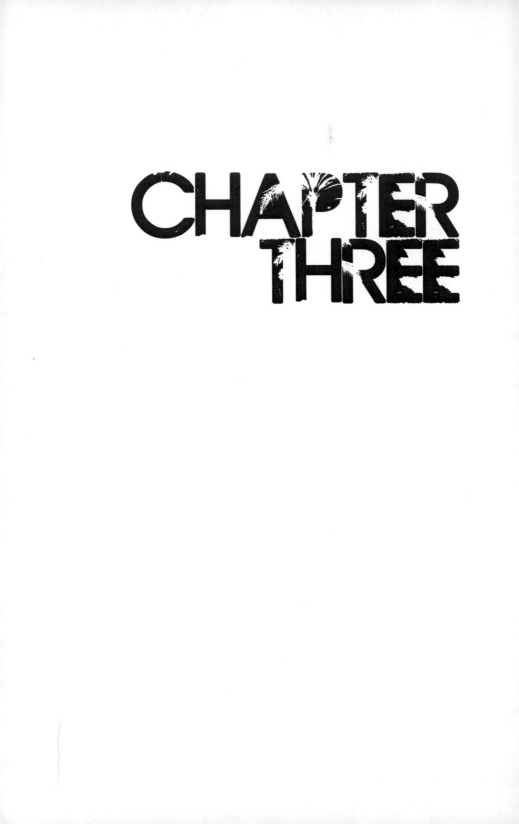

Greg's phone rang as the El Camino sped up the on ramp. He lifted it up to look at the number and nearly swerved into a sparkling green Chevy Impala in the carpool lane beside him. Greg stomped on the accelerator, narrowly avoiding a collision. He waved in the mirror to apologize, but the other car was already fading into the distance.

"Sup Ricky?"

"Did you drop your phone or something?"

"Nope. Just driving."

"Hope you're going hands free. I heard you can get busted for that these days."

His best friend chuckled. Greg didn't join in.

"I'll chance it."

"I'm calling about sound check."

Greg punched the steering wheel. He'd completely forgotten about the gig.

"I don't know, dude. It's been kind of rough today. I might have to bail."

"No way! This show's gonna sell out and most of them are coming to see your ass. There's gonna be a full-blown riot if you no show."

Greg knew it was true. This is what he got for only performing a couple of times a year.

"Yeah, whatever. What's the deal?"

"Show starts at nine. We're on at ten thirty. Junior wants to open doors early, so we have to be done with sound check before eight. I want to make sure we have time to run through all the songs you're gonna sing."

"Cool. See you at Eddie's."

Greg flung the phone across the bench seat after he hung up with Ricky. It was strange how much some things had changed over the years. There was a time in his life when sound checks and punk shows were the only thing he looked forward to. These days they felt a lot more like a twenty-year high school reunion stuck on repeat.

He flipped the turn indicator and sliced across three lanes. Once he was in the fast lane he reached down in front of the passenger seat and fished a CD case from a pile on the floor. The letters BCC were written in Ricky's block letter handwriting across the cover. He slid the disc into the stereo and listened to his own voice screaming at him from across two decades.

The compilation contained just seven songs, a few from each of the albums Greg's band Bad Citizen Corporation released in the nineties. None of the songs were longer than two minutes, and all were played at a break neck tempo that seemed impossibly fast to Greg's middle-aged ears.

Willowy palm trees lined the freeway that sliced through South Central. He was making good time in the early afternoon traffic when he spotted the green Impala again. It was two lanes over and a few lengths back on the right. Even at that distance he could tell the conspicuous car was trailing him, and doing a bad job of it.

Greg never understood why people in LA indulged their road rage when imprisoned in their cars. Still, if this were twenty years ago he knew he would have pulled over and gotten out to fight. Nothing made him feel more alive in those days than driving his fist into another man's face. He pressed his foot down on the gas pedal instead.

He hit *repeat* on the CD player and sang along as he followed the transition from one freeway to the next. Jumbo jets barreled into LAX every couple minutes, their expanding shadows swallowing up the endless line of cars. Heading south on autopilot, the exit came up fast. He had most of the lyrics committed to memory as he rolled down the window and headed toward the glistening Pacific Ocean. It was easily twenty degrees cooler on the coast than in Virgil Heights.

Greg caught a glimmer of green from the corner of his eye as he veered for the off ramp. It didn't take a police badge to know this was about more than just road rage. Turning onto Bay Cities Boulevard, he stayed in the right lane. Eddie's L Bar was only a few blocks away. The green Impala stuck out like a sore thumb in the sea of SUVs and European sports cars.

Greg pulled into the last spot in the small parking lot in front of the bar. His heart almost beat through his chest as he threw the car into park and killed the engine. She sputtered a couple of times, and gave a slight shudder. The green Impala crawled by, taking its time to let Greg know that they had spotted him. He had the feeling they wouldn't be heading back to Virgil Heights any time soon.

EDDIE'S L BAR OCCUPIED a small mini-mall that only had one other tenant—a beauty shop called Junior's. Both storefronts shared a parking lot that faced Bay Cities Boulevard, a four-lane affair that cut through an old industrial district a few miles inland from the beach. Junior's was a small square space with barely enough room to fit three chairs and a wash station. It was the same space where Greg's brother used to run a punk rock record shop back in the day.

Eddie's wrapped around the salon, sharing the side and back walls. The long wooden bar was situated near the front door while the small stage was all the way at the back of the L-shaped room. In between were a couple of small pool tables and a handful of tall tables ringed with stools. On weekends Junior would close the salon a little early to run a punk rock club called "Eddie's HELL Bar."

Greg rubbed his face a couple of times to clear away the cobwebs. He swung the car door open and headed for Eddie's.

"Dude, are you Fred Despair?"

Greg was caught off guard because they'd used his stage name. He was never very comfortable playing the rock star, but knew it wasn't cool to ignore the kids who liked his music.

"You guys here for the show?"

He barely got the words out before the first kid tossed his phone to his friend.

"Dude, get some pictures or nobody will ever believe this!"

He had his arm around Greg's shoulder and flashed a series of hand signals, one after the other. The most Greg could manage was an awkward smile as the camera on the phone mimicked the sound of a shutter clicking. Then the two kids traded places. The posing and clicking went on for another minute before Greg finally pulled himself away.

"Cool, guys. Need to bail. See you at the show tonight."

The star-struck twenty-somethings went inside the bar. Greg hung back, waiting until they were gone. He was checking email on his phone when a shirtless stick figure flew through the door and landed at his feet. His friend Junior came barreling into the parking lot right behind, all balled fists and murderous eyes. Ricky came next. He was trying hard to diffuse the situation, but failing miserably. Greg knew that Ricky was no match for a furious Junior. Nobody was.

Junior lunged at the man on the floor and caught him in the ribs with the tip of a boot.

"I told you to quit dealing drugs in the bar, you scumbag!"

He rolled onto his back, trying hard to laugh through the pain. Greg recognized his old band-mate Marco. He had aged a few years since they last saw each other. His gaunt face was pasty and dark circles ringed his filmy yellow eyes.

Greg took a step forward to shield one friend from another. His kindness was rewarded with a straight arm to the jaw. The blow rocked him backwards and sent him toppling over Marco. He was flat on his back and dazed as Junior advanced again.

"I'm gonna fucking kill you, Marco!"

She was wearing a Black Flag T-shirt that almost stretched to see-through around her hips. A plaid skirt clung to her thick thighs, stopping just above her white knee-high stockings. Her straight blonde hair was cut into an angular bob that perfectly framed a Kewpie doll face contorted with rage. She fell onto Marco and started wailing away, her blue eyes almost glowing with anger. Ricky finally managed to stop her with a flying tackle that sent them tumbling across the parking lot.

Greg jumped up and pulled Marco to his feet.

"Thanks, bro."

"You need to get out of here, like right now."

"That crazy bitch is just lucky I don't hit girls."

He said it loud enough for Junior to hear. She immediately got up on all fours. Ricky caught hold of her ankle before she could pounce.

"You're lucky he's holding you back. Your fat ass hasn't seen the last of me."

Greg grabbed Marco by the shoulders and shook him hard.

"Dude, bail!"

Marco took a couple of hesitant steps back and sprinted around the side of the building. Greg waited until he was out of sight before making his way to where Junior and Ricky lay. He noticed the green Impala idling across the boulevard and jogged toward it instead.

Ricky was right behind Greg as the car lurched forward and merged into traffic. The back window rolled down and a hand emerged holding a blue baseball cap. The two friends stood side-by-side watching the car disappear into the distance. Ricky broke the silence.

"What's up with that?"

"Just some asshole I cut off on the freeway. No big deal."

Greg knew it was a lie, but didn't have the energy to explain. Whatever they had planned for him had nothing to do with any of his friends. They walked over to where Junior was still sitting in the middle of the parking lot. Ricky reached down and helped her up.

Junior slapped his hand away once she was standing. Ricky lifted the trucker hat from his head and ran a palm across his shiny black spikes. His beer belly looked like a beach ball stuffed under his black T-shirt as he grimaced and groaned. He bent forward and made a half-hearted attempt to touch his toes. The letters BCC and a line of four stars stretched across his back.

Junior laughed at all of his huffing and puffing.

"You're getting too old for punk rock."

"My back felt fine until you went crazy on Marco."

"He's lucky you guys were here or I swear he'd be dead right now."

"You just hate him because he isn't afraid of you. And for your information my back's screwed up from lifting fifty-pound bags of concrete all day long. Whatever. Want to get a bite to eat before sound check?"

Junior turned to face Greg, running her fingers through the mop of hair on his head.

"Sorry, but I think I need to do a dye job on 'Fred Despair' before the gig tonight."

Greg twisted out of Junior's grip, stepping back to search her eyes. His brash high school girlfriend was still in there somewhere, beyond the small lines and wrinkles. Lurking below the surface despite the heartbreak of a failed marriage and the all-consuming exhaustion of single parenthood.

Her son Chris wasn't much younger than the kid in the blue hat.

"Earth to Greg. Are we gonna do this or not?"

He snapped out of it and made a weak attempt to defend himself.

"It's a just a couple of greys. You can barely see them through my golden curls. Right?"

Greg flashed a smile that begged for confirmation. Ricky and Junior both folded their arms. He knew he didn't have a choice in the matter.

"Who cares? Everybody knows how old I am. It's not like I have to worry about my street cred anymore."

"It's not *your* cred I'm worried about. I don't want these kids thinking that I book geezers."

"Ouch."

A SMALL BELL ON THE door jingled as he walked into the salon. He took a few steps inside and looked around at the kitschy retro decorations and exposed ceiling beams. It was hard to remember what the place looked like back when it was bursting with record racks. Felt like all he had to do was turn around to see his brother's big goofy smile.

Junior gave Greg a second to get his bearings before motioning to a chair near the sink.

He eased back and enjoyed the feeling of her fingers gently massaging his scalp. It was the most relaxed he'd felt all week.

"How's Chris?"

"Fine, I hope." She frowned at the thought of her son and did a poor job of hiding it. "He's with the neighbors."

"Well I guess that's better than leaving him with his asshole dad."

Her fingers dug into his scalp a little as she rinsed the shampoo.

"Chris can't help it if his father is an asshole. That's pretty much my fault."

Her voiced cracked a little on the last word. Greg could see she was fighting back tears.

"We don't have to talk about this right now, Junior."

"I agree. Let's talk about you. How long is it gonna be before word gets out that Fred Despair is the cop that shot the kid in Virgil Heights?"

"Let's just get through tonight."

"Sounds like a plan. So what color are we doing?"

"Any color, but blue. Not like I have to be at work on Monday."

CHAPTER FOUR

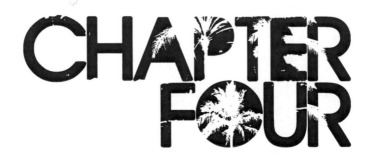

The portly bartender climbed up onto the wobbly barstool. His bulbous gut bubbled out from under a Hawaiian shirt as he strained to stand. He was looming above the loud happy hour crowd, his head dangerously close to the whirring ceiling fan blades. Sweat dripped from the ends of his graying mustache as he made the announcement.

"Last call for alcohol!"

Most of the regulars dutifully flagged down the other bartender to get one last drink. Others pulled their wallets from baggy shorts to settle up. Three young guys pushed their way to the bar. They looked like a boy band lost at a Jimmy Buffet concert. The one standing nearest to the bar was acting like the lead singer. He ran his hand lightly over a carefully crafted coif and tried to get the bartender's attention.

"Can I help you with something?"

"Does this bar always close at six-thirty on a Friday night?"

The young guy doing all the talking flashed a charismatic smile that gleamed like something from a toothpaste commercial. The bartender returned a blank stare that didn't reveal any of his own yellow teeth.

"We have live music here most Friday and Saturday nights, so the bar closes at seven o'clock for sound check. We open up again at eight-thirty, with a cover charge. Now that we cleared that up, can I get you something to drink?"

"Well, where are we supposed to go between now and then?"

The smile was back. This time the bartender responded with a grimace.

"I bet you guys work at one of those computer companies popping up around here."

The three young men traded condescending smiles.

"We all work at *software companies* in the lofts around the reservoir."

"Well, my name is Eddie. I probably own the warehouse your *software company* leases. Just like I own this place and half the buildings around here. The next time you want to go slumming in the local dive bars, maybe you should figure out the lay of the land before you start shooting your mouths off. Oh, and by the way, you're cut off."

"What the hell? Screw you, old man."

The words had barely left his mouth when a few of the locals jumped from their stools. Eddie watched with a blank expression as the three hipsters got dragged outside. They were in for a painful lesson in manners, and a long weekend of licking their wounds.

Eddie headed back to where his friends were sitting. The conversation had completely changed in the couple of minutes he was gone.

"I'll be really surprised if there aren't a few riots."

Roger was short and round with pursed lips and heavy eyelids. He was seated on a barstool next to another regular named Bill, who had his elbows on the bar. Both were retired and spent most weekdays sipping beer and shooting pool at Eddie's.

"The hell are you talking about? People get shot all the time in LA."

"This is something different. The news said that the kid didn't even have a gun."

Eddie walked over and set a beer down in front of Roger. The glass hit the bar with a loud *thunk*. Foam started oozing from the neck of the bottle as Eddie joined in.

"If you two knuckleheads are talking about that bullshit out in Virgil Heights, you can take it somewhere else."

"Calm down, will you? It's on practically every channel around the clock."

"That don't mean I want to hear about it in my bar."

Junior walked in just as most of the happy hour crowd was leaving. She wandered back toward the bar to see how ticket sales were going. Eddie's weathered face lit up in a smile as she approached.

"How's it going, sweetheart?"

"Pretty good, Dad. I think this is going to be a big show tonight."

Eddie had always wanted a son, but changed his mind when his daughter was born. What he didn't change his mind about was naming his first-born child after himself. A heated debate with his wife finally convinced Eddie that he should at least drop one of the Ds. Edie didn't become Junior until she was old enough to help out at the bar on weekends.

"Phone's been ringing off the hook. Everybody wants to know what time Greg goes on."

Her father winked when he said it, but it was hard to deny the concern in his gaze.

"Can I get you something to drink, sweetie?"

"No thanks. It's a little early for that."

Roger and Bill chuckled at her response. Eddie flashed them a dirty look and urged Junior to ignore them. He grabbed her arm and pointed to the empty end of the bar.

"Have you talked to Greg about what happened out in Virgil Heights? A lot of people around here are starting to chatter about it."

"No, but I probably should. I was kinda hoping he would be the one to bring it up."

"We both know that's never gonna happen. He's hanging out in the store room, if you want to talk to him now."

"I think we should just get through the show tonight. Besides, we just…"

Junior let her response trail off. She never liked to tell her father when she and Greg spent time with each other. It always got his hopes up that the two of them would get back together someday.

"You 'just' what?"

"Nothing, Dad. I have to make a call before all the crazies show up."

Every TV screen in the bar was playing the news. A pretty reporter was standing outside an alley in Virgil Heights. Protestors were waving signs in the background, demanding justice for the boy who was shot. The caption at the bottom of the screen said that the officer involved in the shooting had been put on leave, but didn't mention Greg by name. At least not yet.

Eddie brought the remote up and the screens went one black one by one.

CHAPTER FIVE

Greg's curls were a patchwork of amber, black, and red as he waited in the large storage closet next to the stage that night. *Dressing rooms aren't very punk rock*, he thought, cracking the door to scan the hot and sweaty room. Truth was that he never felt completely at ease wandering the crowd before a show either. It was always hard to know exactly where to be.

Ricky and his band tore through a set of original material for thirty minutes in front of the sold out crowd. Greg could see the two kids he had met out in the parking lot pushed up against the stage, shoulder to shoulder with the middle aged punks they would one day become. It was still fifteen minutes before Greg was scheduled to take the stage. Yet he was already filled with the same angry energy he'd felt the very first time he'd played in front of an audience. Part of him hoped that feeling would never go away, but it was getting harder and harder to summon.

He closed the door and turned to check his phone. There were no messages so he texted Junior a single word: "Nervous." Tfhere was no response. He knew she was probably busy pouring drinks behind the bar or checking IDs at the front door.

He slumped into a chair and tried to calm his mind. Next thing he knew the door jerked open and Junior was yelling at him to go on. She stepped aside as he brushed past her, bounding up onto the stage.

Ricky started in on the chords to the first song before Greg even reached the mic. The band kicked in on cue and Greg was screaming his head off. He had no time to worry about whether or not he could remember the lyrics. The song was over almost as quickly as it had started. He was still catching his breath when the drummer counted in the next song. Wooden sticks ticking off like the countdown to a bomb blast.

The room was too narrow for any kind of real slam pit, but little shoving matches were breaking out as the die-hard BCC fans swelled and surged. The band plowed through three songs back-to-back before they finally let the crowd cheer. It was a deafening roar that slowly died down to a hum while Ricky fumbled to replace a broken guitar string. It was taking him a little longer than it should have so Greg was forced to improvise some awkward stage banter.

"What's up Hell Bar?"

The crowd responded with more shouting and shoving. Fans were yelling out song titles that Greg hadn't heard in years.

"If we do that one you'll have to come up here and sing it."

Greg laughed into the mic and turned to see if Ricky was ready yet. He felt like the seconds were passing by in slow motion. The song requests eventually died down, replaced by an increasingly aggressive buzz. Greg could feel the impatient crowd turning ugly when a single voice broke through the din.

"Play a fucking song, pig!"

Greg took a step to the edge of the stage and squinted to see through the blinding lights.

A few people in the crowd started booing. Then he heard it again, that same voice screaming above it all.

"What are you gonna do, pig? Shoot me too?"

There was a swell of motion out in the crowd. Greg could see a group of older guys punching and kicking somebody who was already down on the ground. He went to leap from the stage. Ricky grabbed the collar of his shirt and yanked him back toward the drums.

"Dude! No way. You don't need anymore trouble right now."

Junior rushed from the side of the stage as Greg struggled to get out of Ricky's grip. She quickly motioned for Ricky to start playing another song. The band kicked in as she led Greg from the stage and along the far wall of the bar. He resisted at first, but eventually gave in to Junior's pleading looks. People were streaming out of both doors as the melee grew in size and intensity. The two of them eventually reached the side door and were soon outside of Eddie's.

"We can't just bail!"

"You've got enough shit going on without getting arrested for a stupid bar fight."

"What about Ricky?"

"He can handle himself."

She was right, but he couldn't shake the urge to rush back inside. Even though he knew it would only be a few minutes until The Bay Cities Police arrived and shut the place down. The gig was over either way.

Three men wearing ski masks and waving guns came through the front door right at that moment. The trio pushed their way through the crowd, fanning out like a crack military squadron. The first gunman stopped and leveled a handgun at the bartender. The second went to cover the side door. The third headed straight for the stage where Ricky and the band were still bashing away.

Junior took Greg by the hand and led him up the block. She pushed him into the passenger seat of her car. They were speeding down the boulevard, already several blocks away, when two shots rang out inside of Eddie's.

INSIDE GREG'S APARTMENT, THEY waited anxiously for one of their phones to buzz. He was sprawled out on the bed, staring up at the ceiling. She sat nearby in a wooden chair with her feet propped up on his pillow. He had been texting Ricky non-stop since they left the show an hour before. She had been calling the landline at Eddie's. Nobody was responding and it was making them nervous. Calling Eddie himself was a last resort.

"Do you remember when my dad came home and caught us in bed during senior year?"

Greg could tell she was trying to break the uncomfortable silence.

"I remember him grabbing me by my hair, pulling me down the stairs and throwing me out the front door naked. Do you mean that night?"

"Yep, that night. Mom called me a slut and stomped off. Dad sat down on the edge of my bed and started crying. I mean, like sobbing."

"You were kind of a slut. That's what first attracted me to you."

"Very funny. Did you ever see your dad cry?"

Greg had only seen his father cry two times. The first time was when his mother died. Greg and Tim were both still very young. He could clearly remember his father falling apart when the three of them finally got home after the funeral. The second time was at Tim's funeral. His father never really stopped crying the second time.

"No, my dad didn't cry much."

"I just got this sick feeling in my stomach that night. I promised myself that no matter what I would never make him feel like that again."

"I don't think you've ever told me that story before."

"I kind of feel like I broke that promise tonight."

"It wasn't that bad. There have been plenty of fights at Eddie's."

"It's not about the fight. I just have a really bad feeling. I don't know how to explain it."

His phone started vibrating and he sat up to answer it. Junior could hear her father's voice on the line. He sounded calm, as if he was choosing his words very carefully. Greg said 'okay' a few times and then let out a gasp as he turned to look at her.

"Ricky's dead."

THE EL CAMINO WAS the only civilian car in the parking lot when they pulled up to Eddie's around midnight. An ambulance was pulling away from the side door as they walked up. Greg saw two paramedics working on somebody through the small back windows.

Eddie stood in the doorway with a cigarette dangling from his lips. Junior ducked under the police tape and ran to him with Greg close behind.

"I'm so sorry, Daddy."

"It's not your fault, sweetheart. I'm just glad you two are all right."

Greg gave Eddie a squeeze on the arm and moved past them into the bar. He knew his VHPD badge wouldn't do him much good here, but he still felt naked without it. It was hard to make out the details with the flashing police lights, but the place was a disaster. Tables and stools were flipped over, shattered glass and splatters of blood covered the floor.

From his vantage point just inside the door he had a view of both ends of Eddie's. To his right an officer was talking to a couple of young guys at the bar. He didn't recognize them, even though both were wearing BCC T-shirts. Greg was filled with a rising wave of guilt as he turned away. Up on the stage he saw two officers carefully sifting through the rubble of the band's gear. It was painful to see Ricky's amp tipped on its end with a tear down the front.

Greg started walking in that direction when a firm hand gripped his shoulder. His fists tightened and he stopped in his tracks. He spun around ready to fight and found himself facing Bay Cities Police Chief, Robert Stanley. Or, as he was known to generations of Bay Cities Little Leaguers, Officer Bob.

"Hello, Mr. Salem. Had a feeling you'd make your way back down here tonight. I'm really sorry about your friend."

Greg looked down at his feet and tried to regain his composure. Thinking like a cop was the only way he was getting through this night.

"Got any leads on suspects?"

"That's what I wanted to talk to you about. Why don't we head over there and chat."

Greg followed the thickly built man to the bar. There was a large bald spot at the back of Officer Bob's head that seemed more pronounced than usual. Greg thought he must have gotten pulled out of bed for the investigation. They grabbed two stools and sat face-to-face.

The bags under Officer Bob's eyes were puffy and dark, and his teeth were yellow. Greg felt like he was watching the nemesis from his teenage years decaying right in front of his eyes.

"It seems pretty clear what happened here tonight, but I still have to ask you a few questions. You know the routine, Mr. Salem."

Officer Bob opened his black leather note pad and lifted his pen to write. Greg remained silent, girding himself.

"Before we begin, I'd like to get some understanding about your state of mind. Were you drinking at any point tonight, or taking any other illicit drugs?"

"You know I've been sober for almost a decade."

"Yes, but plenty of drunks fall off the wagon. It's sort of an occupational hazard."

"You want me to do a piss test?"

"That won't be necessary, but thanks for offering. We had reports that you were seen speeding away from the scene with Eddie's daughter shortly before the incident. Witnesses said you were in a pretty big hurry. That true?"

Why were they asking witnesses about Greg instead of focusing on the gunmen? Greg knew he had to choose his words carefully here. Local police departments didn't always appreciate it when officers from other jurisdictions had opinions about their cases, especially officers who were not in good standing. He also knew that Officer Bob still saw him as the punk kid who had a lot of run-ins with the law over the years.

"It's true that we left before the shooting started."

"Any particular reason?"

"Junior was trying to save me from the bar fight."

"Makes sense. She always was protective of you."

Officer Bob let his eyes wonder around the room while he formed his next question.

"Is there any reason for us to suspect that you two knew a robbery was about to occur?"

"Robbery? You can't be serious."

"Please just answer the question and leave the police work to us."

"Come on! These guys were after something other than money, or they wouldn't have gone out of their way to shoot up the band."

"Fine, let's do this your way."

Officer Bob closed his note pad and flung it onto the bar with a slap.

"For one, I don't think they had any idea they were walking into a bar fight. So the gun could have been fired at the stage accidentally. Secondly, assuming that they hadn't bothered to stake the place out first, it's possible the shooter was looking for a second bar and cash register."

"Sounds pretty open-and-shut the way you describe it, but you've been wrong before."

Officer Bob spat out a nervous laugh. Greg was wiping a thin mist of spit from his cheek when the older man leaned in. His voice was a raspy hiss.

"Like it or not, Mr. Salem, I am in charge of all the police investigations in The Bay Cities. And right now I am trying to get to the bottom of a case that unfortunately involves you and a few of your friends. Forgive me if I don't indulge your need to dredge up ancient history."

"What do you want to know then?"

"Let's start at the beginning. What time did you get to Eddie's tonight?"

Greg explained the evening in detail while Officer Bob nodded along. He recounted every second, from the moment he showed up for sound check until arriving back at Eddie's minutes ago.

"I have to ask you a tough question."

Greg nodded. His arms were folded tightly across his chest. Officer Bob checked to see if anybody else around was listening.

"Can you think of anybody that would want to see your friend Ricky dead? Maybe your pal Marco, or somebody from that crew?"

Greg's eyes stung at the mention of Ricky's name. He refused to let himself cry in front of Officer Bob.

"I'll take that as a 'no,' but there is something else I think you should consider."

"What's that?"

"Well, if this wasn't a robbery—and I'm still not convinced it wasn't—it might not have been Ricky they were after."

Greg knew that Officer Bob was right. The shooters could have been there for him.

"There's an obvious motive for wanting me dead, but I was performing under a stage name. Besides, Eddie's is a long way from Virgil Heights."

Greg pictured the green Impala in his head. He wondered if he was the one who had brought this violence down on The Bay Cities. Officer Bob gave him a knowing look before mercifully changing the subject.

"We'll have more questions for you as the investigation continues. Why don't you swing by my office on Monday morning to continue the conversation. Free around ten?"

Officer Bob stood up and walked out the front door, leaving Greg alone at the bar.

CHAPTER SIX

A thin ray of early morning sun sliced through the blinds, slowly making its way across the floor to Greg's bed. He thought about calling Ricky to see if he wanted to go surfing. It wasn't until his feet hit the floor that the previous night came crashing down on him.

Three texts were waiting from Junior, spanning the few hours they had been apart since the shooting. The last message had been sent an hour before. He thought about calling her back, but hoped that she had finally fallen asleep. There wasn't any new information anyway, and there wouldn't be until he had a chance to track down some of the local beach rats.

He walked to the small dresser near the front door. His dingy studio apartment was in a converted garage only a few blocks from the beach. Greg had been renting the place since he officially stopped touring with Bad Citizen Corporation in his mid-twenties.

Three surfboards were mounted on racks above the doorjamb. One of the leashes dangled above his head as he slipped into his boxers. The Velcro from the ankle cuff brushed against his neck when he stood up. He almost jumped into a nearby closet.

Greg watched the leash swinging back and forth like a pendulum as he tried to catch his breath. His eyes scanned the room for the kid with the blue hat. Nobody was there. The light tapping on the front door sent his heart racing again until he heard the soft voice of his landlady, Ruth McMillan.

"Gregory, are you all right?"

He pulled some jeans and a t-shirt on before opening the door. She was standing on his welcome mat stooped forward to listen. At eighty-two she was slow to get herself totally erect again once she gave in to gravity. Greg could see the maternal concern on her face despite the floppy white gardening hat and huge sunglasses.

"Hello Ruth. I'm fine. Just tripped and banged into the closet. No serious damage."

He held his arms up at his sides and gave a little twist to prove he was okay. She lifted her shades and give him a suspicious look, as if considering the evidence.

"You almost gave me a heart attack. I was just trying to finish up my gardening before it gets too hot."

Greg stuck his head out the door to look at the meticulous landscaping.

"Looks perfect, like it always does."

"Jack did all the real work years ago. I just pluck the weeds out."

Greg knew all about Judy's late husband. He made a killing in the local real estate market in the early seventies, back when land was still plentiful and cheap. Jack dropped dead of a heart attack in his late fifties, but Judy never had to work again. Greg knew she needed his company more than she needed the rent.

His phone chirped at him from the bed. Mrs. McMillan took the opportunity to glance at the messy apartment, shaking her head in disgust.

"I'll let you get back to whatever you're doing in there."

"Are you sure you don't want to come in for some coffee?"

"Stop flirting, you're too old for me."

Greg definitely could have afforded a nicer place on his VHPD salary, but nothing this close to the beach. The real estate along the coast hadn't been affordable since before Jack's time. These days those multi-million dollar homes were for superstar athletes, movie stars and their agents. They only let blue-collar locals like Greg and Ricky come around when they needed somebody to paint their walls or shingle their roof.

Squeezing into a snug wetsuit felt comforting to Greg's exhausted brain. He grabbed the fiberglass paddle and hoisted the twelve-foot board under his arm. Seagulls were cawing overhead as he walked carefully along the pebbly street with calloused feet. The sand was still cold so early in the morning, but Greg was moving too fast to notice. He was at the shore and wading out into the calm surf within five minutes of leaving his apartment.

He walked into the water pushing his board beside him until he got waste deep. There was a group of five or six stand-up paddle boarders out beyond the slow rolling waves. They were moving west at a pretty good clip. Greg knew that he could catch them if he hurried.

He climbed on, knelt down and started paddling. Then he stood up and put some muscle into it to build a little momentum. One of the crew spotted Greg and made a wide turn to swing around and greet him.

"I didn't think I'd see you here this morning."

Greg had no time for small talk if he wanted to find Ricky's killer before the police did.

"Hey, Sheila. Have you seen Marco around here lately?"

She lifted the paddle and twisted her wiry torso to face him.

"That's funny. I saw him this morning, first time in weeks. He was getting out of the water with his surfboard when I was getting in."

"Did he say if he was paddling out to the meeting today?"

"Said he was taking off for Ensenada, if you can believe that."

Greg could think of two reasons why Marco might be heading to Baja. He was either making another drug run, or he was just trying to get out of town.

"Did he say anything else?"

"Not really. Didn't seem like he was in the mood to chat. Why do you ask?"

"I just wanted to let him know about Ricky, if he hadn't heard."

"He definitely knows. I asked if he was at the show last night and he seemed pretty sketched out about it. Just kind of shook his head and took off up the sand."

Sheila started paddling again and Greg followed. The two of them reached the group just as the others were swinging their boards around to form a circle. They paddled slowly into place while a grizzled surfer named Pete called the meeting to order.

Greg had been in a lot of recovery groups since getting sober at thirty, but this was his favorite one. They never discussed higher powers or prayed together, and nobody chain smoked cigarettes. It was just a bunch of damaged people bobbing in the ocean and trying to get their shit together. This meeting was also the best place to get the latest dirt about The Bay Cities.

Greg was busy sizing up the newcomers when it was his turn to speak. He hadn't really planned to say anything at all, so he just started at the beginning.

"I was always straight-edge growing up. Never even had a sip of beer until I was twenty-seven. Right after my brother's funeral..."

Talking about Tim made him freeze up. The others waited patiently while he struggled to form his next sentence. He stammered and stopped, daring himself to say out loud that Ricky was dead, too. The words spilled from his mouth like rainwater gushing from a drainage pipe when he finally spoke again.

The group was in a stunned silence when Greg finished fifteen minutes later, so the meeting broke up early. Most of them said their goodbyes and paddled toward the pier for a little exercise. Greg headed to shore with Pete and Sheila.

"Sheila and I were talking about Ricky this morning. It's a real tragedy."

"Thanks Pete. Junior's with his Mom now. I'm supposed to head over there later on."

"She's gonna need your support. You and Ricky were like brothers. Let me know if I can do anything to help."

"Did you talk to Marco this morning too?"

"Nope. He always thinks I'm gonna trick him into getting sober, so he keeps a wide berth. You don't think he had something to do with Ricky getting shot, do you?"

"Not really. Just wanted to see if he knew anything I didn't."

"Not sure if Marco knows anything, but I do know that Ricky had a pretty serious run in with Jeff Barrett last week. I guess they were fighting over some big construction jobs and things got pretty heated. A couple of lifeguards had to drag Barrett off the beach before he ripped Ricky's head off."

"Barrett? Well I guess that's as good a place to start as any."

CHAPTER SEVEN

The early afternoon sun was pounding down on the sand when Greg went looking for Jeff Barrett. He could already feel the beads of sweat forming between his shoulder blades where a BCC logo had been tattooed almost twenty years before. He lifted the black wraparound shades from the bridge of his nose and squinted. Barrett was sitting in his usual spot in the shade of a lifeguard station.

A tablet computer was resting on a round belly that almost obscured his tight red trunks. Flabby arms concealed defined biceps built up over two decades of manual labor. His close-cropped hair was dyed a frosty white but the stubble on his face was dark and thick. A phone was propped between his round shoulder and pierced ear. He motioned for Greg to wait with the flick of his wrist while he finished his call.

Greg watched a group of taut men and women playing volleyball. A ring of spectators lined the court in low-slung chairs, waiting their turn to tag in. Many of them were former high school superstars who bumped, set and spiked their way into lucrative college scholarships. These days they mostly played for fun when they weren't managing hedge funds.

Two teenage boys trotted by with surfboards under their arms. Greg couldn't help thinking of all the times he and Ricky had gone surfing together over the years. His stomach dropped when he realized that it was never going to happen again.

"Greg Salem."

He said it in a booming baritone, sizing Greg up with his words.

"How's it going Barrett? Don't you ever take a day off?"

"No rest for the wicked. But it's hard to call it work when your office looks like this."

Greg had been sparring with Barrett ever since his days as a high school weed dealer. Not long before Barrett did a stint in county jail for aggravated assault. He emerged eighteen months later with a new physique that was primed for hard labor. A local contractor hired him as an apprentice and taught him how to find his way around a toolbox. Barrett bought his first truck within a year of getting out.

Last time Greg checked Barrett had fifty employees, a fleet of trucks and a job yard near the reservoir in North Bay. Most days of the year you could find him running his business via tablet computer from the beach. He was one of the few blue-collar kids from North Bay who could actually afford to live along the beach these days.

Greg sat down next to him on the sand. Barrett wasn't one to pussyfoot around.

"I heard things got out of hand at Eddie's last night."

"Funny you should mention that. I was wondering if you knew anything about it."

"Just what I heard on the beach. Am I supposed to know something more than that?"

Things were getting tense right on schedule.

"Somebody mentioned that you and Ricky got into a fight last week."

The burly man pushed himself back with his feet so that the front legs of his beach chair lifted up. He tilted his face to the sky and let out a loud whistle. Greg waited for the moment to pass, the way he had seen Junior do with her son when he was about to throw a fit.

"Are you fucking kidding me? You think I had something to do with Ricky getting popped just because we were bidding on the same jobs?"

"I'm not sure what to think. I just know that my bro is dead and I'm trying to figure out what the fuck happened."

"So you're here as a bro, and not as a cop?"

"That's right."

"Good. I'll make this nice and simple so you can get your ass off my beach. I didn't have anything to do with Ricky getting shot, but I'm not too surprised that it happened."

"Meaning what?"

"Just what I said. If you want answers about what happened, maybe you should ask around about that little company of his. He could be pretty shady."

Greg sprang, launching himself at the mountain of bare flesh in front of him. Barrett brought his foot up and caught him high up on the cheek. Greg landed hard, his ears ringing louder than usual. He could feel the skin around his left eye swelling up as he covered his head with his arms. The salty taste of blood filled his mouth as Barrett's blows rained down on him. It went on like that until a couple of lifeguards pulled the breathless giant off of him.

They managed to get Greg to his feet while keeping Barrett away. They offered to call for an ambulance, but Greg refused. He took a few careful steps to assess the damage. His left eye was closing up fast and he thought that he might have a couple of bruised ribs. More importantly, he needed to get off of the beach before the police arrived. Barrett was still yelling insults at Greg as he retreated off the sand.

There was a parking ticket tucked under the windshield wiper when he got back to the El Camino. He almost tore it in half yanking it out from under the blade, but smiled through the pain when he ripped it open. The ticket itself was blank, but the name Quincy was on the signature line next to a short message that read, "Call me."

Somebody honked to let Greg know they were waiting for his parking space. He opened the door and slid behind the wheel, dropping the ticket into the glove compartment. NOFX was easing into "Wolves in Wolves' Clothing" as he slid on his sunglasses and pulled out into the light beach traffic.

GREG WAS IN SUCH a hurry to get off the beach, and away from Barrett, that he didn't have a chance to clean up. With his left eye swollen shut and a trickle of blood dripping from his nose, he needed to find a place to stop. There were quite a few boutique restaurants and cafes in South Bay. He knew the wealthy clientele would be shocked when he chose a place at random and walked through the door.

Parallel parking his car was excruciating thanks to the many blows he had taken to the ribs. He slowly managed his way into a tight spot between two European sports cars and paid for the meter with his debit card. Not all of the local parking enforcement officers were as forgiving as Quincy McCloud.

The first place he spotted was a high-end café that served specialty coffee and tea drinks from exotic locales like Thailand, Ethiopia and Vietnam. Greg glanced at the chalkboard menu and noticed that the price of each drink would be considered a small fortune in some of those countries. As predicted, more than a few heads turned as he squeezed past the line of fashionable customers and made his way toward the bathroom at the back. Greg got a small punk rock thrill from bursting the moneyed bubble these South Bay residents lived in.

He was reaching for the handle on the bathroom door when it swung out toward him. The woman who emerged jumped back a step when she got a look at Greg up close. She was wearing a slim-fitting business suit made out of a sleek grey material that clung to her every curve. Her auburn hair was slicked back into a neat bun. The chunky black reading glasses that were perched on the bridge of her nose seemed to magnify her green eyes. Fire engine red lipstick perfectly matched the high-heeled shoes that completed her meticulous ensemble.

Greg managed a half-hearted smile and muttered "excuse me" as he moved past her into the bathroom. The woman lingered a moment and then slowly shut the door behind her. Greg turned the lock and went to work in the sink. The warm water and soft paper napkins felt good on his wounds. He was able to get his nose to stop bleeding and then dabbed the dried blood from his upper lip. He took one last look in the mirror and ran a few hands full of water through his sandy hair before unlocking the door and heading back to his car.

He was out on the sidewalk when somebody called his name. He turned and saw the woman who had almost hit him with the bathroom door. She was seated at a sidewalk table with a hesitant smile on her face. She studied his swollen face, trying to make sure it was him.

"You *are* Greg Salem, right?"

"Yeah. I'm probably a little hard to recognize at the moment."

Greg searched his mind to see if he recognized her. It was hard to imagine that he knew anybody who was that well put together.

"It's okay if you don't know who I am. I've changed quite a bit since high school. Name's Maggie Keane, but I go by Margaret these days."

Maggie Keane, the awkward brainiac with the bad acne that used to sit behind Greg in math class. Last he heard she had gone off to law school on the East Coast. That was more than twenty years ago.

She invited him to sit down. He wondered just how bad her eyesight was given his current state.

"Uh, hey Maggie. It looks like you've done pretty well for yourself."

"Thank you. I wish I could say the same for you… What's with your eye?"

"This? I just had a little volleyball accident on the beach."

He didn't care if she believed him or not. Any other time he would have hung around to see where things could lead. But Greg's ribs were killing him and he badly needed a bag of ice.

"Well, great seeing you again."

He stood up to leave and she stood up with him.

"Going so soon? Here, I'll walk with you."

"Okay..."

"So you're still living the beach rat lifestyle, huh?"

"I guess you could say that. I work in law enforcement, or I did. Otherwise I'm pretty much always on the sand or in the water."

"Still playing music?"

Was it possible that she hadn't heard about Ricky? Probably, given where she was hanging out. Nobody down here cared what happened in North Bay. Greg wasn't going to be the one who broke the news.

"Every once in a while."

"A punk rock cop? That's not something you hear about every day."

"Yeah, well, life will take you funny places."

Greg forced a laugh and it felt like somebody jabbed a knife into his chest. She didn't seem to notice the pained expression on his face, or care if she did. He tried to change the subject.

"What about you?"

"I had my own law firm in DC. Did some lobbying. It got really boring, so I moved back here to start a venture capital firm about six months ago. There are a lot of tech companies popping up along the beach these days."

"That's what I've heard."

"Did Edie ever manage to domesticate you?"

"Junior? No, she married Mikey Fitzgerald and they had a kid together. They're divorced now. We're still good friends, though. At least Junior and I are."

She bristled a little at something Greg said. It was just a small tic, barely noticeable against her perfect façade. Greg couldn't put his finger on it. They reached his car before he could give it another thought.

"Nice seeing you again. Good luck with your new business."

She reached out and offered him a card. He took it and turned it over in his fingers, reading the embossed printing. She waved goodbye as he slid it into his wallet.

"Call me sometime. It might be nice to get reacquainted."

Mrs. McMillan was standing on his doorstep when Greg came through the back gate. She was clutching a large brown envelope to her chest and staring up at the eaves. The package looked heavy in her small spotted hands.

He didn't want to sneak up and startle her in case she was doing something important. A small ocean breeze kicked up and slammed the gate shut behind him. That solved his problem.

"Termites."

She looked miserable. Greg stood next to her, searching the eaves to see if he could see what she was looking at. There wasn't any visible damage, just a few spider webs and some cracking paint. She slapped the envelope into his hands with surprising force and turned to look back up at the roofline.

"That came yesterday. I forgot to give it to you."

The envelope was addressed to "Fred Despair." The return address was from Vancouver, British Columbia.

"We might have to get an exterminator out here. You can stay in one of my extra rooms for a couple of days, but don't get any ideas."

"Okay. I could probably find another place to crash, if that's better for you."

"You kidding? I could use the company."

Greg knew that his landlady was lonely. Her sons were off raising families of their own, and she was going to more funerals than birthday parties these days.

"Are you still getting together with the ladies for breakfast on Friday mornings?"

"Sometimes. A lot of us can't drive anymore so we have to settle for the phone."

Any time Greg was feeling old he only had to spend a few minutes with Mrs. McMillan to get a reality check. His landlady was more than twice his age and still more active than most of his own friends.

"Kind of makes me think that I should just sell this place and move closer to my grandkids."

"Or your sons could come to visit more often."

"Oh no. You'll understand someday when you start a family of your own. They've got better things to do than worry about me."

"I guess that's why you keep letting me hang around."

"Well it isn't because of your incredible handyman skills."

She motioned to the eave once again before turning to walk away. He chuckled as he opened the door and ripped the seal on the package. Three identical copies of the same magazine slid out and dropped onto the floor at his feet. He kicked the top copy over with his toe as he shimmied out of his wetsuit. It was a Canadian hardcore magazine called *CoreNoMore*. They had done a telephone interview with Greg almost two months ago.

The cover featured an old black and white picture of Greg and Tim mid-song at a small, sweaty club. They looked to be in their late teens or very early twenties. Greg couldn't remember what show it was to save his life. They all just kind of blurred together these days. The headline, "Before You Were Punk," was followed by a brief description of the contents: "Catching up with some of the best hardcore bands that you've probably never heard."

Greg was too sore to easily slip out of his wetsuit. He dropped to the floor to finish the job. Down to just his board shorts, Greg picked up a copy of the magazine and started flipping through the pages. He was soon staring at a faded reflection of himself from twenty years ago. Tim was standing behind him, looking off to the side of the frame as though ignoring the camera all together. Further in the background he could make out the blurry silhouettes of Marco behind the drum set and their original bass player J.J. The intro to his interview was spread across two photocopied pages.

Bad Citizen Corporation

This no frills hardcore outfit from Los Angeles released two flawless records in the early nineties. The third and final release was a massive artistic departure that many fans believe was actually meant to be a solo record for brooding front man Fred Despair. The band faded into oblivion in the wake of commercial failure and personal tragedy.

We caught up with the elusive Fred Despair from an undisclosed location in Southern California where he still occasionally pops up to play shows for the lucky locals.

CNM: *Let's start with some of basic info for the readers who are finding out about you for the first time. How did the band form?*

FD: *My brother Tim put the band together. He was a few years older than the rest of us and really into SoCal punk bands like Black Flag, Minutemen, and Descendents. Stuff like that. He wrote most the songs on our first album.*

CNM: *And he owned a legendary hardcore record shop in Los Angeles, right?*

FD: *Yeah, Pretty/Ugly Records. He dropped out of high school in eleventh grade and opened up this little record store that was right next to a bar in our neighborhood.*

CNM: *I don't mean to bring up unpleasant memories, but isn't that the place where Tim hung himself after the band broke up?*

FD: *That's where they found his body. There are some different opinions about whether or not he committed suicide.*

CNM: *What do you believe?*

FD: *Let's just say that Tim wasn't the suicide type. He was pretty intense, like the rest of us were in those days, but he had way too much fun to just check out like that. That's my opinion, no matter what the local police had to say about it back then.*

Greg folded the corner on the page and tossed the magazine across the room. He stood up and wandered into the bathroom, catching his reflection in the mirror over the sink. The dye job Junior had given him really accentuated the lines that were permanently etched into his forehead, and around the corners of his eyes. He slid a drawer open and lifted out his clippers, setting the guide to "2." His curly locks fell to the sink in clumps as he carefully dragged the device across his scalp again and again. His head was covered in uniform fuzz a few minutes later when the phone rang.

It was good to hear the Chief's voice.

"Greg, how're you holding up?"

"Hard to say, all things considered."

"Fair enough. Well, listen. I just got a call from the hospital. The kid just came out of his coma a few hours ago. They think he's gonna make a full recovery."

"Is he talking yet? Did they ask him about the gun?"

"His lawyer got in there before we could. I wanted to give you a heads up because I think things are going to get ugly really fast now."

CHAPTER EIGHT

Greg woke up praying on Sunday morning. His head was throbbing and the shooting pains in his side made it hard to breath. He rolled over carefully to reach for the glass of water on the nightstand, but fell short. The melted ice pack felt warm against his black and blue ribcage. The red numbers on the alarm clock danced as he tried to focus on the time. He let his head drop back to the pillow and groaned as he drifted back to sleep.

He was back in the alley. The blue hat seemed to hover as it spun in the air. Echoes from the gunshots slowly became a loud knocking on Greg's apartment door.

His sheets were soaked through with sweat and he was gasping for air as he sprang upright. The shooting pains made it feel like he was being torn to shreds by a great white shark.

"Greg! Greg, are you in there?!?"

He half growled, half screamed in response. The knocking got more emphatic and then stopped. He heard a key slip into the lock and watched as the deadbolt turned. The door swung open just before Mrs. McMillan poked her head in to look for him. Junior came barreling from behind her and smothered him with a crushing hug. She didn't let go until he whimpered and gasped.

"Jesus, Greg! What the hell happened to you?"

"I had a little run in with Barrett's foot. Followed by several run-ins with his fists."

"Why did that lunatic come looking for you?"

"I actually went looking for him."

He turned slightly and looked back to the door where Mrs. McMillan was still standing. There was a disapproving grimace on her face.

"Hi Ruth. You wouldn't happen to have any ice, would you?"

"You're going to need a lot more than ice, from the looks of things."

She shut the door softly behind her. Junior went to the bathroom sink and ran a washcloth under warm water. He could hear her rifling through his cabinet looking for something to dress his wounds.

She came back to the bed with a washcloth, a box of bandages and a bottle of peroxide. Greg didn't even know he had half that stuff in his medicine cabinet.

"Where's your nurse's outfit?"

"Very funny. Are you gonna tell me why you went to see Barrett?"

"I heard that he got into it with Ricky last week. I wanted to see what the story was."

"You don't think he had anything to do with the shooting, do you?"

"Not sure. Wouldn't surprise me if he did."

"Did you find anything out, or were you too busy getting your ass kicked?"

"We talked a little. Barrett seemed to think Ricky was mixed up in something bigger that could have gotten him...you know. Something to do with work. I couldn't really make sense of it. Did Ricky ever mention anything to you?"

She dabbed a small cut over his swollen eye with healthy dose of peroxide. Every muscle in his body tensed while he tried to breathe through the stinging.

"Can you warn me the next time you do that?"

"What's the matter? Is the punk rock cop afraid of a little pain?"

She giggled and continued to dress his wounds.

"I never trusted Barrett much, but I got the feeling he was telling the truth."

"Officer Bob won't be happy when he hears that you're investigating this."

"Guess I'll find out when I go visit him at the station tomorrow. Are we still on for dinner tonight?"

"I'm not sure I'm up for it with everything that's going on. It'll feel a little weird without Ricky there."

"Well, you know what he would say."

"Yeah. He was always up for a party."

"Come on. It's probably better for us to be around each other right now anyway."

The Sunday barbecues at Junior's house were one of Greg's favorite traditions. It started when they were both still in their twenties and Junior was renting a place with a big backyard. Back then Greg and Ricky would go out deep sea fishing all day. A crowd of people would turn up at Junior's in the afternoon to feast on whatever they caught. Those Sunday barbecues turned into some late nights when Greg was still hitting the bottle. These days it was usually just Junior and her son hanging out in their backyard with Eddie, Greg and Ricky on a lazy Sunday night.

Junior finished cleaning Greg up and headed off to the store to buy provisions for the barbecue. He walked her out to her car and gave her a reassuring hug before she drove away. He saw Mrs. McMillan watching them through the open gate as he headed back toward his apartment. She yelled at him across the backyard as he opened his door.

"You would be stupid not to marry that girl."

Greg woke up sometime in the late afternoon with the magazine face down on his chest. He thought about finishing the *CoreNoMore* article, but he was already going to be late for the barbecue. Standing up still hurt and he was afraid of what he would see when he looked at himself in the mirror.

He felt much better than he had that morning, but he was still moving pretty slow. The thought of a shower and getting out of the house for the first time all day were the only things that kept him going. He just hoped there would still be some food left at Junior's when he finally arrived.

Getting clean was a painful process. He couldn't twist and bend easily to wash himself so he let the running water do most of the work. Toweling off presented the same set of problems, so he went to the barbecue in slightly damp clothes. He was thankful to skip the socks all together in favor of flip-flops.

Greg chased two Extra Strength Tylenols down with a glass of tap water before venturing outside. He shuffled across the backyard and tapped on Mrs. McMillan's patio door to check on her before he went out. She pulled the French door open just as he was ready to give up. He could see the TV on in the background behind her. She was watching the local news.

It felt strange for Greg to see his own face on the screen.

"Sorry, Judy. I wanted to tell you myself."

She stepped forward and wrapped her arms around him. He let his own arms dangle, sure he was unworthy of her sympathy. His mind was racing and he felt like he might throw up. He wanted to kick in her TV screen. Destroy the memories that were eating him alive. She held on tighter as his body shook with fear and rage.

"You don't owe me any explanations, Gregory. I'm just sorry you have to go through this."

They stayed like that for a few endless moments before she finally released him. Her tired eyes glistened as he mumbled an awkward goodbye and shuffled to his car in a daze. He couldn't remember a single thing about the drive over to Junior's house that afternoon. His mind was too busy replaying the shooting over and over again, like waves crashing on the beach.

Junior lived in North Bay, not far from Eddie's L Bar. The house was a small three-bedroom building that was set back from the street. A white picket fence lined the sidewalk at the edge of her enormous front lawn. Chris's bikes and balls were scattered all over the yellowing grass. The barbecue was on one end of a long, faded deck that ran along the front of the house.

Greg pulled into the driveway with Social Distortion's "Mommy's Little Monster" blasting out the windows. He was expecting to see the familiar tailgate of Eddie's truck. He was greeted instead by a vanity license plate that read: **BCDVLPR**. It was mounted on a brand new European sports car—with a frame that read **Bay Cities Developer**, along with a helpful 800 number. He backed out of the driveway and found a spot on the street.

He let the car idle while considering the situation. Any thoughts he was having about himself were obliterated by the sound of Junior screaming from inside.

The fastest way into the house was along the side of the garage and in the through the kitchen door. He gritted his teeth and attempted to jog. That only lasted for a few steps before he settled into a rapid hobble. The unmistakable sound of dishes shattering against the wall greeted him as he charged in.

The door hit Junior's ex husband Mikey in the back, causing him to jump forward a few inches. He turned his head to see who was sneaking up on him and threw his hands up in disgust. Greg could see Eddie holding his daughter back on the other side of the room, her bright red face twisted into a vicious snarl.

Stoneware shards were strewn across the tile floor like tiny shells on the beach. Chris poked his head out carefully from behind his grandfather, flinching every time one of his parents screamed. Greg stepped inside and slammed the door shut. That got everybody's attention.

"What the hell is going on in here?"

"I don't know, Greg. Why don't you ask that crazy bitch?"

Eddie wrapped his arms tightly around his daughter's broad shoulders. She still managed to drag him a few steps into the kitchen. Greg stepped around Mikey and gave Junior a look that said 'chill out'. He waited a moment for her to calm down before he turned to face the wiry man standing behind him. Greg noticed for the first time that Mikey was wearing a pinstriped suit complete with a bright yellow pocket square. A ridiculous outfit by almost any SoCal standard, but especially on a Sunday afternoon.

"Whatever the problem is, nothing gets solved by calling your ex wife names in front of your son."

Mikey drew his hands up to his sides and rested them on his hips. His legs were shifting nervously as he unleashed on Greg.

"You have to be kidding me. I only came here to drop off my alimony check. Next thing I know that lunatic is winging plates at me. Like an animal!"

He screamed the last few words at Junior over Greg's shoulder. She was almost foaming at the mouth when she responded.

"We don't want your money. GET OUT OF MY HOUSE BEFORE I CALL THE POLICE!"

"Do you see, Greg? She's like a broken record. She's always threatening to call the police on me. I just want to see my son."

"I can understand that, Mikey. Here's the problem—she has a restraining order against you. That means that legally you can't be anywhere near this house right now."

Mikey ran his hands through his thick black hair and shook his head.

"Of course. What was I thinking trying to talk sense to the guy who broke my marriage up in the first place? Greg Salem, mister fucking perfect."

"Don't try to make this about me."

"All of you listen to me. My lawyers tell me that this restraining order bullshit is about to come to an end. And when it does my son is going to get a chance to hear both sides of the story. You hear that Chris? You're gonna spend time with daddy again really soon."

"Well, I guess we'll have to let the courts decide that. But right now you to have to go."

Greg raised his arm to escort Mikey outside. Mikey slapped his hand away and shot him a threatening look.

"I don't need any help leaving."

Greg raised his hands in surrender.

"Fine, but I'm still walking out with you so we can have a word in private."

Junior fell to the ground and started sobbing before they even left. Greg watched through the window as Chris tried to comfort his mother. Mikey was already standing next to his car when Greg emerged from behind the garage.

"Mikey, I'm gonna put it to you straight. If you come around here and terrorize anybody in this family ever again I will personally snap your neck with my bare hands. And if I don't, Eddie probably will."

"Really, Greg? I kind of thought shooting innocent kids was more your thing these days."

The words stopped Greg in his tracks. It took every ounce of self-control within him not to smash this weasel's head into the driveway.

"What? You thought people at the beach wouldn't hear about how you screwed up? Looks like you're finally gonna be famous after all."

"I don't have anything to hide from you or anybody else."

"Jesus Christ. Do you know how ridiculous you are? You run around this town like some kind of skateboarding advertisement for the 'good old days.' Well the good old days are dead and buried."

"Expensive clothes and imported cars don't change who you are."

"You're just pathetic, you know that? Grow up, you're not twelve anymore."

"The only twelve-year-old you should be worried about is your son."

"I would love the chance to do that, but my slutty ex-wife—"

Greg grabbed him by the collar before he finished. Electric jolts of pain shot through his body as he spun Mikey around, wrenching an arm up his back. Mikey's forehead hit the hood of the car with a satisfying thud. Greg twisted his fingers into Mikey's hair and drove his face into the polished paint job.

"You never knew when to shut up, did you?"

Mikey tried to talk but the wind was knocked out of him. Greg let him squirm and wheeze a little while longer before finally letting up. Mikey stood and pulled the pocket square from his suit jacket. Greg watched him wiped his brow, checking for blood as he went. Satisfied there was no serious damage, Mikey straightened his suit out and checked his hair in the window's reflection.

"You can throw me around all you want, but this town has changed. Some day very soon there isn't gonna be room for beach trash like you or Eddie."

He opened his car door and climbed in. Greg caught a whiff of the new leather as Mikey rolled down the window to adjust the mirrors. The engine purred to life and he started to back out of the driveway. The car stopped a few feet short of the street. Mikey leaned out to speak.

"Tell Eddie that I'm ready to buy whenever he wants to sell."

Greg took a step toward the car, but it shot backwards into the street. Mikey laid on the horn and yelled something out the window before he shot off for the boulevard. Greg was instantly aware of all the pain he should have been feeling during the altercation. He backed away from the street and inched along to the house.

Eddie was inside with a broom and dustpan trying to clean up the kitchen. Greg knelt down next to him with an old man's groan of his own. Eddie nodded to the living room. That's where Greg's help was needed most.

Junior was seated at one end of a tattered L-shaped couch. Chris was lying along the length of the cushions with his head in her lap. She was running her fingers through his sandy blonde hair. Her eyes were focused on the window that looked out across the front yard. Greg wondered if she had seen him throw Mikey onto the hood of the car. He didn't know where to begin.

"I guess that means no barbecue?"

He lowered himself down on the couch near Chris's feet. The boy's eyes were closed and his breathing was rhythmic. Her voice was soft, but she might as well have been screaming.

"Why are we all so damaged?"

It was a question that neither of them could answer. Forever aimed at the idiot emptiness that surrounded that couch, that neighborhood, their world. He watched waves of regret washing over her as the silence swallowed the words. There was nothing to say in response, but he couldn't say nothing at all.

"I don't know, Junior. I've lived through every second of my life and I still don't know how I got to exactly this moment."

His head throbbed and his mind reeled. It felt like he was buried up to his neck in wet sand, crushing him under its weight. All he could do was wait for the inevitable tide that was coming to wash them all away.

But he couldn't say any of that to her. Not after the night that she had.

"We didn't do anything right or wrong, but that doesn't mean we're innocent. Best we can do is to live our lives without hurting the people around us."

"And just accept whatever bullshit the universe throws our way."

"I don't think the universe has any grand plan for us. It comes down to the decisions we make, and maybe a little luck. We're not damaged, we're just human."

"How is that fair for Chris? He didn't get to choose his parents, but he still has to deal with our shitty decisions."

"He's a kid. Just keep loving him. The rest will work itself out."

A mischievous smile spread across her face. Greg felt a creeping sense of calm. She could do the rest of the talking now.

"You're turning into a hippie in your old age."

Eddie finished sweeping up in the kitchen. He made a little extra noise putting the broom away to let them know he was coming into the living room. Greg couldn't remember a time when Eddie looked so tired. He wondered what his own father would look like if he had lived as long.

Eddie took a seat in the lounge chair and kicked his feet up on the coffee table. He stared at his grandson sleeping peacefully between Greg and Junior. The look on the old man's face made it clear what he was thinking. The same thought had crossed Greg's mind. Is this what their lives would have been like if they were still together? It was too much for Greg to consider.

"Hey Eddie, are you thinking about selling the bar?"

Eddie raised his eyebrows in response. Junior shot her father a look of pure horror. Greg tried to backtrack, but it was too late.

"Never mind. It's just something Mikey said when we were outside."

"Before or after you slammed his face into the hood of the car? For a second there I thought you were going to cuff him."

Eddie flashed a tired smile and shook his head in disbelief. Greg turned to face Junior.

"Please tell me Chris didn't see that."

She shook her head and gently stroked her son's cheek. Eddie let the dust settle a little before he dug deeper.

"What did he tell you?"

"That he was ready to buy whenever you were ready to sell."

Eddie folded his arms and let his chin drop. Greg could see the wheels spinning in that grey head of his. He didn't dare to look over at Junior. She had almost stopped breathing all together.

"Dad?"

"It's not just him. The neighborhood is changing and these developers—they're really aggressive. Always coming around making offers that seem too good to be true. I'm talking about a lot of money. I used to throw them out, but now…I don't know. Maybe he's right. Maybe it is time to cash in and retire."

"Dad, please don't talk like that."

"Honey, with the money they're offering we could both retire."

"It isn't just about the money. I can't stand the thought of the bar you built—where I grew up—getting turned into some hipster lofts, or a soulless coffee outlet."

"The thing is, I might not have a choice after what happened the other night."

CHAPTER NINE

There was a loud crash in the alley behind Greg's apartment. He lay perfectly still in the pre-dawn darkness, listening. Something or someone was scraping and scratching along the pavement, tearing the bags apart. Silent seconds passed before he exhaled. It could have been a raccoon. Or maybe it was one of the local homeless population, scouring the nighttime streets in search of unwanted treasures.

He rolled over to look at his alarm clock without much pain. His sore ribs were already starting to heal. It was only 5:30 when he got up to brew a cup of coffee, easing into a couple of light stretches while the water boiled.

It might be possible to catch a couple of sunrise waves before he had to meet with Officer Bob. The wetsuit hanging from the shower rod seemed like a positive confirmation, just like it always did. He slipped it on and grabbed one of the surfboards from the rack. It was still and dark in the garden, except for the chirping birds. He could hear the sound of waves crashing in the distance, calling to him as the back gate swung shut.

A rectangular brown trashcan was on the hood of the El Camino. Broken trash bags were scattered on the roof and in the bed of the car. There was a long, thin crack reflecting from the windshield in the harsh glow of a streetlight. A folded piece of paper was tucked neatly under one of the windshield wipers. He leaned his surfboard against the open gate and stomped over to grab it. Little puffs of fog accompanied every curse that came from his mouth in the brisk morning air.

Sorry we missed you at the show the other night. We'll be sure to get there a little earlier next time.

xoxo,

Your Biggest Fan

The note was printed in color ink on everyday copier paper. The font mimicked letters that had been cut out of newspapers and magazines, like the cover of the first Sex Pistols album. Greg almost had to laugh at the ridiculousness of it all. He took a step out into the middle of the alley to make sure that nobody was watching him. Barrett and his gang of knuckle draggers would get a real kick out of watching him clean their mess up, but the coast was clear in both directions.

Greg went back inside the apartment to grab his phone. He took some pictures of the scene before hosing his car down. Not that the BCPD would ever do anything about it. Greg didn't make the kind of money it took to buy their protection.

He read the note a few more times to see if he had missed any obvious clues. Nothing new jumped out at him. He crumpled the paper up and threw it away with the rest of the trash. He wasn't going to let Barrett keep him from going surfing.

The beach was empty aside from an old woman searching the sand with a metal detector. Seagulls were retreating from the tide on webbed feet as he dropped his surfboard into the shallow water. He attached the leash to his ankle and dove under a frothy wall of whitewash. The salty water felt cold and sticky on his head and neck. He slid the board under his body and started paddling. The sun was already up by the time he caught his first wave of the day.

THE BAY CITIES POLICE Station looked like a recreation center compared to the dump in Virgil Heights. Manicured bushes lined a circular walkway where two flags snapped in the light ocean breeze. A colorful mural featuring whales and dolphins filled an entire wall outside the glass doors. A grizzled old desk jockey greeted Greg with a sneeze.

"I'm here to see Officer Bob."

"Assuming you mean Chief Stanley. Is he expecting you?"

"Tell him Greg Salem is here to see him."

The officer did a double take and quickly reached for the phone. He mumbled a couple of things in a whisper that Greg couldn't make out. He snuck a glance at Greg before croaking into the phone a few more times. That was followed with a few "mm hms" before he hung up.

"Chief's running a little behind. Have a seat."

He motioned to a couple of concrete benches near the door, and busied himself on the computer. Greg took a seat and settled in for a long wait.

A female parking enforcement officer appeared behind the counter. She was dressed for work, but could have easily been headed out to the beach. The requisition polo shirt and loose fitting khaki shorts did nothing to obscure her curves. A tangle of thick curls was pulled into a messy ponytail at the back of her head. Her chocolate brown eyes sparkled and danced when she spotted Greg. White teeth beamed through plump pink lips as she walked his way.

"I didn't think I would see you here today. Did you get my note?"

"Hi Quincy." He caught a whiff of her coconut-scented sunscreen as she bent down to hug him. "I'm actually here on business. Meeting with Officer Bob. Sorry I haven't called you."

She took his hand in hers and gave a little squeeze.

"Oh my God, Greg. I'm so sorry about your friend."

"Thanks. Can I call you later on? It might do me some good to get out tonight."

"I'll keep my phone on, but only if you're up for it."

Greg flashed a weak smile. She bent down to give him a quick peck on the cheek. He watched as she walked down the path and climbed into her small parking enforcement vehicle. Greg reached for a stack of newspapers by the door and grabbed a copy of the free weekly.

The Bay Cities News had fallen on hard times in the internet age. A huge drop in readership resulted in declining ad revenue that forced the original owners to fire half the staff. Real estate interviews, real estate listings and real estate ads soon replaced the features on pancake breakfasts and city council meetings.

He flipped through the pages of coupons and finally found a small pocket of local content in the middle of the paper. He skimmed the surf report to get an idea of what the waves would be like that weekend before turning to the obituaries. There were three pictures along with short blurbs stuffed into one skinny column, all of them memorializing senior citizens. What would it be like to see Ricky's picture sandwiched onto that page? He flipped the paper onto a nearby chair and folded his arms across his chest.

"Mr. Salem. The Chief will see you now."

Greg followed the officer around the front desk and along a paneled corridor that led to the back of the building. Officer Bob occupied a large corner office that overlooked a small patch of grass and a private sand volleyball court. Some officers were playing a game of three-on-three as Greg shook his hand. Officer Bob was staring straight at the fading purple ring around Greg's eye.

"Thanks for showing up. Can I offer you a coffee, or some sparkling water?"

"Have you found anything out about the murder?"

Officer Bob plopped down into his leather chair and leaned back.

"I had an interesting conversation with your Chief in Virgil Heights this morning. He seems to hold you in pretty high regard."

That last comment sounded like a question. As though Greg should explain how a no good punk like him had fooled so many cops. He considered giving Officer Bob an answer, but decided it would just prolong their time together. There were a lot of other places he would rather be at that moment. Hanging out with Quincy was currently topping the list.

"Were you checking up on me?"

"Actually, he called me. I wouldn't expect anything less from somebody as experienced as he is. It's a real shame to see him wasting away in Virgil Heights. How exactly did you end up on the force?"

"The usual way. Lots of training, lots of tests. You?"

"I was actually wondering what would have driven somebody with such a colorful past to pursue a career in law enforcement."

"Let's just say that I wasn't always impressed with the police officers I encountered. I guess at some point I decided I could do it better."

Officer Bob frowned, but nodded along in agreement.

"And how's that going for you, Mr. Salem?"

"Let's just get this over with. You got any leads on the shooters, or what?"

"I'm going to remind you again that you are not a police officer in this town. Come to think of it, you aren't a police officer in any town these days. So let me ask the questions."

Greg was exhausted and his nerves were shot. He tried to swallow, but it was becoming more and more difficult. There was still no way he would accept anything from Officer Bob. Not even a bottle of water.

"While we're on the topic, I better not hear about any more run-ins between you and Jeff Barrett. If I do, I will have you arrested for obstruction. Is that clear?"

"Crystal."

Officer Bob leaned forward and opened up a notebook.

"Right. Let's go over the events of that evening again. I want to make sure we didn't miss anything important when we last spoke."

Greg went through the night again, starting from when he arrived for sound check. Officer Bob listened attentively, scribbling down some notes and nodding here and there. He put his pen down when Greg got to the part about the two fans that stopped him in the parking lot.

Officer Bob had a look of deep concentration on his face. He spun in his chair until he was facing the window. They both sat in silence and watched the volleyball game outside. The uncomfortable pause went on for a minute or two before Officer Bob finally spoke again.

"I haven't forgotten you Mr. Salem. I'm just trying to fit the pieces together. There's something about these two fans of yours that isn't sitting right with me."

"What part? It isn't that weird for kids to ask for autographs outside of shows."

"I don't doubt that, it's just—" He stopped mid-sentence, as if he caught himself sharing too much information. Greg could sense the internal debate that Officer Bob was struggling with. In the end, common sense seemed to win out. "I think there's something I should show you."

Officer Bob spun around quickly and opened a drawer low down on his desk. He pulled out a light colored folder and placed it between the two of them. Greg wanted to grab it, but knew he would never see what was inside if he did. Officer Bob was choosing his words very carefully now.

"On the night of the incident, you and several other witnesses stated that a fight broke out in the audience during the show. That fight was instigated when somebody in the crowd yelled out an insult at you. Is that accurate?"

Greg hadn't given it much thought since he was on stage. Now he could almost hear it again in his head. He could feel the muscles in his shoulders and back tense up at the memory. He nodded and Officer Bob went on.

"The person who was attacked sustained significant injuries during the fight that followed. He has been in the hospital since the night of the incident. Yesterday we obtained a warrant to search his personal belongings, including the pictures on his phone."

Officer Bob flipped the folder open and turned it so that Greg could see the print on top. It was one of the shots he had posed for with those two kids outside of Eddie's.

"Is that the guy that got jumped?"

"Yes. He was released from the hospital earlier today." Officer Bob turned the folder back to flip through the stack of prints. He got to the picture he was looking for, but stopped short of sharing it. "But that's not what has me confused. Did you recognize him when he approached you that night?"

Officer Bob handed the picture over before Greg could answer. It was a little blurry after being transferred from a phone, enlarged and reproduced on a desktop printer. Still, Greg didn't notice anything familiar about the kid next to him in the shot. Officer Bob seemed disappointed when Greg shook his head.

"Technically I am not supposed to show you this next picture since it doesn't directly relate to your investigation—at least not that we know of. Once you see it I think you'll understand why I'm concerned."

He slid the next print across the desk. Greg's hands were starting to shake a little as he saw the same kid again, wearing the same clothes as in the previous picture. This time he was posing with a gaunt older man. His stringy, blonde hair dangled limply down to bony shoulders that almost poked through a tattered BCC T-shirt.

"Marco? He wasn't even at the show."

"That picture was taken earlier in the day, around one o'clock according to the date stamp. I know this puts you in a tough position since Marco and Ricky are both friends of yours. But I have to ask—can you think of any reason why Marco would want either of you dead?"

Greg was in a daze when he finally emerged from the police station. After showing him the second picture, Officer Bob had gone on a rant about Marco and the cast of characters he ran with. How they'd taken over most of the rooms at a rundown motel under the freeway ramps in North Bay. The place had once been a respectable family establishment that catered to tourists making the drive between Ventura and San Diego. In recent years it had become a residential motel that charged cheap weekly rates for half the rooms, and hourly rates for the rest.

Officer Bob said he'd been watching the place very carefully since Marco and his crew moved in. Recent raids had turned up a meth lab in one of the rooms and a sophisticated marijuana growing operation in another. It sounded to Greg like Officer Bob was on a one-man crusade to get the place condemned.

Greg couldn't figure out how things had gone so wrong for Marco after he left Bad Citizen Corporation. Sure, he had some pretty serious habits while he was still in the band, but his parents had thrown him into a rehab the minute they got off the road. He simply disappeared. When he reemerged a year later he looked positively human with his shiny hair, chubby cheeks and ear-to-ear grin.

That only lasted a couple of years as far as Greg could remember. Then the rumors about his drug use started spreading again, just as Greg found his way into that world himself. They even spent some long weekends together during that time, surfing all day and partying all night.

Marco seemed to fade into the background again once Greg got sober. Greg would ask around about him once in a while, but their paths had definitely split. Marco's struggles with addiction had been on again, off again ever since. Greg still tried to stay in contact with him, even when Marco made it clear that he would rather be left alone. Which was most of the time.

All the information that Officer Bob gave him was swirling around in his head, filling him with doubt. Greg wanted to believe that Marco would never do anything to harm him or Ricky. But he also knew that you could only count on a drug addict for one thing; to absolutely destroy the lives of the people who loved them the most.

Greg needed to go for a drive. Just some time alone to get his thoughts straight and plan his next move. He climbed into the El Camino and cruised along the coast. Jimmy Cliff was singing "The Harder They Come" as he wound his way through Malibu and kept going north.

CHAPTER TEN

Twice in one week is aggressive, but you can't always rely on your partner to get the job done right.

The dog kept barking and charging along the length of the white picket fence. Then the sedatives from the tainted piece of rawhide finally kicked in. It was laying on its side panting when the front gate swung open. It was just a few steps along the flagstone path that wound through the wildflowers. This house had real curb appeal, which is why it got moved up the list.

The front door was always propped open during the day so that the dog could easily get in and out. The caregiver came daily, but made frequent trips to the pharmacy during lunch.

The old man's baldhead was poking up just above the top of the leather reclining chair. Wisps of grey hair were combed up the sides in a vain attempt to cover the brown sunspots on top. Right wing talking heads were shouting from the flat screen television mounted on the far wall. It was loud enough that he didn't hear the screen door squeak open. It wasn't anything that a few drops of oil couldn't fix, but enough to put a potential buyer off. *First impressions are so important.*

The old man was wheezing despite the oxygen tubes that ran under his nose. Two more steps across the hardwood floor and just turn the knob on the oxygen tank. He was already semiconscious to begin with, so this shouldn't take long. His body eventually stiffened and his legs flailed a little. Just a few more seconds now until the oxygen ran out. It was beautiful the way his eyes rolled back in his head as he reached for the tank in vain. And then a final gasp and shudder.

The lug nut on the tank's valve eventually came loose. The gauge showed the tank was a little more than half full. It was just a matter of turning the knob full blast and letting the oxygen rush out until it was all gone. It was a shame that the caregiver would be blamed for the death, but that's what insurance was for.

Tighten the lug nut back down. Check the pulse for good measure. The doggy sedatives would be wearing off any minute now, if the dose was right. *Soon none of this will be necessary.*

CHAPTER ELEVEN

Greg almost made it all the way to Santa Barbara before he turned around. He watched the sun setting over the Pacific Ocean through the passenger window on the way home. His mind was much clearer now, but he wasn't any closer to figuring out who killed Ricky. It was starting to eat him alive.

He was heading down Bay Cities Boulevard an hour later with Lagwagon belting out "Violins" on the stereo. Eddie's was still open as he passed the half empty parking lot. Flowers and candles were piling up just outside the front door where many of the locals had come to pay their respects. He considered stopping in to see if any of his friends were there, but knew it wouldn't help him find the murderer.

The boulevard wound its way to the beach. Greg hit red light after red light, giving him time to indulge in memories of Ricky at every intersection. He passed the coffee shop where the two of them used to hang out late into the night all throughout high school. The sandwich place where Ricky used to work. A baseball diamond where they played little league together.

And a liquor store on almost every block. Greg kept his eyes focused on the road in front of him while a debate raged in his head. One beer wouldn't kill him, but it might take the edge off. And a six-pack would probably help him get to sleep. That's all he was really after, just a good night's sleep. One night without any nightmares. Greg gripped the steering wheel harder and stepped on the accelerator.

It was 12:30 a.m. when he threw his car into park and made a quick dash to his apartment. The sweat on his temple was starting to build as he fumbled to get the key in the lock. There was only an hour and a half left before the liquor stores and bars would close for the night. He knew from experience that the intense urges would be gone when he woke up in the morning. Or at least he hoped so. They hadn't been this bad in years.

His clothes were off in a matter of seconds and he dove for the comfort of his bed. The issue of *CoreNoMore* was waiting for him as he pulled the covers up and gritted his teeth. He flipped to a random page and tried reading himself to sleep.

CNM: *What about your manager?*

FD: *Mikey? He was some dorky guy from our high school who got a business degree in college. The next time we saw him he was telling us how he was going to make us "gazillionaires." I think he actually used that word.*

CNM: *Who hired him?*

FD: *I guess I did, since everybody else was strung out.*

CNM: *How did the rest of the band feel about it?*

FD: *Tim was pretty pissed off. The last time we were in the studio together he swung his guitar at me and started yelling about how I was "selling out." That was one of the last times we ever spoke.*

When that didn't work he flipped the TV on. The first thing he found was a rebroadcast of the local news. They showed a picture of Greg before he could hit the power button on the remote. The screen went black, but not nearly as black as the thoughts in his head. Maybe a midnight run on the beach would do the trick.

Or maybe he could still make it to the liquor store before they closed.

SOMEBODY WAS SNORING LOUDLY nearby. Greg tried to open his eyes, but they felt glued shut. And the throbbing in his temples made it impossible to force them open. His tongue was bone dry, the tip of a Saharan thirst that made his entire body pucker.

He could tell that they were inside, he and whoever was making all the unbearable fucking noise. But where? It wasn't his apartment, the odor just wasn't right. The air was too musty and without the comforting undercurrent of ocean air. He tried to sit up to see where he was and immediately vomited onto the multicolored bedspread.

The tears in his eyes were giving him a kaleidoscopic view of the room. It wasn't helping his dizziness. A second wave of nausea produced toxic yellow bile that spilled from his slack jaw and dribbled down his chin. He tried to breathe through his nose to fight back the convulsions, but couldn't catch his breath. His ribs ached and an acrid odor was wafting up into his nostrils. He slumped forward to rest his forehead on shaky knees. His brain was throbbing rhythmically in his shattered skull.

Minutes passed before he attempted to move again. He leaned back and lifted his hands to gently rub the tears from his eyes.

It took a couple of seconds to focus after he brought his hands down onto his lap. His knuckles were swollen and covered in jagged little cuts. The sight of his own blood filled him with enough adrenaline to overcome the pain. He gave the landscape a quick scan, but his misery was the only familiar thing.

He was in a queen-sized bed that occupied most of a small hotel room. He jumped back a little when he realized that the snoring was coming from right beside him. This mystery person was turned away from him under the same comforter he had just destroyed. Long blonde hair was flowing out from under a stained pillow.

Early afternoon sunlight was fighting its way into the room through several cigarette burns in the blackout curtain. The tiny dots were like cockroach spotlights on the threadbare carpet. Next to the window he could see that the front door was dead bolted, locked with a chain and secured for good measure with a chair jammed up under the knob. A small round table was upended and laying on the floor amid a sea of empty bottles and aluminum cans.

His jacket was draped over a tall floor lamp across from the bed. A bulky TV from another era was mounted precariously on top of a tattered dresser. The screen was bashed in and crumpled. His eyes followed the wall into the darkness where a small closet butted up against the bathroom.

He looked down at his hands again and tried to piece the previous night together. The unmistakable whirring sound of midweek freeway traffic was constant in the background. Everything after he left the liquor store was a total blank.

"Good morning, sunshine." Marco's normally raspy voice was more of a croak as he sat up next to Greg in the bed. "Seems like you're a little out of practice when it comes to partying."

"What the fuck is happening here?"

Marco cackled maniacally as he slid from the covers and headed toward the bathroom. He nearly tripped over an unconscious figure propped up against the wall. Greg listened as Marco pissed in complete darkness. It sounded like he had pretty impressive aim for an addict. He stumbled back to the bed with a half empty bottle of cheap vodka in his hand.

"Jesus, Marco. Do you keep booze hidden in the bathroom?"

"Yep. In the tank. What?" He seemed genuinely offended by the look of horror on Greg's puffy face. "It's clean water, and none of these losers ever think to look in there."

Marco popped a few pills into his mouth and tilted the bottle up with purpose. Greg watched as the clear liquid drained out. He was disgusted at first, and then a little amazed at how much abuse one body could take.

"Was that aspirin?"

Marco brought the bottle down and wiped his mouth with the back of his hand.

"Way stronger than that. You interested?"

Greg wasn't interested in the pills, but he was gripped by a wave of panic when he saw that the bottle was almost empty. It was a familiar feeling, although he hadn't felt it this acutely since he first got sober. That's when the horrible realization sank in. He had let a decade of sobriety slip through his fingers. The worst part was that he didn't remember any of it.

Now he was salivating as he watched Marco guzzling vodka first thing in the morning.

"Dude, save some for me!"

The bottle came down slowly. There was a still a few ounces left as Greg yanked it from the hands of his old band mate. Marco smirked proudly.

"Not so high and mighty now, huh? Go ahead and polish it off. We can always get more."

Greg forced down a couple of shots worth of vodka in a single gulp. He let the bottle roll from his hand. It came to rest in his puddle of vomit on the bedspread. The spreading warmth calmed his nerves enough so that he could ask Marco a question that was worrying him.

"Please tell me that isn't a dead body over there."

He pointed in the direction of the bathroom with his thumb.

"No, but he might be if I hadn't pulled you off of him last night. You went from zero to ape shit when he accused you of being a cop, *which you fucking are.* Do you think my room looked like this before you showed up?!"

"How did I end up here last night?"

Greg fell back. His head hit the pillow with a thud.

"I can't really help you there. You just came barreling through the door out of nowhere." He cackled in fits and starts trying to get his next sentence out. "Fucking freaked everybody in the whole place out. They scattered like roaches when you ripped this place up!"

"Was I alone?"

"Alone like Jekyll and Hyde. Dude, you were shitfaced and looking for a fight. First thing you did was threaten to kick my ass if I had anything to do with Ricky getting shot. Then you kept asking me 'who the guy in the picture' was. I'm still not sure what the fuck you were talking about."

"This is a fucking nightmare. I need something else to drink."

"I'm right there with you. There's probably beer left in some of the cans around here, or we can head over to the Lo Bar for something a little fresher. We can stick that bedspread in the washing machine on the way over."

Greg managed to stand up, certain that his balance would have been much worse without the vodka. He stepped over the motionless body on the floor and went into the bathroom. A shower would probably help, but the bathtub was filled half way to the ceiling with cardboard boxes. He settled for splashing some water on his face in the sink and squeezing a dab of toothpaste onto his tongue.

Marco was sitting on a cracked and faded plastic lawn chair in the parking lot smoking a cigarette when Greg emerged. The transition from the dingy motel room to broad daylight was jarring. He squinted his eyes and scratched at his t-shirt where it clung to the dried sweat on his skin. The day was just getting started, but it already felt way too long.

Everybody at the Laundromat seemed to know Marco, and he stopped to bump fists or chat with all of them. It took the two of them almost fifteen minutes to finally get the wretched smelling bedspread soaking in the washer. Marco made the rounds one more time on the way back out to the sidewalk.

The front door of the Lo Bar was propped open with an unoccupied stool. A black curtain was hanging from the jamb. They pushed their way into the room and it instantly felt like the sun had set forever. The only light in the cramped space was coming from the votive candles on the tables and a few florescent bulbs down low behind the bar. A rotating fan was pushing flies around the room in currents of warm air as the two of them leaned up against the bar and ordered. They grabbed two drinks each and headed to a booth in the darkest corner of the room. Marco drained his first glass before Greg could sit down.

"I thought you were in Baja."

"Dude, we went over this last night."

"It's safe to assume that I've already forgotten anything you told me last night."

Greg took a pull from his drink. Amazing. He swore he had seen the bartender pour juice into the glass, but all he could taste was vodka. It was easily the best drink that he had ever had in his entire life.

"No shit, right? I was down in Baja, but just for a day. You know, taking care of some business."

"You'll do serious time if you get caught smuggling pills across the border."

"Dude! That is exactly what you said last night..." Greg flashed him a menacing look. "Okay, fine. Anyway, I brought my board down with me, but the shipment was bigger than I thought it was gonna be. So I decided to head back up."

"Is that what's in the bathtub back at the motel?"

"Do you really want to know?"

They both drained their glasses. Greg sent Marco back to the bar with a couple of twenties for another round. He realized his phone was missing when he went to shove his wallet back into his jeans. There was no reason to believe he would ever see that phone again. Marco returned with a tray full of drinks and a proud smile on his face.

"I don't want to have to get up every five minutes."

"Did we talk about Ricky at all last night?" His chest tightened as a he spat the words out. "I mean, about what happened to him."

"You kidding? That's practically all we talked about. You had me crying like a baby. It was fucking embarrassing."

"Right. Well, I have to ask you a few questions about that."

"Okay, stop that bullshit right there. I know you want to pretend like last night didn't happen, but don't start acting like a fucking cop again. This is me you're talking to, Marco, not some fucking…" His eyes rolled back in his head while he searched for the word. "Perp."

"Did you seriously just say 'perp'?"

"What, isn't that a real thing? They say it on TV all the time. Back when I had a TV."

"You know I'll replace your fucking TV. Now answer my question."

"For the last time, no. I didn't have anything to do with Ricky getting shot. If you ask me, I think it had something to do with Barrett. He and Ricky had some seriously bad blood."

"What do you know about any of that?"

"Just what I overheard when I was picking up odd jobs with Ricky. Barrett and a couple of his bros showed up at one of the jobs I was on and accused Ricky of raiding his job sites. They said he was breaking in at night and stealing his supplies. I guess they were both bidding on some huge job and Barrett thought Ricky was trying to trash his reputation. It was pretty gnarly."

"Was there truth to any of it?"

"I never helped Ricky raid Barrett's job sites, if that's what you mean."

"Okay. What about the guy from the picture?"

"Are you seriously gonna start that shit again?"

"This is a fucked up situation. If Ricky really was your bro then you need to help me figure out who did this to him. The Bay Cities police showed me a picture of you and some guy that they got from his phone. I took a picture with that same guy right before the show the other night. There has to be a connection."

"That guy with the fucked up skin? He was just some BCC fan that heard I lived in town. He asked me for my autograph and everything. You think he had something to do with Ricky getting shot?"

"No idea. Did he say how he found you?"

"Somebody down at the beach told him. Not sure who."

"Did he say what street he was hanging out at?"

"Uh, no...but he mentioned something about volleyball."

"Well, in that case I have one more question for you. Where's my car?"

Greg grabbed a glass from the tray. He gave Marco a little toast before sucking it down.

THERE WAS A LOUD crack as somebody broke a rack of balls at one of the pool tables. A couple of regulars were playing cards at a round table, and a few others were milling around the jukebox in the corner.

"The carpool lane is not the fast lane."

Roger and Bill had been arguing for the better part of an hour. Eddie leaned in to listen as Bill jumped back in.

"So you're telling me that, by your own logic, you drive up the freeway ramp and accelerate to merge into the first lane. Then you accelerate and merge again and again, gaining speed each time until you are finally in the fast lane. At this point you're probably going a little faster than the speed limit."

Roger was trying to ignore him, like usual. Bill was on a roll.

"Then, when you finally merge into the carpool lane—*the lane furthest to the left*—you slow down? That just doesn't make any sense."

"No, that's not what I'm saying. I'm talking about the assholes that tailgate me in the carpool lane. It isn't the fast lane. If they want to go faster than the posted speed limit, then they should get back in the fast lane."

Eddie wandered over and dropped a couple of fresh beers down in front of them. He leaned in to listen for a moment before he joined in.

"What did you two figure out?"

"The carpool lane is not the fast lane."

Roger nodded triumphantly and took a drink from his beer. Eddie started polishing beer mugs with a tattered bar towel. Bill looked over Eddie's shoulder to watch the muted TV mounted on the wall.

"Hey, Eddie. Your boy Greg's on TV again."

They all looked up at the screen. A local talking head was giving some kind of commentary on police violence. Eddie yanked the power chord right out of the wall. Bill was already too drunk to notice.

"You hear anything from the police about the shooting here the other night?"

"I'm supposed to follow up with them in a day or two."

"Shame about Ricky. Have you spoken to his mom?"

"Edie's been spending some time with his family. I don't really know them that well. Not since the kids were in school together."

"Maybe we should set up some kind of a fund. You know, get some money together to help his family with funeral costs. I'm sure everybody around here would chip in a few bucks. Right Roger?"

"Count me in." Roger patted the bar gently with the palm of his hand to get Eddie's attention. "How's Greg doing anyway?"

"I saw him for a minute yesterday. Seems to be holding up okay."

"Gotta be tough for him, especially after everything he went through with his brother."

"That thought crossed my mind, too. Hopefully the police will get some real answers this time around."

Roger turned his attention to a newspaper spread out on the bar. Bill picked up where Roger left off.

"I heard that happened next door."

"I forgot you didn't live around here back then, Bill. Why'd you move here anyway?"

Hard to say if Eddie was actually curious or just wanted to change the subject. Bill didn't seem to notice or care.

"Real estate, same as everybody else. This is about the only place where the property values go up anymore. Greg's brother committed suicide, right?"

Eddie threw the towel down and started pacing behind the bar.

"Bullshit. That wasn't a suicide. Timmy wouldn't do that to Greg and his dad. No matter what the police said. He was a good kid, just a little screwed up from the drugs."

Bill could see that Eddie was getting agitated, but didn't let up.

"What do you think happened?"

"Nobody knows. The police overlooked a lot of things that made it seem like a robbery. All the money was missing, for one thing. And there was no note."

Eddie's voice was hoarse and his cheeks were flushed. He was getting short of breath as he went on talking.

"Greg thought the police weren't interested in investigating the death of a junkie. I'm not sure he ever really got over it. And now this happens."

Roger was the one who finally stepped in.

"Take it easy, Eddie. You don't look so good."

CHAPTER TWELVE

Marco made a pretty good partner, after a little coaxing. The two of them finished their tray of drinks and then stumbled back to the motel like a couple of binge drinking frat boys. The room was completely empty when they arrived, much to Greg's relief. They both fell into bed side by side and tried to sleep themselves sober throughout the afternoon. It was already early evening when Greg finally sat up hours later. He was still drunk, but filled with a renewed sense of urgency.

"Marco. You awake?"

He gave his companion a couple of shoves. When there was no response he punched him hard on the shoulder. Marco came to life with a howl.

"What?"

"Get up, man. We have some work to do."

Marco pulled a pillow over his head as Greg jumped up. He was already fast asleep again when Greg grabbed him by the ankles and yanked him from the end of the bed. He was on his feet and chest to chest with Greg as soon as he hit the floor.

"Don't mess with me!"

Greg brushed past him and opened the door. The room instantly filled with the smell of exhaust fumes. A battered taxi was idling in the parking spot just outside of Marco's room. The driver was sitting in the front seat speaking on his phone when Greg approached and tapped on the window. The driver eyed him suspiciously and then pointed up with his index finger. The sign on the roof of the car said "Off Duty." Greg pulled the car door open before the man had a chance to lock it.

"My friend and I need a ride. Name your price."

The driver barked a few hushed sentences into his phone and hung up.

"How far?"

"A couple of miles. Over by the reservoir."

"Fifty."

"Fine." Greg told the driver to hold on while he went back to grab Marco. "Let's go. There's a taxi waiting for us."

"I'm staying right here."

"Okay, but I would ditch those boxes in the bathroom if I were you. The police will be on their way over as soon as I can get to a phone."

"Seriously, dude?"

"Get in the taxi, Marco. I need your help figuring out what jobs Ricky and Barrett were bidding on."

"So we're just gonna go jump Barrett and beat the truth out of him?"

"No. We're gonna go to his job yard and break into his office. He has to have files for all of his bids."

"Bummer. I was kind of hoping we were gonna kick his ass."

"It might come to that eventually." Greg stepped aside and let Marco leave the room first. He closed the door behind him, but didn't bother to check if it was locked. "Especially if he catches us in his office."

They climbed into the backseat of the cab and immediately started formulating a plan. The driver pulled the taxi out into traffic and they inched their way along the boulevard. This end of North Bay was populated with mini malls and car dealerships. The commercial sprawl eventually transformed to suburban housing tracts as the boulevard wound toward the beach. In between was a small industrial area that surrounded a reservoir. Eddie's was on one side of the tiny expanse of water, and Barrett's job yard was on the other side. The area that lined the reservoir in between was rapidly being converted from workshops to business complexes.

Greg had the driver stop a few blocks from Barrett's place and dropped three twenties into the front seat. They watched as the taxi flipped a U-turn and headed back along the reservoir in the direction of the boulevard. The silence overwhelmed them as they started walking along the frontage road. There were a few lights on in the offices around them, but the neighborhood was otherwise dark at that time of night.

The emptiness reminded Greg of Virgil Heights on the weekend. The mirrored office complexes eventually gave way to older brick buildings a few blocks down the road. Guard dogs were barking at them from behind chain link fences as they passed. Neither of them had considered the possibility that Barrett might have guard dogs.

"You ever been bitten, Greg?"

"Not since I was a kid."

"Well, I can tell you. It hurts like hell."

Barrett's job yard looked like a messy parking lot. Boxy white trucks lined the fence along the street. Gear of various shapes and sizes were stacked in neat piles around the lot between the trucks and the office. Curls of barbed wire lined the top of the fence and the gate at the entrance was chained and locked.

Greg grabbed hold of the chain link and gave it a couple of vigorous shakes and waited to see if dogs would appear. He was trying to figure out how to lift his partner up and over the barbed wire when Marco pulled the two halves of the gate apart and slipped between the bars. It was a tight squeeze, even for his thin frame.

"Something tells me that wasn't the first time you've done that. You know there's no way I'm getting through there."

Marco turned and dashed off between two trucks and into the dark yard. He reappeared a few minutes later with industrial bolt cutters. The chain resisted at first, but eventually snapped under the incredible tension. Greg pulled the gate open and followed Marco into the yard. Marco was rounding the corner of a truck when Greg grabbed him by the elbow and yanked him back.

"Look up at the corner of the building. Cameras."

Years of police work in an industrial district had taught Greg a thing or two about security. The camera was mounted high up on the wall and pointed at the open space between the trucks and the front door of the office building.

"No wonder he doesn't need a guard dog. I bet he sits on the beach and monitors everybody from his computer all day. What should we do?"

"I'm going to pull my T-shirt over my head and run over to that truck near the wall. There's a ladder in the back. I'll climb up and cover the camera lens. He'll know somebody was here, but he won't know it was us."

"You're a criminal mastermind, Marco. Let's do it."

Marco scampered off while Greg hung back in the shadows. He could hear metal scraping against metal as his partner removed the ladder from the back of the truck and carried it across the yard. There were footsteps and then the sound of the ladder coming to rest against the building. Marco whistled loudly to let Greg know the coast was clear.

The camera was pointing up at the sky as Greg approached the front of the building. The door was unlocked and all the lights were out.

"Do you think somebody's inside?"

"I doubt it. They probably just don't bother to lock it since the front gate is chained."

They entered the building and took a few tentative steps into the darkness. Greg could see two office doors along the far wall. "Barrett" was engraved on one of the nameplates. The door didn't budge, so Marco used Greg's credit card to jimmy the lock.

Greg would have killed for a police-issued flashlight right at that moment. Even the flashlight app on his smart phone would have been better than turning the office lights on. He didn't think anybody would be able to see into the office window from the street, but he still felt exposed. The fluorescent lights flickered and revealed a small space with a couple of steel filing cabinets lining the wall on their right. A large wooden desk filled most of the room. There was a computer monitor and a keyboard on top of the desk.

"Check those filing cabinets and see what you can find. I'll check the desk."

Marco sprang into action again. Greg pulled open the three large desk drawers. They were mostly full of office supplies. He found a box of nicotine patches in the top drawer along with an enormous rubber band ball. 'Desk jobs must be miserable,' he thought as he continued to rummage through the clutter. The monitor came to life as he jostled the drawers. Whoever used the computer last had logged out and it was password protected. He knew they were out of luck if Barrett only kept digital files.

"I found something. Check it out."

Greg jumped up and grabbed the file from Marco. The tab at the top was labeled "New Bids." There were only a few stapled packets inside. The first couple of bids were residential, all of them in South Bay. The last one was for what looked like a big commercial job. The address was only a couple of blocks away from Eddie's. The client's name was at the top of the second page, Sand Castle Estates Realty.

"Isn't that one of Mikey's companies?"

Greg did a double take at his friend's comment. Marco didn't have time to explain himself thanks to the rapidly approaching sirens. They couldn't be sure the police were headed their way, but it didn't seem smart to wait around and find out.

"There must be a silent alarm."

Marco shoved the folder into the back of his pants. Greg went for the light switch. They both bolted back across the outer office as the wailing got closer. It sounded to Greg like two police cruisers approaching from the direction of the boulevard. He flew through the front door of the building and started heading toward the back of the yard and the reservoir. Marco went straight for the front gate.

"Marco! This way..."

"We gotta split up. If one of us is getting arrested tonight it ain't gonna be you. I'll keep them busy. You try to find a way out to the water. I'll meet you back at the motel if I can."

Greg watched Marco sprint to the gate and out of sight, and then followed the building around to the back. The sirens came blaring up the street and stopped just outside the front gates. He heard an officer yell "Freeze!" in the distance as he headed toward the reservoir. There were a few young trees in large wooden boxes lined up against the fence. He climbed the tallest one to the top and then jumped from the uppermost branch over the barbed wire. He landed hard on the gravel utility road that surrounded the reservoir. He stopped for a second to catch his breath and then jumped up and started running away from the job yard.

His heart was pounding as it tried to pump the alcohol through his bloodstream. The urge to stop was overwhelming. He knew that he had to get some distance between himself and the police officers. It was only the thought of another drink that kept him running until he was on the other side of the reservoir. He knew Eddie's was nearby, but stopping in there was one of the worst ideas he could've had. They probably wouldn't even serve him, at least not without a lecture. His El Camino would have come in handy right about then.

He decided to head back to the boulevard and catch a taxi home. It wasn't likely that his partner had gotten away. And even if he had, Greg didn't want to be caught in a motel room full of illegal drugs when the police came looking for Marco. *Maybe another drink isn't the best idea*, he thought as he scaled the fence around the reservoir and dropped down to the street on the other side. *Not if I'm going to pay Mikey a visit tomorrow.*

CHAPTER THIRTEEN

It was a relief to see his car parked outside of the apartment when he stepped out of the taxi. He slipped in through the back gate in case Mrs. McMillan was waiting up for him, and let himself into the apartment quietly. He headed straight for the bathroom and a hot shower, undressing as he walked. The water hurt his skin at first, but he let it wash over him until it ran cold. He stepped from the tub and wiped the steam from the bathroom mirror. There were dark circles under his eyes and the skin on his face looked pasty and puffy. He needed a shave, along with another drink.

He found his phone sitting on the floor near the bed. There were fourteen text messages and two voicemails waiting. The first message was from Quincy, and all the rest were from Junior. He opened her latest text and responded with a simple, "Hi." He could see that she was responding immediately and kept his eyes on the screen until words appeared.

"Where have u been???"

He didn't want to lie, but there was only so much he could tell her for now.

"Needed some time alone."

"Please don't ignore me next time. I was REALLY worried."

"I'm fine. You?"

"Better now. A little tired."

"Get some sleep. Let's talk tomorrow."

"K."

He set his phone down on the bed beside his leg. The *CoreNoMore* magazine was there next to him, but he wasn't in the mood to read about himself. Not while Marco was probably being processed down at The Bay Cities Police station. Besides, he knew it was going to be a long sleepless night without any alcohol to knock him out. The magazine might be a handy distraction in a couple of hours when he was fighting the urge to make a run to the nearest liquor store. In the meantime he grabbed the remote and decided to watch a little TV.

The local station was replaying the eleven o'clock news. Greg was hoping to catch a few sports highlights and maybe the surf report. The anchor was just wrapping up coverage of the national headlines when they cut to a reporter live in the field. Greg recognized the alley immediately and sat up in bed to take it all in. The camera was capturing a vigil in Virgil Heights where a small group of local residents were calling for an investigation into the police shooting of a young man who was in critical condition at a local hospital. The story was starting to gain momentum. He knew that he was running out of time.

Sleep was out of the question now, and he tried to convince himself that another night of drinking was a bad idea, too. He got dressed, grabbed his keys and headed out to the El Camino without any kind of real plan. The sight of the cracked windshield hit him like a punch to the gut.

So much had happened in his life since he had rebuilt that car with his brother and his dad. There were ups and downs, but the world had always seemed right when he was behind the wheel of the El Camino. Until now. Right at that moment he was wishing that his brother and dad were with him to help him fight the sickening urge to go back out and drink. He was the last Salem standing.

He started the car and slipped it into neutral, letting gravity pull the weight down the sloping alley. He found it ironic that he could really only think of one place to go at that moment. Anything to avoid making the phone call he knew he had to make.

Greg made every light on the boulevard and was back at the motel in less than fifteen minutes. The door to Marco's room was open slightly as Greg swung the car into the lot. He took that as a good sign, but also knew that it wouldn't necessarily be Marco that he found inside. He got out of his car and approached the motel room, stopping to listen before he actually went in. There was no sound coming from inside.

"Marco, are you in there?"

There was no response so Greg pushed the door open and went inside. The place had been completely ransacked. Every drawer was pulled out of the dressers and the miscellaneous contents were strewn around the floor. The mattresses were flipped over and sliced open to reveal coarse gray stuffing. The closet doors were ripped off of their hinges and the cheap paintings were torn from their mounting on the walls. Greg stepped through the wreckage and quickly made his way to the bathroom. The boxes in the bathtub were gone just as he had suspected they would be. He couldn't help wondering how much money Marco had just lost and how dearly it would cost him when the people he was working for found out. His phone started buzzing in his pocket just as he was leaving the room. It was Junior.

"Hello?"

"Greg, I think that you should come over here right away. There is somebody here who really wants to see you. Right now."

The line went dead before he could even respond. He thought about calling her back, but knew it would go straight to voice mail.

The El Camino went tearing from the parking lot a few seconds later. It was hard to keep from flooring the gas pedal, but he wanted to make sure he didn't draw any attention to himself on the way to Junior's. He parked on the street down the block from her house just to be safe. The living room lights were on but the curtains were drawn as he crossed the lawn and rang the bell. Junior opened the door and grabbed him by the wrist to pull him inside. She slammed the door shut behind him and quickly locked the dead bolt.

"Junior, what's going on?"

"All I know is your friend Marco showed up here a little while ago and scared the crap out of me. He's convinced Barrett is trying to kill him."

"What? Where is he?"

She motioned with her thumb toward the hall closet and rolled her eyes. Greg went over and opened the door. Marco was hiding behind a row of jackets on hangars. He exhaled loudly with relief when he saw Greg's face.

"Dude, are you alone?"

"Why did you come here? I don't want Chris or Junior involved in any of this."

"I didn't have a choice. Barrett knows I broke into his place. I don't know how he knows, but he knows. I saw a couple of his trucks outside the motel." Marco gave Junior an obvious sideways glance. "You know, after we split up earlier"

"I know, I just came from the motel. They tore the place up pretty good. And they took all those boxes you had in the bathroom."

"You two better stop the cloak and dagger act if you're gonna use my house as some kind of hide out."

The two of them traded looks and silently agreed that they had to let her in on the secret. Greg conveniently began the story from after he woke up that afternoon.

"I went to the motel to make sure Marco knew about Ricky. We got to talking about the shooting and there were a few things that didn't add up. Long story short, we ended up breaking into Barrett's office."

"What the hell were you thinking? That guy's a lunatic."

"Believe me, I know. it just seems like he might be involved with the shooting. We're just not exactly sure how. Hey Marco, how did you get away from the police anyway?"

"The police? Okay, both of you on the couch. I want to hear the whole story."

Greg did most of the talking and carefully left out any information that either might upset her or potentially incriminate her later on. Junior listened carefully. She didn't say another word until after Marco explained how he had gotten away.

"So Greg went around the back and escaped through the reservoir. I went out the front and just bolted past the cop cars. One of them nearly hit me, so I just kept running. A fat cop started yelling and chasing after me, and then threw in the towel after a couple hundred yards. Once I got some distance I started going bush-to-bush, and complex-to-complex. I thought for sure they would call the helicopters in, but they never showed up."

"So then Barrett somehow finds out it's you and sends his goons to come find you?"

"Seems like it. I honestly didn't stick around once I saw those trucks. This seemed like the safest place to hide out and get a hold of Greg, so here we are."

Greg let the info settle in before he spoke again. He was working hard to control the anger that was rising up inside of him like a geyser about to blow.

"Do you at least have the folder?"

"Not with me. It's totally safe where I stashed it. I'll get it for you tomorrow."

"Okay, good. Say goodbye to Junior."

"What?" She seemed more confused than when he arrived. "Where are you going?"

"I'm not sure. I already told you that I don't want you or Chris involved in any of this."

"It's really late and I don't think Barrett will come looking for you here. Where did you park?"

"Down the street a little ways."

"Good. I think you two should just stay here tonight, I'm too freaked out to be alone now. We'll have to come up with some kind of plan in the morning. Marco, you can sleep on the couch. Greg, into my bedroom."

"Greg Salem always gets the girl."

"Shut up, Marco. And good night."

"Good night, Junior. If you guys get up early, please be quiet." Marco fell back on the couch with a satisfied grin on his face. "I like to sleep in."

"You're getting up when Chris gets up, probably around seven. And then you're playing video games with him until he gets bored."

"Whatever, dude…"

Greg's tired eyes locked with hers the moment they were alone in the bedroom. A small smile was forming at the corners of his mouth as she flipped the bathroom lights off and shuffled to the bed. His right hand was tucked underneath his head and four tattooed stars were bulging on his bicep. He patted her side of the bed with his free hand, moving it just in time for her to lie down on her side facing him.

"I'm sorry you got dragged into this."

"I wasn't exactly stoked to get a surprise visit from Marco, but I'm glad you guys are all right."

"He's not a bad guy."

"Maybe not right now, but if you let him hang around long enough something will go wrong. Guaranteed."

He wanted to reach out and touch her face, and knew that he couldn't. That he shouldn't. There were so many things that had gone so wrong between them for so many years. Somewhere in the back of his mind he knew there was a world where the two of them ended up together, just not in this world.

His self-restraint felt comforting in the most frustrating way possible.

"What are you thinking?"

"Nothing."

She reached out and stroked his cheek with the palm of her hand. He closed his eyes and smiled.

"I'm worried about you, Greg."

"Don't be. I can handle Barrett."

"I'm not just worried about Barrett, I'm worried about all of it. About the kid you shot, and about Ricky and my dad's bar and this whole mess. I know you love Ricky, I really do, but part of me thinks that you have to let go of solving his murder and just be sad that he's gone."

He opened his eyes. Their faces were inches apart.

"You know I can't do that, right?"

"I know. I just don't want to lose you, too."

"I've always been around. And I'm always gonna be around–"

She stopped him with a kiss. It was light at first, her soft lips parted and hungry for a response. Her hand slid up behind his ear. He moved his body forward so that they were pressed against each other. His hand found her hip and he traced the curve of her thigh with the tips of his fingers. She let out a soft groan as he kissed along her jaw and down the length of her neck. He felt the palms of her hands on his chest, squeezing gently at first before pushing him back a few inches.

"No sex." She whispered it under her breath. It was unconvincing, but he lifted his hands and rolled onto his back. "Not like this, not after so long."

She swung her hand and brought a pillow down on her face with a smack. Her frustrated laughter was muffled as she rocked her head back and forth underneath it.

"Junior, it's okay. If it's meant to happen, it doesn't have to happen right now. And if it isn't meant to happen, well…that will have to be okay, too."

Her face was bright red when she flung the pillow off the end of the bed. He could see the deliberation in her eyes. Sex is easy compared to everything that it's supposed to mean. She brought her leg up and slid it across his thighs, lifting herself up until she was straddling him. His belt came off with a loud, leathery slap. He helped her out of her tank top and sat up to kiss her.

"It hasn't been all right, Greg. I've wanted this for too long."

CHAPTER FOURTEEN

"Greg. Wake up. You're having a bad dream."

His eyes shot open. He was crouched on a pillow with his back against a cold wall. A fan was blowing a cool breeze across his naked body. Junior was on her knees in front of him, gently shaking him by the shoulders.

"He had a gun."

"Who had a gun, Greg? Barrett?"

"The kid with…" The room snapped into focus. "Never mind. It's just a nightmare."

"A nightmare about the shooting?"

"Yes and no. Something's not right."

He brought his forehead down on his knees and tried to collect his thoughts. What if there hadn't been a gun? Had he over-reacted? Let the adrenaline from the chase get the best of him?

"I'm going to make some coffee. Unless you want me to stay."

"It's okay. Coffee sounds good. But come right back, okay?"

She flashed a small smile and slid off the end of the bed. He studied her curves as she stood up and got dressed. She slipped out of the room and pulled the door closed quietly behind her. Chris and Marco were probably both still asleep, so there might be a chance to continue where they left off the night before.

He let his right leg drop to the floor and pushed himself up with his arms. A soft light was peeking through the blinds as he made his way to the bathroom. The toilet seat hit the tank a with crack as he flipped it up. He remembered to wash his hands before he turned to make his way back to the bed. Junior was standing there with a folded piece of paper in her hand.

"Marco's gone. Your name was on this note." She held it out for him. "He must have left right after we got into bed last night."

Greg thought he saw her blush as he grabbed the note from her hand. Marco had remarkably neat handwriting for an addict.

G–

Had to bail. Too much shit going on right now. I checked in at the motel and Barrett's already been there looking for me. I'm heading over there to see if I can figure out how to get my stash back. I won't stick around longer than I need to. I'll find you at Junior's later on, after I get a few things figured out. Good hanging out with you again, even if you almost got me arrested. And killed.

Later, M

P.S.—You still owe me a TV.

"God damn it."

"What's that idiot up to now?"

"Nothing you want to know about. I'll probably have to track him down today before he gets himself killed."

She snorted and shook her head.

"Greg Salem to the rescue. You haven't changed a bit since high school."

Greg knew what she meant, but she was wrong. A lot had happened since they were kids. Things that had changed him forever.

"I'm the reason he's involved in any of this."

"He was Ricky's friend, too."

"Right, but he wouldn't have gone looking for the killer on his own. That's the difference between the two of us. He's a junkie, I'm a cop."

He was lost in thought when she pushed him backwards onto the bed.

"Well, right now Chris is still asleep so we've got a little time to kill…"

CHRIS WAS SITTING CROSS-LEGGED on the floor in front of the TV playing a video game when Greg finally emerged from the bedroom. The boy greeted him with a nod as he passed through the living room. Greg tried to make sense of the action on the screen as he passed. It looked like some kind of first-person shooter game. The coffee in the kitchen smelled too good to be ignored so he kept moving.

The mugs were hiding in plain sight, dangling on hooks from under the cupboard. It took Greg several minutes to locate them. He had been here a million times, but couldn't remember ever making coffee. He guessed correctly that the creamer was on the rack on the inside of the refrigerator door, and missed the mark on the sugar. He poured two cups and stirred in the ingredients until it was the color of wet sand.

Greg took it slow going back through the living room. He didn't want to spill coffee on Chris when he walked by.

"Can you make me breakfast?"

Greg stopped in his tracks. The coffee sloshed around and almost spilled over the lips of the mugs. Chris still had his eyes fixed on the screen before him.

"Um, okay. What do you want?"

"Cereal."

Still no eye contact.

"Let me put this coffee down in the bed—in the other room—and I'll make you breakfast in a second. Cool?"

Greg handed Junior a mug and set his down on the nightstand. She took a sip and watched him heading back to the kitchen.

"Forget something?"

"Chris wants cereal."

"It's in the cupboard next to the fridge."

Greg scratched his head and shuffled back through the living room. The TV was still on, but Chris was gone. He found the boy seated at the dinette digging into a bowl of cereal. The box and carton of milk were standing at the ready on the table next to the boy's pumping elbow.

"Couldn't wait?"

"Uh uh."

Milk was dribbling down his chin as he shoveled multicolored pebbles into his mouth. His round cheeks were scrunching up and down as his jaw fought to keep up with the endless stream of food. Greg grabbed a bowl from the cupboard and took a seat next to him. Chris didn't flinch as Greg made himself a matching bowl and immediately got to work.

Chris got up without another word and dropped his bowl and spoon in the sink. The video game came back to life with a barrage of gunfire in the living room. Greg rinsed both bowls and went to join his breakfast companion.

"Wanna play?"

"It's a little early for a gunfight. You got baseball?"

The boy bent forward and pressed a few buttons on the gaming console. The screen flickered as he took one disc out and inserted another from a nearby pile. He handed Greg a second controller without looking up.

"Homerun derby?"

"Sounds good."

Long before hardcore music, Greg and Ricky had bonded over baseball. If they weren't hanging around the little league diamond, they were playing tape ball out in the street. Or trading baseball cards during recess at elementary school. They even went to the batting cages a couple times as adults. Greg couldn't imagine that he would ever go again now that Ricky was gone.

Junior came into the living room eventually and set Greg's coffee mug on the floor beside him. She sat on the couch and watched the two of them hitting homerun after homerun. It was Chris who finally put his paddle down to signal that he was ready to move on.

"What are we doing today?"

"You're hanging out with grandpa. I'm running errands with Greg."

Greg turned to look at her, but she just returned his stare. Chris started whining.

"You said you would take me to the beach."

Junior's tone was something Greg had never heard her use before.

"Not up for discussion. Now go get dressed."

Greg felt the need to jump in, although he couldn't explain why.

"You and I can go surfing together this weekend. Sunday morning."

"Seriously? Awesome."

Chris shuffled off to his bedroom. Greg waited until he was gone before speaking again.

"You can't come with me today."

"You sure as hell aren't going alone. Besides, I can handle myself."

He knew she was right, but he didn't care. Whatever was going on was bigger than some bar fight at a punk show.

"Ain't happening."

"You've brought this bullshit into my house. Am I supposed to just sit around here and wait for Barrett to show up?"

Greg had no choice. He had to bring her along.

"Fine. But you're staying in the car."

"Stop pretending like your opinion matters."

Greg fumed as she went to take a shower. Truth was an extra pair of eyes might come in handy, especially now that Marco had split on him.

With time to kill, Greg went outside to make the call he'd been avoiding.

"Chief, it's Greg."

"Great to hear your voice. How's your vacation going?"

"So-so. Any word on the gun?"

"Jesus. Get to the point, why don't you?"

"Sorry. I'm just a little on edge."

"We're working on it around the clock, so stop worrying. Is that why you called?"

"What about the kid?"

"He's in stable condition."

The long silence that followed was painful. Greg wanted to tell the Chief he'd relapsed, but the words got stuck in his throat. He probably never would have enrolled in the Police Academy, or gotten sober, if it weren't for the man on the line.

"That's all. Just checking in."

"You'll be the first to know when we find something. Listen, I have a few things to finish up here. Why don't I come out there later this week and we can grab a cup of coffee."

He could hear the hesitation in the Chief's voice and it made him feel better. He knew the old man hated the beach.

"Sounds good."

Greg hung up just as Eddie's car pulled into the driveway. The old man climbed out and shuffled over to where he was standing.

"Hey, Greg. Surprised to see you here so early, but glad I've got you alone for a minute."

Greg could still smell last night's whisky on Eddie's breath. He wished it didn't make him want a cocktail so bad, but it did. Eddie gave him a slap on the shoulder and made his pitch.

"Listen, there's something I need to talk to you about. I heard from Mikey again today. He made a pretty serious offer for the property. Really serious."

"The bar?"

"All of it, Greg. The whole kit and caboodle."

"Jesus, Eddie. That's gotta be worth millions."

"Said he's willing to make it worth my while if I move fast. I don't know how much longer I can hold out. It seems too good to be true, but part of me thinks that maybe now is the time to cash in and just get out. Take it easy for a few years and enjoy Chris before he turns into an asshole teenager. Unless..."

"Unless what?"

Eddie seemed to reconsider. Greg knew he wouldn't be getting the answer to his question any time soon.

"I'm gonna meet with him in the next couple of days at his office. I was hoping you'd come with me. I could use some outside perspective, and I don't dare mention it to Junior."

"You know I'll be there, Eddie. Just name the time."

The two men headed inside together. Junior was dressed and ready, but Chris had started another video game. He wanted them to wait until he completed the level he was on. Greg and Junior took that as the cue to leave.

They said their goodbyes and went out to Junior's car. She tossed the keys to Greg and got into the passenger seat.

"Where are we headed?"

"If I know Barrett, he'll probably be up at the tidal pools. They surf there pretty much every morning before work. Best break in The Bay Cities."

Greg backed out of the driveway and practically let the car steer itself to the beach. It was a warm day and they could see three-foot waves breaking on the shore between the buildings as they headed east. The tidal pools sat just below a steep cliff face along a couple miles of coastal bluffs that separated South Bay from the urban sprawl further down the coast. There was a small zoo up there when Greg was a kid. These days it was all golf courses and estates.

The tidal pools were hard to spot from the small road that wound along the cliffs. Locals knew to look for parked cars with empty surf racks. A narrow trail led from the side of the road for a thousand yards before opening up to a small, rocky beach. A short walk across the smooth boulders along the base of the cliffs revealed a collection of jagged peaks that split the powerful waves and sent sprays of whitewash up into the air. Twice a day the tide receded leaving small pools of ocean water that became a living museum of starfish, sea slugs and crabs. Further down the beach, where the towering cliffs seemed to loom over the water, was one of the most consistent surf breaks in The Bay Cities. Most days there were more surfers in the water than there were families enjoying the tidal pools.

They pulled up and found a spot close to the trailhead. Greg recognized a few of the cars parked along the curb, including Barrett's huge Suburban. He waited until she got out and crossed the street before reaching over to the glove compartment. His Glock was tucked into the back of his pants when he went over to join her. There was only a small chance that he would need it, but it wasn't a chance he could take with Junior around.

It was a switchback trail, but generations of impatient surfers had carved out shortcuts that made it possible to more-or-less descend in a straight line. It just took sure footing and the kind of energy that neither Greg nor Junior could muster that morning.

Greg helped Junior navigate the ankle-breaking walk across the rocky beach once they reached the bottom. There was no sign of Marco, but he wasn't always easy to spot among the caves and rock formations. They got to the tidal pools just in time to see Barrett catch a wave on his long board. Junior plopped down on a small patch of sand and pulled a flimsy straw hat down over her head. There was nothing to do but stay visible and wait to get noticed.

"Do you think he saw us?"

"Just a matter of time. There isn't much that happens here without Barrett finding out."

"Remember when those idiots used to throw rocks from from up on the cliffs at any surfers they didn't recognize?"

"I saw it with my own eyes. They got out of the water in a hurry after that. And Barrett and his crew were always waiting for them at the top of the trail. Total bloodbath."

"What an asshole."

"Lots of weird stuff has happened up here. Suicides, shark attacks, whatever."

"There's no way all of that stuff is true."

"Did I ever take you into the underwater caves?"

"I am way too claustrophobic. Didn't somebody drown under there?"

"A couple of people, depending on who you talk to. It's pretty sketchy the first couple of times you try it, but it's an incredible rush to be standing under the tidal pools listening to the waves crashing overhead."

"You have to swim under the water to get in?"

"You can wade in at low tide. The problem is getting caught in there when the tide starts rising. If that happens you better be really great at holding your breath or you're screwed."

"Yeah, no thanks."

Barrett came bounding across the tidal pools until he was looming over them. His hair was matted with salt water and there was a grin smeared across his face. Greg told Junior to stay put, but jumped up himself.

"Waves look fun today."

"You got balls showing your face around here. You think I won't kick your ass again just because you brought your girlfriend?"

Greg kept his distance. He was still sore from the last time he got too close to Barrett.

"I'm just looking for Marco."

"That makes two of us. I know that little prick broke into my office."

"And I know you had something to do with what happened to Ricky."

Barrett took a step forward. Three more of his bros walked up and started spreading out. Greg knew it was time to make his point. He might not get another chance.

"I'll make this really simple for you. Keep away from Marco."

Greg motioned for Junior to stand up. Barrett was clearly in the mood to fight.

"Or what?"

Greg brought the gun out from the back of his pants. None of them even flinched.

"Or you'll have to answer to me."

"Haven't you shot enough innocent people lately?"

Greg's finger tightened on the trigger. This wasn't the first time he'd wanted to kill Barrett, but it was as close as he'd actually gotten to doing it.

"I could ask you the same question."

"Don't start that shit again. I had nothing to do with Ricky getting shot. Ask Officer Bob if you don't believe me. He knows the truth."

"That's funny. I trust him about as much as I trust you."

"Fine. You're the cop, Greg—or at least you were. Prove it."

"Give me a few days."

"You're in way over your head, but do whatever you want. I'm done with you."

Barrett turned around and walked away. Greg kept his gun up until the rest of the crew did the same. He gave Junior a hand as they scrambled across the rocks for the trail.

She was the first to notice that the passenger side windows on her car had been shattered. Two rocks the size of bowling balls were resting on the seats amid a sea of glass pebbles. The words "Locals Only" were scratched into the paint on the side of the car as well. She shot Greg a few disappointed glances as they worked together to sweep the glass out onto the curb.

The sound of the wind whipping through the windows made it hard to speak. Junior was practically yelling at him as they wound their way back to North Bay.

"Where to now?"

"I think we should stop by the motel and see if Marco's there. If not, we can look at a couple of places around there."

"Didn't his note say he'd come looking for you at my place?"

"Yeah. Why?"

"Nothing. It's just, my dad's gonna have Chris the rest of the day. We'd have the place to ourselves…"

"Jesus, Junior. You have a one track mind."

"Sorry. I guess guns turn me on."

THEY COULDN'T FIND MARCO at any of his usual hangouts that afternoon, and he wasn't anywhere on the beach. Greg knew addicts had a knack for disappearing when they needed to, but Marco was like a junkie chameleon. They were down on the boardwalk scanning the beach for any sign of him when a voice called out.

"Are you stalking me?"

Greg just ignored her. People say stupid things to cops all the time, trying to get a rise out of them. Experience taught him that it was better just to leave it alone. But Junior had no police training. She walked straight over to where the bikini-clad stranger was sunbathing.

"Do we know you?"

The woman stood up, revealing a lean body that was white as milk. She stepped forward and pulled down her sunglasses to study Junior's face.

"Edie? Is that you?"

Margaret Keane was already reacquainting herself with Junior when Greg joined the reunion. Junior couldn't believe her eyes.

"Wow. Maggie. It's been years."

"I go by Margaret now. What a nice surprise to see you together after all this time."

Maggie gave Greg a sideways glance that Junior picked up on right away. Greg shuffled his feet and tried to change the subject.

"We were just looking for a friend. Do you remember Marco?"

"Of course I do. I had a little crush on him back in the day. What's he up to?"

Junior answered for him.

"Nothing good. That's kind of why we need to find him."

"I honestly don't think I would recognize him."

"You would know if you had seen him. He's kind of hard to miss. Is this your place?"

Maggie spun and gave the beachfront mansion the once over.

"I wish. No, I'm just staying with a...friend."

She leered at Greg, biting her lip this time. He grabbed Junior by the arm and tried to hurry things along.

"Great seeing you, but we have to get going."

"Leaving so soon?"

Greg and Junior waved in unison and walked away. They were almost out of earshot when Maggie called out.

"Edie. I meant to tell you that I ran into your ex at an investor's lunch. Seems like he's done pretty well for himself. Can't believe you let that one go."

"You should ask him out some time. I bet you two would have a lot in common."

Maggie flashed a frozen smile as Junior muttered 'bitch' under her breath. They were back at her car when Greg thought it was safe to ask the obvious question.

"What was that all about?"

"Don't you read the papers? Maggie—sorry, *Margaret*—was involved in some embezzlement scandal last year. I'm surprised she's not in prison."

Junior was finally ready to call it a day after their encounter with Maggie. He thought about just walking back to his place from the beach, but wanted to make sure the coast was clear back at her house. So he drove her home and searched every inch of the house before letting her inside. Then one thing led to another and soon Marco was the furthest thing from their minds.

Greg got home a little after nine that night. He was exhausted and needed to clear his mind. Between Junior and Marco he barely had time to think about everything else that had gone sideways in his life. The kid in the blue hat filled Greg's thoughts the minute he settled into bed.

Two pillows were wedged under his head and The Surfaris was playing quietly on the stereo. He turned the lights down to darken the corners of the room. There was a rapid knocking on the door just as he was dozing off.

Greg slammed the *CoreNoMore* magazine down and got up to throttle Marco. A large fist connected with the bridge of his nose as he pulled the door open. His knees went weak and he fell to the ground face first. They shoved him back inside and shut the door. Somebody jumped on his back and slipped a plastic garbage bag over his head, twisting the flaps around his neck.

He struggled to get out from under his assailant. The extra energy he expended quickly ate up his oxygen. His face was sticking to the inside of the bag as the sound in the room gave way to a pulsating rhythm inside his head. It sounded like a helicopter approaching. *Whuh whuh whuh whuh.* "Get him into the trunk" was the last thing he heard before everything went black.

CHAPTER FIFTEEN

Virgil Heights. Even with the blindfold on, Greg recognized the permanent smell of boiling meat wafting from the nearby food-processing plants. His head was throbbing as he struggled to steer his mind through the fog. He could feel a thin layer of sweat coating his whole body and running in streams from his temples. It seemed they must be inside one of the warehouses, but which one? He knew them all like the back of his hand. If he could only get a peek under the blindfold. He lifted his head painfully and heard somebody whistle nearby. There was a scuffle and some chains rattled behind him. The chair that he was tied to jerked upward so that he was swinging in the air.

"Somebody get me a stick for this *piñata*."

There was a chorus of riotous laughter. It sounded to Greg like there were ten or more men in the room with him. He could hear the links of the chain grinding against the wooden beam above him as he swung back and forth.

"Actually, I changed my mind. I want him back on the ground. *Odele!*"

His feet swung forward as the chain went slack. The back of the chair almost crushed his arms when he crashed into the ground. He was lucky that he managed to shift his weight at the last moment so that his left shoulder and bicep took the brunt of the fall. The rickety wooden chair splintered on impact and left him in a heap on the warm concrete floor.

Somebody stepped forward and yanked the sweaty blindfold from his face. The diffused light coming through the yellow windows made it hard to adjust his eyes. A circle of young men slowly came into focus all around him, a rainbow coalition of thugs. All of them were standing at attention with their chests out and their chins up. The disembodied voice was behind him now.

"Nice of you to drop in."

Nobody laughed this time, except Greg. His sarcastic chuckling eventually gave way to a series of painful coughs. He could taste the tang of blood in his mouth. The rope that kept his arms tied behind his back was digging into his wrists. It was impossible to do a complete survey of all the damage that had been done to his body.

"Is somebody gonna tell me what I'm doing here?"

"You fucked up, pig." The voice was rotating to Greg's left, taking his time coming into view. "You shot the wrong kid."

There was nothing he could say in response. He let his cheek drop to the floor and closed his eyes. Images of Chris unexpectedly flashed in his mind.

"What's up, boss? Pleading the fifth?"

"He had a gun."

"'He had a gun.' You hear that fellas?" The voice was right beside him now. "Does anybody here have a gun?"

Feet shuffled in unison. It was followed by the unmistakable sound of ten people racking the slides on their semi-automatic handguns in unison. Endless hours on the shooting range had permanently etched that sound into Greg's brain.

"*Those* were guns. Did you hear anything like that in the alley that night? I don't think so, because nobody found a gun on that kid you shot." Greg felt the tip of a sneaker tapping on his forehead. "You still with us, pig?"

He opened his eyes to see a short, wiry figure looming over him. Greg's eyes followed the khaki pants up to a loose fitting white t-shirt. His face was a deep caramel color and a thin black mustache lined his upper lip. He looked like one of the neighborhood kids that used to hang around the police station back when Greg was a rookie. A kid named Manny. Greg wasn't totally sure it was him, but he seemed about the right age.

"I was asking you about the gun." He dropped to his knees and brought his face down in front of Greg's. Manny was all grown up and doing a passable impersonation of a gangster. "I think you might have your story mixed up."

"Fine. He didn't have a gun. Is that what you want to hear?"

"That is definitely what I want to hear, but not here." He sprung up and started to walk away. "Somebody untie him."

One of the men slid a knife between Greg's wrists. It took a few tugs, but the binds finally came free. Greg flexed his fingers to get the circulation going and then rolled onto his stomach. He pushed himself up slowly until he was squatting. Searing pain was shooting across the left side of his body from the fall. He took a couple of deep breaths through his nose and let the air out through gritted teeth.

The circle of men had gotten a little wider. Manny was standing inside with him now, just a few feet away. He pulled a handgun from the back of his pants and offered it to Greg.

"I'm not sure that will do me much good. It seems like I'm a little outnumbered."

"Take the gun. It ain't loaded anyways."

Greg brought his right arm up slowly and took the 9mm. It felt light without the clip.

"Hold it up like you were holding your gun that day."

There was no point in resisting, so Greg did as he was told.

"*Perfecto.* Let's pretend that I'm that kid you shot. It shouldn't be hard since everybody always said we looked the same."

Manny lifted his arms up, palms down, and started to slowly spin in place. He made two complete turns and then stopped facing Greg again.

"Did you see a gun?"

"No."

"Exactly. So when you go to testify, that's exactly what I want you to tell the judge."

"Got it. But I think we can skip all the theatrics—"

Manny took two steps forward and brought an effortless roundhouse kick across his face. Greg staggered to his left and dropped the gun that went clattering across the floor. He managed to stay on his feet but his eyes felt like they were bouncing around in their sockets. Somebody pushed him back into the center of the circle from behind.

"You're not in charge here, pig."

"Fine. Let's do it your way. 'There was no gun, your honor.'"

"Good. Just keep saying that until it's automatic. Now, let's talk about my brother."

Greg searched his mind. He couldn't remember ever meeting Manny's younger brother.

"I didn't know he was your brother. I didn't know anything about him at all."

Greg was trying to keep the pleading out of his voice. It was getting harder as Manny circled him. He wasn't sure how much more punishment he could take.

"I was just responding to a call, doing my job."

"I know, pig. I actually feel for you. Cops are like a necessary evil where I come from."

"You mean Virgil Heights?"

"What do you know about that. So you do remember me?"

There were a million things Greg wanted to say in response. The thought of another kick to the head helped him keep his mouth shut.

"You know, it was only a matter of time before that little shit got himself shot. I'm just glad it was a cop and not another *homie.* Those dudes shoot to kill."

"I'll tell the judge whatever you want. It won't matter because the woman he attacked will testify about the gun. There's nothing I can do about that."

"Last I checked nobody found a gun, so it will be your word against hers."

More chuckling from the peanut gallery. The truth was slowly starting to dawn on Greg.

"You guys got to the gun before the police arrived. You were in the crowd that night..."

"Maybe we were, maybe we weren't."

"Well your brother will still do time for the sexual assault and robbery."

"Sexual assault? Shit, I bet that bitch loved every minute of it. But that don't matter, he was just following orders."

"What kind of animal would order a kid to rape an old lady?"

"'Old lady'? Dude, you should get a mirror. I bet you two are the same age."

It was Manny's turn to laugh.

"We were just sending a message to her stupid son."

"Well, I hope it was worth it."

"My brother didn't plan on getting shot by a cop, but you know what? I think prison will be good for him. He'll have protection in there and when he gets out in a couple of years he'll be ready to join the family business, *for reals.* Just like his big brother."

Greg's time on the force had taught him that prison could be like college for wannabe gangsters. They go in young and weak, and come out angry and strong. Or they don't come out at all.

"It sounds like we have an understanding. Ain't that right, pig?"

Greg gave a tight-lipped nod.

"Good, but don't fuck with me. If you do anything stupid I'll take my anger out on your girlfriend and her kid. Could be fun. It seems like you're into big girls just as much as I am."

Greg's head snapped up at the mention of Junior and Chris.

"Just like you did with Ricky?"

"You mean that mess at the bar? I got nothing to say about that."

A forearm slid around Greg's throat before he could respond. Several men swooped in and spun him in the direction of the loading dock doors. The green Impala was waiting with the trunk propped open like the gaping mouth of a leviathan. He swung his head to the side to get his bearings. All he could see was an empty parking lot before they pulled a blindfold over his eyes. The trunk lid slammed shut and the engine roared to life.

Greg was unconscious for the ride in, but he had a feeling it was no Sunday drive. He pulled the blindfold off as the driver took the first corner at full speed. He got lucky that his hands were free this time, it meant he could brace himself. Greg kicked the inside of the trunk for effect. He was pretty sure that the foursome in the car would be disappointed if they didn't think they were banging him up on the road home—if that's where they were going.

They continued careening between the empty factories for longer than it should have taken to reach the freeway ramp. Probably having too much fun playing their vehicular cat and mouse game with Greg, which was fine by him. He knew that every minute they spent in town was another chance for VHPD to pull the car over and save him. He waited for the wail of a siren. The only sound was the guttural rev and grind of the engine.

Their driving was getting more erratic. Greg imagined a bottle being passed around inside the cab. It was hard for him to hear them talking over the constant rumbling in the trunk, but he could make out a loud laughter every couple of blocks. His arms and legs were starting to cramp from trying to hold his body in place through all the swerving.

And then the car took a wide, squealing turn that caused the tires to stutter across the pavement. Greg was momentarily weightless, like a diver on his way back to the surface. He felt the back of the car pull into a slide that sent them spinning. It seemed to last forever. The ride came to an abrupt stop when the driver's side slammed into a brick wall.

The spinning had slowed the car down, but the impact sent him pinballing around the inside of the trunk. The passenger side wheels lifted up into the air simultaneously and then came down to the curb with a creaking crash. A hissing sound was coming from the front of the car and filled the silence. He heard the four men inside the Impala pile out the passenger side doors. Their footsteps echoed off the walls as they took off running down the in the empty midnight streets of Virgil Heights.

The sound of approaching sirens brought a smile to Greg's face, even of they were a little behind schedule. He lay there in the darkness praying that they found him before the car went up in flames. The police cruiser had barely come to a stop before he started yelling and kicking.

"Officer down inside of the trunk!"

There was no immediate response. He knew that the officers standing outside of the car had their guns drawn and were taking stock of the situation.

"Officer down!"

"You. In the car. This is officer Coleridge with the Virgil Heights Police Department. Identify yourself."

"Goddammit, Mark. It's Greg Salem. Open the fucking lid before I suffocate!"

THE POLICE CHIEF WAS already waiting at the station when they pulled up. He greeted Greg at the door wearing sweat pants and a windbreaker. It looked like he had been woken from a very deep sleep.

"Jesus. You're a mess. Do we need to get you to a hospital?"

"Just get me some ice and a couple dozen Ibuprofen."

He threw his arm around the nearest officer's neck and they walked a few yards into the tiny station. Greg took a seat on a small sofa in the Police Chief's office. It was painful to lower himself into a reclining position, but he couldn't bear the thought of staying upright. The second officer came in a few minutes later and helped Greg choke down a couple of pills with a glass of tap water. Greg brought his head back down on the arm of the sofa. The Police Chief dropped a sandwich bag full of ice on his forehead once he was settled.

"You mind telling me how you ended up in the trunk of a totaled car?"

"It's a long, very painful story."

"I'm guessing it had something to do with that friend of yours who got gunned down last week. I'm really sorry about that. Just doesn't seem fair."

"It hasn't really sunk in yet, but that's not how I ended up here. I got shanghaied from my apartment in South Bay by a bunch of gangsters."

"From Virgil Heights? How did they find you?"

"Not sure. I should have known something was up when that green Impala trailed me home from here last week."

"God damn it. When were you planning to tell me about that?"

Greg didn't have a good answer so he didn't say anything.

"Fine, let's concentrate on tonight. Was one of them a Filipino with a stoner mustache?"

"Yep. His name is Manny."

"Did he tell you that?"

"No, but he used to hang around here sometimes. He would have been ten or eleven years old back then. Do you remember him?"

"Hell no. But my memory's for shit these days."

"It seems like he's a little pissed off that I shot his kid brother."

"I was really hoping they wouldn't find you. There's no way of knowing what he'll do if his brother gets locked up."

"Well, if it makes you feel any better, he doesn't seem all that worried about the prison time. He was a lot more wound up about the gun."

"Makes sense. They're going to hold the preliminary hearing Tuesday morning."

"When were you planning to let me know?"

"Tomorrow. If we can't prove he was armed, 'assault with a deadly weapon' goes right out the window. He'll do two years max if he pleads on the lesser felonies."

"He had a gun, Chief."

"Only if we can find it. We both know that's pretty unlikely at this point."

"I wouldn't have shot him if he wasn't armed."

"Do you want to stay here at the station tonight? We've got a few empty cells."

"Thanks, but I really want to go home and sleep in my bed. Can one of your new guys give me a lift?"

Greg slept the entire ride home. The VHPD cruiser dropped him off outside of his apartment shortly before dawn. The officer offered to help Greg get inside, but he declined.

"Thanks for the ride. I think I've got it from here."

He climbed out and strained to straighten out his back. The officer gave him a concerned look as he pushed the car door shut and turned to walk through the back gate. His apartment was unlocked and the lights were still on when he got inside. He gulped four more Ibuprofen down and drank a glass of water before easing himself onto the bed. The cold sheets felt good against his sore muscles and bruised bones. Sleep came easy despite the pain.

CHAPTER SIXTEEN

Greg's sheets were soaked through with sweat and every joint in his body felt locked up. It took him the better part of thirty minutes to make his way to the bathroom. His body felt racked and his stomach was growling. He only had enough energy to make a bowl of instant oatmeal that he devoured.

The food hit his shrunken stomach like a brick that left him feeling nauseous. Another handful of Ibuprofen seemed like the only solution to his mounting problems. He started a pot of coffee and nursed a glass of orange juice while it brewed. The mixture of medicine and sugar, combined with the smell of coffee, gave him the energy he needed to find his phone.

There were too many text messages to count, most of them from Junior. She had also left a few phone messages, along with his Police Chief and a couple of Virgil Heights finest. He deleted almost all of them without reading or listening to them. There was also a message from Ricky's mom. He decided to save that one until he was in a better frame of mind. The last one was from Eddie earlier that morning.

"Mikey called and wants to meet this afternoon around four thirty. I would really appreciate it if you could join us. Give me a call when you get this message."

The thought of seeing Mikey on a good day was almost too much to handle. In his current condition it seemed almost unimaginable. But Greg knew he had to go to the meeting, even if Eddie wouldn't take his advice in the long run.

He tapped the Call Back button and told Eddie he would meet him around four o'clock. Mikey's office was only a few blocks away from the L Bar. He guessed he could get some more information out of Eddie on the walk over.

His next call was to Junior. He hoped he might get away with leaving a message since she was probably still at work. She picked up on the first ring.

"Where the hell have you been?"

"In bed."

"Hm. Anybody I know?"

"Just me, myself and I. How's it going?"

"Well, the funeral's tomorrow. Did Ricky's mom call you? She wants you to say a few words. I mean, if you're up for it."

"Jesus, I didn't even think about that."

"What, the funeral?"

"No. That people might expect me to get up and say something."

"Well, you were—I mean, you *are* his best friend. But I'm sure everybody would understand if it was too much for you to handle right now. You kinda have a lot going on."

"Would you consider standing up there with me?" The words were as much of a surprise to him as they were to her. "I mean, in case it's too hard."

Her response sounded a little too quick to both of them.

"I don't think so. I mean, I'll have Chris with me so I should probably stay nearby. He's never been to a funeral before, you know?"

"I get it. I'll figure something out. There are a ton of good memories to share."

He heard her catch her breath on the other end of the line. It was probably best to get off the phone before they both broke down. There would be plenty of time to cry tomorrow.

"I should probably jump. I've got a meeting in a couple of hours."

"What's the meeting about?"

Greg knew she was making small talk, but decided to dodge the question anyway.

"I'll try to call you later on if that's cool."

"I hope you do."

He hung up and swiped the screen to reveal his unheard messages. He let his thumb hover over the message from Ricky's mom, but couldn't get himself to hit play. It was going to take a little soul searching to find the right words about his best friend. The shower seemed like the best place to start collecting his thoughts.

The cracked windshield on the El Camino seemed brand new every time Greg saw it. He had planned to squeeze in a visit to the motel to grab Barrett's file folder on the way to Eddie's, but getting dressed turned out to be a real chore. It took a full fifteen minutes just to get an accurate inventory of all the scrapes, cuts and bruises that now covered his entire body.

Traffic was mercifully light so he still managed to arrive at the L Bar a few minutes early. He could see Eddie sitting on a stool and chatting with a couple of the regulars. Part of him expected to see Ricky come bounding out of the front door toward him. He closed his eyes tight and tried to indulge in the memory, but it was already slipping away. Just like it had with his brother. Like he hoped it eventually would with the kid in the blue hat.

He stepped inside and made his way over to the bar.

"Greg, I'm glad you made it."

“Wouldn’t miss it.”

“Let me grab my jacket out of the back. You know Roger and Bill, right?”

The three of them shook hands while Eddie scuttled off. Roger went back to sipping his beer. Bill kept his eyes on Greg.

“Sorry about your friend. It’s a real shame to lose somebody so young.”

“Thanks. I think I’ll go see what’s taking Eddie so long.”

Greg walked the length of the bar, back to where the room took a hard right. The door to the storeroom was right in front of him and he could see the entire stage. It was the last place that Ricky would ever play guitar. Right there, at the back of Eddie’s, where both of them had played so many times over the years. He couldn’t imagine ever playing on that stage again.

Eddie came out of the back and stood beside Greg for a moment.

“Are you sure you’re up for this? I know that you and Mikey have a colorful history.”

“Don’t worry about me, Eddie. You were his father-in-law. If you can see past his relationship with Junior, then I can see past everything else.”

They both turned and headed out the side door. Neither of them spoke again until they were half way to Mikey’s sleek office building along the backside of the reservoir.

“Are you seriously considering selling?”

“I’m not getting any younger. Mikey might be an asshole, but he’s also the highest bidder.”

“There just aren’t many places like the L Bar left in The Bay Cities. It’s an institution.”

“It’s nice to know that somebody else cares about it as much as I do.”

Eddie slowed down and gave Greg a searching look.

"Eddie, please. If you have something to say, just spit it out."

"You know you're like a son to me, right?" Greg nodded, keeping his mouth shut tight. "Would you ever consider taking over the bar? You know, maybe running it with Junior after I'm gone."

They came up to the front doors of the gleaming glass office building just as Eddie finished asking the question. There was a soft buzzing sound followed by a click as they were granted access to the lobby. Greg gave Eddie a surprised look that was met with a sheepish smile.

The receptionist greeted them from inside her circular desk in the lobby and offered them cappuccinos while they waited. Both men declined and took a seat on the stiff leather couches near the small indoor Koi pond. Mikey came bounding down the swooping industrial staircase to collect them a few minutes later. He led them up to a massive office with floor to ceiling views of the reservoir.

"I'm glad you could make it, Eddie, but you didn't need to bring security. Did Cheryl offer you two drinks?"

"We're good, thanks. Greg and I are considering a business arrangement so he needs to be here. I have to get back to the bar before too long, so let's just get down to business?"

"No foreplay. I like that. But before we move on, I have to ask—don't you ever get tired of spending every waking moment at that little bar?"

Greg shifted in his seat and Mikey made a show of covering his tracks.

"Don't get me wrong. I have a ton of respect for anybody who can build a business with their own two hands, but it must be exhausting to keep it running year after year. I'm not sure our generation has the same work ethic. Am I right, Greg?"

"I wouldn't know."

"Yeah. I guess you gave your dreams up pretty young, didn't you? You look like shit, by the way. Rough night?"

Mikey's tone was playful. He seemed pleased to be getting under Greg's skin. Eddie grabbed Greg's wrist just as he went to get out of his chair. Mikey flashed a cocky smile and turned his attention back to the older man.

"So, have you considered my offer? I doubt you'll get anything nearly as generous."

"I have considered it, but I have a few questions."

"Shoot."

"I mostly want to know what you plan to do with all the property if I do decide to sell."

Mikey swiveled his chair slowly from side to side, his eyes raised to the ceiling in thought. Greg could hear his former manager doing deep breathing exercises to keep himself calm. He turned to make eye contact with Eddie and noticed beads of sweat starting to form on the old man's forehead. His chest was rising and falling roughly and his knee was pumping like a piston in front of him. Greg was just about to ask Eddie if he was doing okay when Mikey chimed in.

"I've known you for a long time, Eddie. It hasn't always been an easy relationship, what with Junior and the boy—my son. But we're going to have to keep this a business conversation if we hope to get anything accomplished. In that spirit, I'm just going to be as straight with you as I can. When you sell me this property, at a price that I'll remind you is way above market value, what happens to it will be between me and my business partner."

"Which is who?" Eddie wasn't going to let up on his line of questioning, and it was clearly starting to wear on Mikey. "I deserve to know."

"None of your business."

"What if I make it a condition of the deal that the bar and salon have to remain in business with a guaranteed twenty year lease for my family and me?"

"Then we won't have a deal."

"You're bluffing. I know you're desperate or you wouldn't be throwing money around like you are."

Greg was trying to let Eddie take the lead, but he couldn't stop himself from speaking up.

"He isn't bluffing, Eddie. He doesn't have a decent bone in his body. Not for the L Bar or anything else in The Bay Cities. He told me so that night outside of Junior's house."

Mikey gave an uncomfortable smile when Greg finished talking.

"He's right about one thing. This is purely a business transaction for me. And the offer I gave you is final. Take it or leave it."

"Come on, Eddie. Let's get out of here." Greg's voice remained even, but his fingers were digging into the ends of the armrests on his chair. "This deal isn't worth your time."

"Isn't this interesting? You're getting pulled in both directions by your former son-in-law, and by the son-in-law you always wished you had."

Eddie was a little wobbly standing up.

"I need a second to clear my head. Where's the bathroom?"

Mikey nodded toward the office door and pointed left with his thumb. Eddie eventually managed to shuffle across the polished wooden floor and out into the hall. Mikey sprang from his chair and turned to stand in front of the window overlooking the reservoir. Greg stayed put in his chair and enjoyed the scene that was running through his head, the one where he leaps across the desk and snaps Mikey's neck.

It was Mikey's voice that brought him out of his reverie.

"It's not true, you know. What you said a minute ago."

He was still facing the window with his hands in his pants pockets. Greg thought his posture was unnaturally perfect, like somebody who was a little too militaristic about his yoga.

"What's that?"

"About me not caring what happens to The Bay Cities. I think you've got me all wrong. I might have outgrown my love of punk rock and wasting time on the beach, but nothing matters to me more than what happens to this town."

He glanced over his shoulder to see if Greg was paying attention before he went on.

"I know for a fact that I'm not the only developer that has approached Eddie about selling, but I do know that I'm the only local developer."

"What difference does that make? You said it yourself, this is strictly business."

"It makes all the difference in the world. Most of these guys represent corporations looking to turn a buck without any concern for what happens after they're long gone. They don't work here, or live here, or have kids in school here. Like I do."

Greg watched as a flock of birds flew into view from the left and swooped down low over the reservoir. Their silhouetted wings danced across the marbled blue and white sky like musical notes. Mikey gave a little sigh.

"Do you remember when we were kids and dared each other to swim across the reservoir?"

"Of course. All those stories about sharks scared the crap out of me."

"Chris is about the age we would have been when we tried to make that swim."

"I don't think you have anything to worry about, he does just fine in the water."

"It isn't that, it's just…I don't know what I'll tell him when he asks if I ever swam across the reservoir, because I never did. I chickened out, because of a shark that didn't exist."

"I doubt it will matter to him very much. I'm not even sure if kids around here care about the reservoir anymore. I barely ever see them outside."

"It matters to me. I want him to be proud of his father."

"Seems like you're pretty successful, from the looks of things. That's something he can probably be proud of."

Greg motioned around the spacious office. Mikey kept his eyes on the water.

"That's the problem. I spent so much time focusing on building my business that I pretty much ignored the most important thing in my life."

"He isn't that old. You still have time, if it really is important to you."

"You're probably right, but kids grow up really fast these days. That's why this development project is so important. I want to close one big deal—one massive deal—so that I can just retire and focus on what matters. That's why I need your help."

"My help? Get real."

"I know it sounds ridiculous coming from me."

Mikey turned to face Greg just as his receptionist came racing through the office door. Panic was written all over her face.

"Come quick! Your other guest, the older man, he collapsed in the bathroom. It seems like he can't breathe."

Greg kicked his chair out from under him and sent it skidding back across the floor. He was through the bathroom door moments later with Mikey just behind him. Eddie's face was red. He was clutching at his chest and gasping for air. Greg was down on the floor beside him and trying to dial 911 on his cell phone.

EDDIE SEEMED TO RELAX a little once the paramedics arrived. They did a couple of field tests on him and assured Greg that it wasn't a heart attack. The snap diagnosis seemed to be that he had some kind of heart spasm that was brought on by stress. He definitely wasn't out of the woods yet, but it was a good sign that he was alert and talking. Greg was about to climb into to the back of the ambulance to ride along to the hospital when Eddie raised his hand.

"Greg, I need you to do me a favor. Can you go back to the bar and let them know what happened? I was supposed to cover for Randy until eight tonight."

"I'll take care of it. And I'll have Junior meet you at the hospital. Just take it easy."

"Think about what I said."

The paramedics pushed Eddie and the gurney into the back of the ambulance. The old man waved and tried to brave a smile as the doors closed. Greg took out his cell phone and started to text Junior. He changed his mind and dialed her number instead.

"How was your secret meeting?"

"Good as could be expected. Listen, are you at work right now?"

"Just finishing up. Why?"

"You're dad is going to be fine. That's the first thing. But he's on his way to the emergency room in an ambulance right now."

"What?"

"He's fine, Junior. He was talking and smiling when they carted him off. They just need to do some tests. I think you should go be with him."

"Oh my god! Okay, okay. I'm going."

"Wait! What about Chris?"

"What? Oh, he's at a sleepover tonight."

"Okay. Good. Do you need me to lock up the salon?"

"That would be great. I'll leave the key with the bartender."

Greg slid the phone into the back pocket of his jeans and then headed upstairs to look for Mikey. He felt the need to finish their conversation, despite their history. There was a part of him that was intrigued by what Mikey had to say, even if his bullshit meter was going off during their little swim down memory lane. He found the office empty when he reached the top of the stairs. The last rays of sunlight danced across the surface of the reservoir while he waited. He tried to imagine a shark fin breaking the glassy water, but was too old to conjure childhood monsters.

"There you are."

Greg spun around to find Mikey standing in the doorway with a small grin on his face. He looked like he was standing in the spotlight as the afternoon sun came through the window. He motioned for Greg to take a seat as he swung around the desk and dropped heavily into his own chair.

"I have the exact opposite view from my living room. It's almost a perfect mirror image."

"What, over there on the other side of the reservoir? There aren't many locals who can afford one of those houses."

"I thought it would be a nice place for my son to grow up, but I won't bore you with all of that. What did the paramedics say about Eddie?"

"They don't seem to think it was anything serious. Just severe stress."

Greg locked eyes with Mikey as he delivered the diagnosis. Mikey brought his hand up across his brow and shook his head quickly from side to side.

"You know I wouldn't want anything bad to happen to him, right?"

"It sure would make things easier for you, having him out of the way."

"Easier how? You think it would be 'easier' dealing with my ex-wife?"

There was a growing edge to his voice that Greg would recognize anywhere. It was a cross between breathless sarcasm and nervousness that Mikey seemed to originate from somewhere deep in his throat. Greg had heard that voice countless times back when Mikey was still in charge of his music career, and it almost always signaled the beginning of an argument. This time Mikey seemed to fight back the bile just as quickly as it rose up inside of him.

"Impressive. How much yoga did it take to get that under control?"

Mikey pulled a sealed bottle of water out from under his desk. He twisted the cap and drank down half the contents before speaking again.

"I guess it's hard to hide your emotions from somebody who has known you for so long."

"Look, Mikey. I have to get back to the L Bar. Why don't you just finish what you were trying to ask me earlier?"

"Okay…I guess I'm just asking for your support. I know Eddie and Edie trust you. It would mean a lot to me if you try to remind them every once in a while that I'm not such a bad guy. If you won't do it for me, do it for Chris."

"Nobody would think you were such a bad guy if you didn't go out of your way to prove it all the time."

Greg stood up and placed his palms on the edge of the desk. Mikey was biting his lower lip and nodding in response to Greg's last comment, waiting for whatever came next.

"For what it's worth, I never really fell for your tough guy routine. So show me that you really want to be part of your son's life again and I will do what I can to help you. Deal?"

"Deal."

CHAPTER SEVENTEEN

Greg waved to the receptionist and mouthed a "thank you" as he passed through the lobby. His thoughts turned to Eddie's offer as he walked. Would working in a bar all day put him in constant danger of drinking again, or make him immune? The whole idea was absurd, but there was something appealing about running his own business.

He couldn't imagine going back to work with VHPD after everything that had happened, but he wasn't cut out for construction. And working side by side with Junior everyday seemed perfect somehow. As if he could live the kind of life his brother had lost so young.

Happy hour was in full swing when Greg walked into Eddie's. He made his way through a small crowd of well-dressed professionals and stepped behind the bar. Randy the bartender was moving faster than Greg had ever seen him move before, popping bottle tops and mixing drinks in a dewy silver shaker. Greg grabbed an apron and started clearing empty bottles and glasses from the bar so that Randy had more room to work. It was few minutes before they got caught up enough on drink orders so that they could talk.

"Where's Eddie?"

"At the hospital. He's going to be all right. He sent me over to help you out."

"Shit. I have to be at my kid's school for a parent teacher deal tonight. My wife is gonna kill me."

"I got you covered. Let me go lock up the salon and then I'll come back over. Where's Junior's key?"

The bartender pointed to the register and went back to taking orders. Greg opened the drawer and pulled out a simple ring with a single key on it. He tried to squeeze behind Randy, but the taller man stopped him.

"Do you even know how to mix drinks?"

"Not really, but I can wing it."

Greg wound through the crowd and out into the parking lot. The door of the salon was locked, but the lights were on. He let himself in and got to work dropping combs into jars of blue liquid and sweeping hair off the floor. The place was in pretty good shape before he turned his attention to the drawer where Junior kept her cash box.

He knew the combination to the dial lock was 3-2-1. Inside he found a stack of twenties that he counted off and paper clipped in a couple one hundred dollars stacks. He ran the daily report on the credit card terminal by following handwritten instructions that were taped to the wall next to the machine. The print out went into the cash box last. He closed the lid and set the dials to 6-6-6.

Greg couldn't shake the feeling that he was inside of his brother's record shop, closing up for the day. The sensation was so familiar that he didn't want to ruin it by confronting the reality. He deposited the cash box in a small floor safe in Junior's office, the same one that had always been there, and flipped the lights off. He was back inside of Eddie's thirty minutes later. There were handwritten notes all along the bar that said: "Beer Only."

"Thanks, Randy. That should make things easier."

"Domestics are three dollars. Imports are four dollars. You can do shots for four bucks too, if somebody really needs a snort.

There's a white line on the shot glass, but go ahead and fill it to the top. It's good for tips."

"I think I can manage that."

"I'll be back before eight."

"Take your time. Looks like it's already dying down."

Randy had obviously taken a lot of orders before he left because the first fifteen minutes flew by. Then, as the bottles started to empty and the crowd got drunk, Greg found himself buried in a twenty-minute rush. It took him a couple of tries to figure out how the different beer brands were stacked in the various reach-in coolers. And he was instantly thankful for the customers who were running a tab, because it kept him from having to work the register too often.

He was surprised to see the tips piling up on the bar considering how bad we was at this. There is a way to casually sweep the cash out of sight, but Greg didn't know how. So he started grabbing it in his fists and dropping it to the sticky ground.

The ground was littered with bills when he looked up and saw Quincy standing there.

"Moonlighting?"

She gave a nervous laugh and pursed her red lips.

"Just helping Eddie out. Get you a drink?"

He motioned to the bar with both hands. She eyed one of the handwritten signs and wrinkled her nose.

"No wine?"

"I think I can handle that. I'm just not great with mixed drinks. Red or white?"

"Chardonnay would be great."

He spun around to pour the wine into one of the stemmed glasses. The golden liquid nearly reached the lip of the bowl before he stopped. It made it difficult to get the drink to Quincy without spilling. Barrett was standing behind her with a hand on her shoulder. Her voice climbed an octave as she tried to diffuse the situation.

"You two know each other?"

"Sup, Greg?"

"Barrett."

The two men locked eyes for a long moment. Barrett broke the silence first.

"Where's your gun, tough guy?"

"Close enough if I need it. Drink?"

Barrett placed his order and Greg went to fetch it. Quincy was standing a few feet away at a tall table when he returned. He could see that she was preoccupied with her phone when he set the bottle down on the bar. Barrett pulled a giant wad of cash out of his pocket and started flipping through the twenties.

"What do I owe you?"

"I'll get this round. You kids have fun."

Barrett ignored him, throwing forty dollars onto the bar. One of the bills landed on its side, standing up. Barrett swelled with pride, as if he had done it on purpose.

"Make sure you tell Marco that I'm still looking for him."

"I'll keep it in mind."

Barrett laughed and took his bottle over to where Quincy was standing. He put his hand on her hip and gave her a peck on the nape of the neck. He was watching Greg from the corner of his eye the whole time, like some giant demented parrot.

Quincy smiled but seemed to recoil a little at the public display of affection. Greg winked and went down the bar to take a few orders. He'd finally hit his stride by the time Randy came back to take over.

"Dude. There's money all over the floor."

"Wasn't that there when I started?"

Greg considered sticking around just to make things uncomfortable for Barrett, but he couldn't risk another fight. His body was still bruised and beaten from his joy ride the night before.

He also wanted to check in with Junior, in case she needed him at the hospital. He was leaning on the El Camino texting with her a few minutes later. She told him that Eddie had been admitted. He was dehydrated and they needed to run some tests to check his arteries. Otherwise everything was fine. He got in the car and headed up the boulevard to the motel. Marco wouldn't be surprised that Barrett was after him, but he would probably appreciate the heads up.

The windows in Marco's room were dark when Greg pulled into the parking lot. He left the car running and climbed out to knock. Nobody answered, so he slipped a note under the door before heading home. He could hear Mrs. McMillan chatting with somebody in the garden as he opened the back gate.

"And there he is now." Mrs. McMillan was seated at a small table, facing the gate. The second woman had her back to him. "You have a guest, Gregory."

Quincy spun in her chair and batted her eyes theatrically. Mrs. McMillan quietly excused herself and slipped back inside her house. Greg opened his door and invited Quincy inside.

"This is a surprise. I thought you already had plans tonight."

"Well, I did. Then I met this really hot bartender."

There was only one chair in the small apartment and it was covered with a pile of Greg's clothes. He went to clear it off for her. She plopped down on the bed instead.

"You can join me up here. Don't be shy."

She patted the mattress beside her. Greg walked over to accept her offer.

"I wasn't expecting any company tonight. How did you get out of Barrett's clutches?"

"He's been asking me out for months and I finally gave in. Oh my god, you're jealous!"

"What is there to be jealous of? Date whatever brain dead gorilla you want."

"Well, I'm still flattered—even if you don't return my phone calls. Maybe you're the relationship type after all."

She brought her hand up and placed it on his thigh. Her head was resting on his shoulder. He could smell the Chardonnay on her breath as she exhaled.

"I'm just not sure if I'm up for a late night with the funeral tomorrow."

The words were jumbled as he forced them from his mouth. She slid her hand up his thigh and under his shirt.

"It doesn't have to last all night. Why don't you just relax? You look so tired these days."

She said, "Tired," but Greg heard "old." He couldn't disagree either way.

"I'm really sorry. I'm just not up for it tonight."

He stood up and headed for the refrigerator. She fell back on the bed and focused her gaze on the whirling ceiling fan. He returned holding two glasses of water, handing one to her.

"First funeral?"

The question caught Greg off guard. He realized in that moment that there was still so much they didn't know about each other. How old was she? Where did she grow up? Why did she move to the Bay Cities? The truth was that they had spent very little time talking since they first met a couple of months before.

Greg was getting out of the water with his board when she jogged by and tripped on his leash. And now here they were, chit-chatting with each other on the night before they buried his best friend. He should be working on his speech, but he didn't want her to go. Not yet.

"Definitely not my first."

He was still in diapers when his mother died, so he didn't remember anything about her service. His dad's funeral was one of the best parties that Greg had ever been to. Just a room full of men telling stories until the sun came up.

And Tim.

Tim's funeral felt like heart surgery without all the scalpels and saws. Like somebody reached straight down his throat and squished his heart in their fist. His chest still hurt whenever he thought about it, almost twenty years later.

"How about you? Been to many funerals?"

He was half fishing to figure out her age. No time like the present.

"I've seen my share of people go into the ground."

"I'm really sorry to hear that."

"They say it gets easier with time, but that really isn't true. For a while it was all I could think about. Now I feel guilty if a day goes by and I haven't thought about him."

"I know what you mean. I lost my dad, too."

"It was actually my brother."

A silence fell between them. Greg tried to think of something to say, but felt powerless to change the course of the night. It didn't take long before his thoughts turned back to the funeral and his unwritten speech. Ricky was gone and now everything was so complicated with Junior. A night with Quincy would be a relief, but would only keep him from what he had to do.

She tried to change the subject, but they both knew it was too late.

"Why don't we talk about something a little more cheerful?"

"I think I should get my thoughts together for tomorrow."

CHAPTER EIGHTEEN

"Hey, everybody. Glad you could all be here today, despite the circumstances. I know Ricky would be pretty stoked that he managed to sell out his last gig."

Greg was choosing his words carefully. It was impossible to speak above a whisper without dry heaving. The microphone squealed a little when somebody brought the volume up.

"Ricky's mom asked me to say a few words today, but before I do that I want to say 'thank you' to her. Thank you for introducing me to Ricky on the first day of second grade. And thank you for making the most amazing snacks for all our Little League games. And thank you for asking me to come up here and speak today. I wouldn't have done it on my own. I'll never forget your son, and I promise that you will never be alone in missing him every single day."

Greg welcomed the silent response. He knew that he was on the edge of a complete breakdown. He couldn't even look up from his notes to make eye contact with any of the two hundred people in The Bay Cities Community Center.

"I wrote down a few thoughts and I'm gonna try to read those to you now. You'll have to excuse me if I can't make it all the way through."

He swallowed and took a deep breath.

"I met Ricky in elementary school. I remember his mom pushing him toward me during lunch. His family had just moved to town and it was his first day. His eyes were bugging out of his head and he looked like he was ready to bolt. His mom made him introduce himself. I'm not sure why they chose me, but I remember that he had this awesome bowl cut and he was wearing a Puka shell necklace with a lightning bolt hanging from it. So I gave him half of my package of peanut butter crackers and that was pretty much it."

"We started skateboarding together in sixth grade, after I got the cast off of my arm. I remember he had this plastic yellow board that his mom got him at a garage sale. He used to get gnarly speed wobbles whenever we tried to bomb a hill. I got tired of picking him up every time he wiped out so I stole one of my brother's decks and made him a new board. After that we were unstoppable, going on adventures all around the neighborhood.

"We started getting in a little trouble around that time, too. There are some secrets from those days that we both promised we would take to our grave. I'm the only one who knows those secrets now."

"Ricky was the first one to introduce me to a skateboard ramp. He knew some older kids that had built one in their backyard and he convinced them to let us ride it. I might have been better at bombing hills, but Ricky totally mastered that ramp in one summer. I've never seen anybody fly that high and land the board so often. I know that a lot of you here today know what I'm talking about because you were there, too. Skateboarding was the thing that he was most stoked about all during junior high. I really hope that's what he's doing right now."

Greg reached for a bottle of water Junior had left on the podium for him. He could see her sitting a few rows back with tears streaming down her cheeks. Chris was right beside her with a blank expression on his face.

"It was all about music by the time we got into high school. I bet half the people here today played in one band or another with

Ricky over the years. And the other half of you were probably in the crowd at a few of those gigs. It didn't matter to him whether he was playing in a backyard or on tour at a random club in Germany; Ricky was always high energy when it came to playing his guitar for a crowd. I am proud and honored that I got to share the stage with him for his last show. And I know he's already setting up the gear for our reunion on the other side."

Greg stopped and studied the room for a few moments. All of these people were here today because they loved Ricky. Not because he was a good skateboarder or great punk rock guitarist. Those were things he did, not who he was. These people were here because Ricky was one of them, because he lived like them and he loved them—loved The Bay Cities—with all of his heart. Greg folded his notes and let them drop to the floor.

"I wrote down a few more things to say, but all these stories I'm telling you about Ricky, they're just my memories. Just some of the experiences I shared with a really great guy over the many years that I was lucky enough to know him. I have some pretty ugly stories about Ricky too, but this didn't seem like the place to share those kinds of memories. I just think it's important to remember that above anything else, Ricky was probably one of the most human people I have ever known. He was terribly flawed in so many ways, but you always knew where you stood with Ricky. Come hell or high water, I can't imagine I will ever meet another person who I could trust so completely. I'm not sure there is any better compliment than that when it comes to describing your best friend."

Greg heard a loud shuffling of chairs and looked up to see Junior hurrying down the aisle. She had one hand over her face and was sobbing convulsively as Chris chased after her. Greg followed her silhouette as she flung open the front doors and got swallowed up by the sunlight. An usher closed the doors behind her and all eyes returned to the podium.

"I, uh, I'm sure you all have your own stories to share and I honestly hope I get to hear all of them at the reception. Because that's what this is really supposed to be about, a celebration of Ricky's life. He died too young and I'm pissed off about that. He would have been the best man at my wedding. We should have taught our kids how to surf together. And we could have grown old together.

"None of that is going to happen. But look around. Any one of us would be lucky to have this many people love us so much. We probably already do. We just don't always realize it."

THE RECEPTION TOOK PLACE at Ricky's mom's house. It was a simple two-bedroom bungalow that skirted the line between North Bay and South Bay. The house itself was small, but the property it sat on was long and narrow. There was ample room for a local caterer to set up tables across the lawn that stretched from the back door to the back fence. Eddie had a couple of his guys from the L Bar set up a table to serve drinks. Junior made sure that there was a small PA system and a couple of amplifiers in case anybody wanted to play some of Ricky's music.

Greg gave Ricky's mom a big hug when he came through the door. Junior and Chris were already seated at a table with Eddie near the makeshift bar. Greg pulled up a chair next to Junior and put his arm around her shoulder.

"You all right?"

"Better now. That was a really beautiful, what you said up there. I'm sorry I made a scene in the middle of it."

"You don't have anything to be sorry about. Funerals suck."

"I'll drink to that." Eddie lifted his glass and polished off a few fingers of Scotch in one gulp. "No parent should ever have to bury their child."

"You should probably take it easy, Eddie. You just got out of the hospital this morning."

"At my age it doesn't matter what the tests say, the diagnosis is always the same. Did you know this is my third funeral this year? Three people I've known for forty years or more."

"That's terrible, Dad. I'm so sorry."

"Happens to the best of us. One minute you're singing and dancing with your friends, and the next minute—POOF!" He stood up and steadied himself on the edge of the table. "Anybody else need a drink?"

Junior held up her empty wine glass. Chris just stirred his soda with a straw. Greg waited for Eddie to get out of earshot before he turned to Junior.

"What's gotten into him?"

"I'm not sure. Why don't you tell me?"

"I'm sworn to secrecy."

"Well, whatever that meeting was about yesterday it's got him in a really weird mood. He asked me if I wanted to take over running the bar on the ride over here from the funeral."

"And?"

"I can't run a bar and the salon, and try to raise a kid on my own. Did he ask you too?"

"Let's talk about this later. I'm going to grab a bite to eat and then there are a few people here that I want to talk to."

Greg stood up and made his way to the buffet table. He took a plate from the top of the stack and grabbed some silverware from a basket. The caterer had prepared a selection of Ricky's favorite dishes including fish tacos, bacon wrapped scallops, and mac and cheese. Greg took some of each and ate standing near the back fence so he could watch the crowd. He knew that Barrett wouldn't dare show his face, but there were plenty of others who might have information to share. He spotted a couple of Ricky's employees smoking cigarettes by the garage and decided to start there.

Even showered and dressed in clean clothes, the trio of beach rats gave off a distinctly blue-collar vibe. One had blonde hair that was slicked back, dark roots making a thick black line across the top of his forehead. The second one was wearing a short-sleeved plaid button-down with a black concert T-shirt poking up underneath. The third had a cigarette tucked comfortably behind one ear while holding a lit one between his fingers. All three were wearing pressed work pants and suede tennis shoes. They greeted him with a series of quick nods as he approached.

"Glad you guys could make it."

"It's a real bummer about Ricky. Pretty cool to hear those stories you told about him."

"Thanks. That was probably one of the hardest things I ever had to do."

"I would have freaked out, bro."

"Did you see Ricky's mom on the way in?"

"Yeah. That was pretty harsh. She started crying the minute she saw us."

"Do you know her very well?"

"You kidding, she was like our team mom." He gestured to his two friends who silently nodded in agreement. "We pretty much completely rebuilt this place last summer. She used to cook us dinner and shit every night."

"I knew Ricky was doing some work around here. I just didn't know how much."

"Pretty much went all the way down to the studs. We even put in a new roof."

"That must have been expensive. Where did Ricky get the money for that?"

The three men exchanged glances. Two of them took long, time-killing drags off of their cigarettes. Greg's relaxed posture and grin made it clear that he would wait patiently for an answer.

"Come on, guys. There's no way his mom could afford it."

"Ricky kept a lot of the left over materials from other jobs. Mostly odds and ends. We made it work."

"Last I checked he didn't have a yard. Where was he keeping all this stuff?"

"He stashed most of it in the garage right here." He pointed over his shoulder with his thumb. "And, well, pretty much anywhere he could get free storage. There's probably still some stuff over at his rehearsal space. That was kind of his office."

"Do you know if he had a computer at the rehearsal space?"

The foreman stood up straight and gave his pals a slap on the shoulder to get their attention. Their eyes were focused on a point just behind Greg. He spun around to see what was so interesting. Officer Bob was standing a few feet away with a drink in his hand. He was wearing khaki pants and a light blue dress shirt. The three guys from Ricky's crew said their goodbyes and then quickly excused themselves to the buffet.

"Beautiful speech, Mr. Salem. I didn't know you had such a gift for public speaking."

"There're probably a lot of things you don't know about me."

"That might be true. I do know you've been sticking your nose where it doesn't belong."

"What makes you say that?"

"I had an interesting talk with Mr. Barrett. Were you aware that he had a break in over at his office a few days ago?"

"Barrett might have mentioned it last time I saw him."

"You mean at the beach?"

"Hard to say. I've been kind of busy."

"His security company notified us that a silent alarm had been tripped, so a couple of my officers responded. When they arrived they saw a shirtless man running from the yard. Apparently he looked an awful lot like your friend Marco."

"There's lots of guys in North Bay who look like Marco."

"There was also a second suspect who escaped out the back of the property." Officer Bob turned so that they were standing side by side facing the reception. "Mr. Barrett came out and did a survey of the office. He was reluctant to allow a thorough investigation of the premises."

"Well then, case closed I guess. Listen, I would love to stand here and chat about this fascinating police work, but in case you hadn't noticed there's a funeral going on."

"You're right, Mr. Salem. I guess I'll let you go—for now."

Officer Bob took a few slow steps backwards before he started mingling with the other guests. Greg was walking back to where Junior and her family were seated when a strange sound came from inside of the garage. He listened for a second, convinced that it was just his mind playing tricks on him. Then he heard it again. It sounded like a cross between a whistle and a hiss. He went over to the side door and took a tentative peek inside. Marco was standing there, leaning against a stack of plywood sheets that went half way up to the ceiling.

Greg made sure the coast was clear and slipped inside. The room was almost totally dark once he closed the door. Marco lit a cigarette and almost tripped over his own shoes.

"I just got done talking to Officer Bob about you out there."

"I heard him, and he doesn't have shit on me. Besides, you know I never miss a party."

Marco reached up on top of the stack of plywood and produced a half empty bottle of whisky. The smell of it hit Greg like a ton of bricks. Marco tilted the bottle up and took a long drink. Greg kept his eyes on him, his thoughts alternating between disgust and envy. Marco offered the bottle to him through the gloom, but Greg waved him off.

"You go ahead."

"Back on the wagon, bro?" He laughed and took another chug. "Guess you're gonna have to start all over again at those meetings of yours."

"We'll see. Either way, you need to get out of here."

"Yeah, yeah, yeah. I'll leave when I'm ready. I wanted to let you know that I did some checking around. Ricky wasn't exactly an angel."

"What'd you find out?"

"For starters, half the shit in this garage was stolen from Barrett's job sites."

"That's not a good enough reason for Barrett to hire somebody to kill him."

"No, but there could be another reason in here." Marco produced the folder they had taken from Barrett's office. Greg grabbed it out of his hands and tucked it into the back of his pants, under his dress shirt. "And I found a couple of other things out from a few of my friends."

Greg flipped the folder open and scanned the first page.

"I didn't know if you were actually able to hold onto this or not."

"I stashed it between two dryers at the Laundromat near the motel. Pretty rad, right?"

"That was a couple of days ago. Where have you been since then?"

"Laying low. The guys I was doing those deliveries for—you know, those dudes from Mexico? They weren't too thrilled that the whole shipment got snagged from my hotel room."

Just then somebody tried to open the side door to the garage from the outside. Greg pressed his heel against the base. He yelled 'I'll be right out' while urging Marco to hide.

"Greg?"

It was Eddie.

"You in there? Ricky's mom is looking for you. Let me in."

"I'm on the phone. I'll be right out."

The old man grumbled, but backed off. The garage was empty when Greg turned around.

"Marco? Where'd you go?"

His response was an exaggerated whisper.

"You fucking told me to hide. So I'm hiding."

"What did you find out from your friends?"

Greg barely finished the question before Eddie started pounding on the door again. It sounded like he was drunk enough to make a scene. Maybe even attract the attention of Officer Bob.

"Marco. Get out of here before you get arrested. Meet me on the beach first thing tomorrow morning."

He waited in the silence for a few moments and then let himself out. The buffet was looking pretty picked over, but people were still eating. A line extended several guests deep from the bar where Eddie had jumped in to help. Ricky's crew had picked up guitars and were strumming a few chords.

Junior was sitting at the table with Chris and Ricky's mom when Greg arrived. She immediately stood up and threw herself into his arms. He pulled her in tight and stroked her hair while she sobbed into the collar of his shirt.

"What you said today was just so beautiful." She pulled back and wiped her eyes. "Ricky was so lucky to have a friend like you."

"We were all lucky to know him. Is there anything I can do for you?"

"Oh, not tonight. I imagine this will just go on until the booze runs out."

"Okay, well let me know. I can stay as late as you need me, too."

"I'm actually going to need your help over the next couple of days. Somebody has to get all of his things out of that apartment before the first of the month, and you're the only one I trust. I hope it's not too much to ask, I just don't think I could bear to do it myself."

Her words faded into sniffling and tears. Greg waited while she tried to overcome the waves of sadness.

"We don't need to talk about this right now."

"Yes we do. I just want it all behind me." It was getting harder for Greg to understand her through the tears. "I can't imagine waiting, just leaving his stuff sitting there to collect dust."

Her wailing became inconsolable as Greg pulled her into his chest again. Junior came up from behind and placed a shawl across her shuddering shoulders. She motioned to Chris with her eyes before leading Ricky's mom off in the direction of the house. Greg slumped down into the seat next to the boy and took a sip of water.

He was disappointed that it wasn't a beer.

"How're you holding up?"

"Okay, I guess." The boy kept his eyes on the table where he was playing with a small ball of dried candle wax. "He really isn't coming back, is he?"

Greg placed a reassuring hand on Chris's back.

"Doesn't seem like it. This is all pretty confusing, huh?"

"Yeah. It's just, well, Ricky was teaching me how to surf the last few months."

"He was? I didn't know that. I bet he was a pretty awesome teacher."

"The best. I just hope my mom keeps taking me surfing."

"We're still on for dawn patrol this Sunday?"

Chris perked up and they exchanged smiles. Greg stopped short of mussing the boy's hair, but the urge had definitely struck him.

"Did you get a chance to eat anything?"

"A little. I'm still pretty hungry."

"I'll get you a plate before the vultures eat it all."

He stood up and headed back to the buffet. Officer Bob was standing there eating a spoonful of mac and cheese directly from the chafing dish.

"I love the little crusty parts that stick to the pan."

"Knock yourself out."

"What were doing in the garage?"

"Oh, just now? I had to make a phone call."

"Anybody I know?"

"Probably."

Junior and Eddie were both back when Greg returned with the food. He set the plate down in front of Chris and went to squat between the adults. He looked at Eddie first and instantly knew the old man was a lost cause.

"Why don't we call it a night soon and get some rest? Looks like I have to start clearing Ricky's apartment out tomorrow."

"You think we can drop my dad off on the way? He shouldn't be driving."

Greg stood up, grimacing through the pain in his knees and back. He offered Junior his hand and then gave Eddie a pat on the shoulder. Chris didn't need any prompting at all.

Greg would normally just sneak out the back gate, but that was hard to do with four people. At least Ricky's mom was already safely tucked away in her bedroom. It made him feel better about leaving so early.

They hugged and kissed their way to the door. Junior did most of the kissing while Eddie hugged Greg tight to keep himself upright. They poured Eddie into the back seat of Junior's car and Greg got into the driver's seat. It took all three of them to strip the old man's clothes off and put him to bed. He was snoring loudly as they locked the door and closed it tight behind them.

Chris fired up his gaming console the minute they got home. Junior told him he had fifteen minutes to play before bed. He grunted and started obliterating aliens on the TV screen. Greg poured himself a glass of water and took a seat on the couch behind the boy. He noticed an electric guitar leaning in the corner of the living room just as Junior came back in wearing sweats and a loose fitting T-shirt.

She curled up on the other end of the couch and closed her eyes. Chris finally turned the game off an hour later and shuffled off to bed. Greg gave Junior a peck on the cheek and slipped out the kitchen door.

CHAPTER NINETEEN

Greg didn't have a single drop of booze at the reception, but he still felt hung over the next morning. His head throbbed, his mouth was dry and the thought of coffee made his stomach turn. It could have been all the stress from the last few weeks finally catching up with him, or it might have been all that trashy food. He had to get up and meet Marco either way.

Mrs. McMillan was already working away in the garden when he went outside. She was a little too chipper for his current state of mind.

"Good morning. Are we still on for breakfast?"

"I wouldn't miss it."

"Good. Have fun in the water."

He lifted the paddleboard on top of his head and started toward the beach. There was a steady wind blowing as he crossed the sand and dropped his board in the water. The waves were breaking close to shore and there were small whitecaps dotting the seascape. Marco wasn't anywhere to be seen.

Greg looked for him under a boarded up lifeguard stand, and checked the stalls in the public bathroom. He knew that Marco might be crashed out somewhere, sleeping off his bender. Or maybe the previous night never ended and he was still going strong with some of his friends.

The possibilities got darker as Greg went down the list. What if Officer Bob had finally caught up with him? Or the Mexican mafia? He scanned the horizon on the off chance that Marco was already out in the water. A few members of the sober paddleboard group were making their way across the rugged surf at a slow clip. Greg's best option at the moment was to paddle out and ask if they had seen Marco.

He found seven people bobbing up and down on their boards when he caught up. It took him a minute to realize there was an eighth board a little beyond the rest of the group. Somebody was lying down on their back with their arms over their face. Greg recognized the stringy blonde hair immediately and paddled over to say hello.

"Marco?"

The man on the board didn't move, but Greg heard a muffled response.

"I can't move or I'm going to puke again."

"Don't. It'll attract the sharks."

"That might be less painful."

Greg heard members of the group starting to talk. He needed to get Marco out of there before he made a scene.

"Let's paddle back to shore and grab a cup of coffee."

"I'm staying for the meeting."

"Seriously?"

Marco rolled off of his board and submerged himself in the water. He re-emerged seconds later and climbed up onto his board looking a little too much like a wet rat. His emaciated frame was glistening in the morning sunlight as they paddled toward the others. Pete couldn't contain his surprise as they joined the meeting.

"Welcome back, you two. Quite a surprise to see you here together."

"Nobody was more surprised than me."

Greg paddled the last few strokes and then let the board glide to a wobbly stop. Marco was a few yards behind him, huffing and puffing.

"Holy shit dude. I am so out of shape."

Marco curled up on his board with his paddle and moaned quietly under his breath. It was a little painful for the others to watch because they had all been there at one time or another. Pete tried to lighten the mood.

"Anybody have anything they want to get off their chest?"

Nobody expected Marco to start talking.

"I'm almost forty years old and I don't have shit to show for it. I couldn't even go to my friend's funeral yesterday because the cops are after me…again." He pronounced it "uh gain" for emphasis. "And I would have been too wasted even if the cops weren't after me. I've got drug dealers breathing down my neck and, and…I don't know dude. I think I just need to get my shit together. Like for real this time."

Nobody said a word during the pregnant pause that followed. It felt as if he was daring them to doubt him.

"And to top it off I stole this board off the beach this morning."

Even Greg had to laugh at this last line. There was no greater sin on the beach than stealing somebody's board, but Marco's story was just getting worse by the second.

"Yuck it up. But you guys aren't gonna have to fight your way off the sand later on."

"Calm down." An exasperated edge was beginning to undercut Greg's tone. "We'll make sure you get home okay."

"That's another thing. They're closing the motel down. We all got thrown out last night."

"You can crash with me until you figure something out."

Greg knew it wouldn't be easy sharing a studio apartment with an addict who was going cold turkey. He also knew that Marco had nowhere else to go.

"Seriously, bro? That's awesome."

Greg watched a squadron of pelicans gliding effortlessly along the water as Marco finished up. A couple of the others said a few things afterward, but nothing like the complete wipe out that Marco described. The two of them were paddling back to shore together less than an hour later.

Marco managed to get the stolen board back onto the sand without getting noticed. His T-shirt and tattered jeans were still buried where he'd left them. He dug them up and they made a beeline for the boardwalk.

Mrs. McMillan was setting out breakfast plates for two at the garden table when Greg and Marco came through the back gate.

"Oh. I didn't realize we were expecting company. I'll get another setting."

"It's okay. He's just needs to use my computer for a while..."

"I don't want to hear it. You're friend should absolutely join us for breakfast. It's been a while since I've had a threesome."

Greg pushed Marco inside the apartment and told him to get in the shower.

"Dude, what did she just say?"

Once Greg heard the water running he went into his closet and found some old clothes that were too tight. Marco toweled off and eyed the pile suspiciously, but agreed to put them on. They were baggier than Greg thought they would be.

Breakfast was already set up when they went back outside. There was a basket of homemade muffins in the center of the table along with a steaming bowl of scrambled eggs and plate full of bacon. Mrs. McMillan instructed them to take their seats and immediately started serving her ravenous guests. She nibbled at a muffin and waited patiently while the two men shoveled forkfuls of food into their mouths.

"Is this a friend of yours from the paddleboard club?"

"I'm so sorry." Greg set his fork down and forced down a mouth full of food. "This is Marco. He's an old friend of mine. From the neighborhood."

"It's Marco Johnson, correct? You look a lot like your father."

"That's what people tell me. I didn't know him too well. But nice to meet you anyway. This food is fu… Uh, it's really delicious."

"I'm glad you're enjoying it. Please, keep eating. I hate left-overs. How was the funeral yesterday, Gregory?"

"Good as can be expected, I guess. Didn't stay too late."

"I understand Eddie had a little emergency a couple of nights ago."

Greg knew that nothing happened in *The Bay Cities* without old timers like Mrs. McMillan finding out. He still had no idea how she got such accurate information. It made him curious about the things she knew but didn't mention.

"It was just stress. They're doing some tests, but everything seems all right for now. He was the same old Eddie at the funeral yesterday."

"I'm very glad to hear that. I've known him for more than forty years. Sweet man."

"Really? I had no idea."

"Oh, sure. We sold him all his property, back when Jack still had the real estate business. First the bar, and then the other properties nearby a few years later. It would have to be worth a mint these days."

Marco jumped into the conversation without any warning.

"Wow. If he bought that property in the early seventies and held onto it for all this time the capital appreciations alone would be mind blowing."

"I'm sorry, Mr. Johnson. I didn't realize you were in real estate?"

"Oh, I'm not. Not really. I just read The Bay Cities News a lot."

"Sorry, I should've warned you about Marco." Greg shot him a look while attempting to steer the conversation back to the topic at hand. "What's that you were saying about Eddie?"

"There are plenty of things you don't know about me, Gregory. It's what makes me so mysterious."

She lifted her goblet and took a dramatic sip of orange juice. Greg served himself another plate of food.

"He's actually been thinking about selling some of it off. Somebody made an offer that he might not be able to refuse."

"That would be Robert Fitzgerald's son, I assume."

"Right. Mikey. He's a big time real estate developer now."

"His father was one of my husband's closest friends. At least they were back in the seventies. They used to go deep sea fishing all the time. Male bonding, and all of that. It was just an excuse to drink beer and complain about their wives."

"That's funny. Mikey and I used to be pretty close, but I never met his dad."

"He was a polite little boy. Very soft spoken, just like his father. I almost didn't recognize him when he first approached me about selling. He's so well put together now. Very successful from the looks of things."

"We're not really that close any more, but I guess I can see what you mean." Greg was trying to be polite. Was it possible that he was too close to the situation to see the real Mikey? That soft-spoken kid she described might have grown up a little too ambitious, but he was there for Greg when the band fell apart. "He definitely has cash to burn."

"Oh, I know. I sold my last piece of property to him about a year ago. He gave me more than what the appraiser said it was worth, in cash. I'm not sure where he's getting his money from, but I know he has been on something of a buying spree. I can't imagine there's much property left over near the reservoir that he doesn't own at this point."

"That explains why he's giving Eddie the hard sell. I imagine he'll just build around him if he doesn't cave in soon."

"I'm afraid that wouldn't be possible. Not if Jack had anything to say about it."

She pursed her lips and picked at her mostly untouched muffin, savoring the moment. Greg kept his eyes locked on her. Marco's loaded fork was frozen in mid-air somewhere between his plate and his mouth. It felt like an eternity before she finally spoke again.

"My husband was a very smart man, but he had some peculiar ideas about certain things. We held the deeds on most of the land around the reservoir back then. It wasn't really worth all that much because they were just open fields. Beautiful, really. It's hard to imagine now." She let her eyes drift up to the trees for a moment as she reminisced. "So much has changed around here over the years. It's barely the same place it once was."

"Tell me about it. A lot of my friends from around here will never be able to afford a house in their hometown. It's a pretty harsh reality."

"Well, this place might be available soon. I'm thinking about moving up north to be near my grandchildren. They're growing up so fast and they barely know me. It hardly seems fair to deprive them of that pleasure."

"Are you serious?" Greg was trying hard to contain the panic that was welling up inside of him. "I mean, that would be great for you, but a big loss for this town."

"That's sweet of you to say, but my friends are dropping like flies. It's just not the same place it was."

"I would really like to discuss that with you later, when we can chat alone."

He motioned to Marco with his head and gave her a quick wink.

"Of course, dear. Where was I?"

"You were telling us about your husband's real estate strategy."

"Yes, that's right. Real estate wasn't just about money for Jack. He didn't want somebody coming in and building one of those ugly suburban housing developments that were so popular at the time. So he created what he called a 'Checkerboard.'"

"What's that?"

"You know how the squares on a checkerboard alternate so that no two squares next to each other are the same color?"

Greg and Marco nodded in unison. Her point was slowly dawning on both of them.

"That's how Jack sold off the property around the reservoir. It didn't matter to most of the buyers because they were only interested in a single piece of land. It was a different story if anybody wanted more than that. Jack would only sell them parcels that weren't side by side."

"So Eddie's properties are all spread out?"

Mrs. McMillan smiled and nodded. Greg turned to address Marco.

"That means that all the properties Mikey has been swooping up at a premium won't be worth much in the grand scheme of things if Eddie doesn't sell."

Then back to Mrs. McMillan.

"Does Mikey know all of this?"

"I never really discussed it with him. I'm sure he's figured it out by now."

"Well, I hope you can keep this our little secret."

"Don't be silly, Gregory. I haven't spoken to Mr. Fitzgerald since I cashed his check."

Breakfast wound down once the conversation turned from real estate to the weather, and eventually found its way to gardening. Greg did his best to give Mrs. McMillan the impression that he was interested in her choice of fertilizers, but his thoughts turned to the rest of the day.

Marco was polishing off the last slice of bacon when Greg took advantage of a lull in the conversation and stood up. He threw his napkin down on the table and thanked Mrs. McMillan for the delicious breakfast.

"You are welcome. Where are you two off to now?"

"We promised Ricky's mom that we would clean out his apartment today."

Greg started the sentence with his eyes on Mrs. McMillan. He finished staring at Marco.

"Wait, what?"

CHAPTER TWENTY

Apartment number eight was always hot and dark. It was situated in the bottom half of a two story building, all the way in the back. That meant that it got very little sunlight during the day, but still managed to absorb all the heat from the units around it. The only bright spot for Greg and Marco was that it was located conveniently close to the driveway and carports. Greg backed his El Camino under Ricky's bedroom window and they both went inside to investigate.

Everything was pretty much just as Greg remembered it. The living room was sparsely furnished, with anything of value—TV, stereo system, gaming console—propped up on plastic milk crates near the door. There was a small, lopsided futon against the opposite wall that served as a sofa. A square black guitar amplifier was face down on the carpet in front of the futon with a bong and a couple of empty beer bottles on top of it.

A twenty-gallon fish tank was propped up on cinder blocks under the window. A modified desk lap provided harsh light that shined down on a medium-sized iguana. The large lizard was basking in the warmth on a slab of granite, head cocked and one eye sizing up the two intruders.

"Marco, meet Godzilla. Godzilla, Marco."

"Sup Godzilla?"

"That thing always creeped me out."

Marco went into the adjoining kitchen to see if there was anything to feed Ricky's pet. The cupboards were mostly empty expect for a stack of red plastic cups and a few mismatched plates. There were frostbitten blocks of fishing bait in the freezer and a collection of sketchy to-go boxes scattered around the refrigerator. The shelves on the inside of the door were lined with bottles of light beer. He came back with a few wilted pieces of lettuce that he found in the crisper and dropped them into the aquarium. The iguana and Marco were engaged in some kind of intense staring contest as Greg went to investigate the rest of the apartment.

There was nothing out of the ordinary in the bathroom so he headed for the bedroom. A brand new king sized bed took up almost every inch of floor space. A large flat screen TV was mounted on the wall across from the pillows. Greg knew that Ricky was always happiest when he was sleeping, but he had no idea how he had managed to squeeze the box spring into the tiny room. More importantly, he didn't have a clue how he and Marco would manage to get it out.

He was formulating a plan when he slid the closet door open. The clothes on hangars were packed tight from one end of the closet to the other. The shelf up above was filled with folded T-shirts and pants. Tucked into the corner on one end of the closet he saw a two-drawer steel filing cabinet.

"Marco, get in here."

Marco came into the bedroom with the iguana resting on his forearm. It was nibbling on the piece of lettuce in his other hand.

"Are you the iguana whisperer or something?"

"It's either the iguana or I pound all those beers in the fridge. What'd you find?"

Greg pulled open the top drawer. It was filled with glossy photos of every shapes and size. He reached in, grabbed a stack and started shuffling through them. There didn't seem to be any rhyme or reason to how they were sorted. Pictures of Ricky from elementary school were mixed in with shots from a recent club tour his band had done in Europe. In between there were photos of Greg and Ricky together on a surfing trip to Mexico during high school, prom photos featuring awkward poses with long forgotten girlfriends, and a short series featuring Ricky's long-dead pet dog. He even found a couple of wrinkled black and whites of Ricky's mom and dad on their wedding day.

Greg was tempted to sit down and go through all of the photos right then, but knew it would take up most of the morning. It was probably best just to have Marco start loading them into a box that they could deliver to Ricky's mom. He knew it was important for her to have the photos, even if she would never have the strength to go through them.

The bottom drawer seemed stuck, as though it was caught on something inside. Greg managed to get it open about an inch and then slide his other hand in to rearrange the contents. The drawer came sliding open on his next tug. He removed a couple of small cardboard boxes from the top of the pile and found stacks of shrink wrapped CDs underneath. Ricky had saved a pristine copy of every record that he or Greg had ever played on, including European and Japanese versions. It was like a tiny punk rock shrine and it almost took Greg's breath away.

"Marco. Put your friend down and load all this stuff into boxes. Put the pictures in one box and the CDs in another box. Then use one of the black markers we brought to label them."

"I know how to move, dude."

Greg wandered back into the living room. One of Ricky's guitars was leaning in the corner. He grabbed it and took a seat on the futon. He was picking out a simple pattern when Marco came back in holding a stack of file folders.

"Mother load!"

"Where did you find that?"

"In the same drawer as the CDs. It looks like he kept records of all his jobs."

Greg grabbed the stack from his partner's hands and started leafing through the papers. Marco took a seat beside him on the futon and scanned the documents over his shoulder. Greg closed the top folder and gave Marco an exasperated look.

"Those boxes aren't going to pack themselves."

Sometimes keeping an addict busy during the first days of recovery was the only way to work off the nervous energy. Greg knew his friend had some tough days ahead.

An hour flew by while Greg searched through Ricky's business records. Marco spent his time sliding Ricky's belongings out the bedroom window and into the bed of the El Camino. The place was almost empty when Greg went to find Marco. He was curled up on the stripped mattress rubbing the iguana's belly.

"Break time?"

"There's only heavy shit left. I need help."

"Why didn't you say something?"

"You need to get your ears checked, bro. Find anything interesting in those files?"

"Nothing yet, but I'm only half way through. There is one sheet of paper that has a bunch of addresses written in Ricky's handwriting. Everything else is just invoices and receipts. Come on, let's knock this out and get whatever we're keeping over to the rehearsal space."

Marco groaned. He rose to his feet and took Godzilla back to the aquarium in the living room. The dumpster near the carports was brimming by the time they pulled away from the empty apartment a couple of hours later.

Greg could feel the El Camino's shocks groaning under the weight as they headed for Ricky's rehearsal space. Marco kept his eyes fixed on the aquarium in his lap.

THEY MADE IT TO Ricky's rehearsal space in a few minutes. Marco complained about his sore back the entire ride over. Greg was too busy dealing with his phone to give his friend's whining too much thought. A disturbing string of text messages was coming across at regular intervals; each of them was sent from a different number that Greg didn't recognize.

The first one was just an exterior shot of Junior's house. It took a moment for him to recognize himself coming out her front door in the picture. It had obviously been taken from the window of a parked car.

His phone buzzed again about two minutes later. This time it was a picture of Greg and Junior sitting on the rocks at the tidal pools. She had her head tilted back in laughter and he was smiling at her.

Greg tried to call Junior, but got no answer. He left a message and hoped she would get back to him right away.

They arrived and he started pacing around the parking lot like a caged tiger. Marco was chasing after him asking what was wrong. Greg was too freaked out to respond. Instead he tossed Marco the keys that Ricky's mom had given him and told him to unload the El Camino. Marco's protests fell on deaf ears.

Greg could remember when this building was used as a storage facility. That was back when this North Bay neighborhood was still a sought after suburban oasis. Since then a new freeway extension had gone in and the property values had plummeted. Now the storage units were primarily used by bands looking for a cheap place to keep their gear set up around the clock. A few of the band members even slept in their units when they weren't embarking on break-even, cross-country van tours.

Another picture was waiting when he checked his phone again. He made up his mind that if the next call or text wasn't from Junior they were getting in the car and driving straight to her house. His phone buzzed again, but it wasn't Junior. This picture was taken at the tidal pools, too. It showed Greg outside of Junior's vandalized car. The picture was a little out of focus, like it had been taken from a distance and then cropped.

He was trying to wrap his head around it all when the phone rang. He still had it cupped in his palms and almost jumped straight out of his sweaty clothes. The name 'Junior' appeared on the screen and he tapped the 'Answer' button repeatedly.

"Where are you?"

"I'm at the salon. Where are you?"

"Where's Chris?"

"Fishing with his grandpa. I got your message. What's going on with you?"

Greg exhaled and let the phone drop from his ear. He could hear Junior screaming at him in the background. He needed a moment to get his thoughts together.

"Sorry. I just thought something was wrong."

"Okay… How'd it go at Ricky's place today?"

"Good. We're just finishing up at the rehearsal space."

"Who's 'we'?"

"Me and Marco. And Godzilla. Call me and let me know that you got home okay."

MARCO WAS SPREAD OUT across Greg's bed with the iguana on his bare chest. The wet towel at his waist was dangerously close to slipping off. He was too tired and sore to move.

Greg was in a T-shirt and board shorts sitting on a chair with his feet propped up on the end of the bed. He was staring up at the ceiling and thinking about the text messages and pictures. He had been so preoccupied at the studio that he never even made it inside, and he was feeling as if he had missed band practice.

I will take my anger out on your girlfriend and her kid.

That's what Manny had said that day in the warehouse. They were watching him and his friends, probably all of the time. Everybody would be in danger if he went to the preliminary hearing on Tuesday morning. And for what? They didn't have a gun so it would just be his word against the word of the kid in the blue hat. It was a no win situation for everybody involved, but the cop in him didn't want to cave in to threats.

"Are you gonna tell me what's got you all twisted up, or what?"

"I have to make a tough decision, and I can't figure out the right thing to do. Somebody gets hurt either way."

"I think that's called a moral dilemma."

"Right, 'a moral dilemma.' Please spare me your junkie philosophy."

"Look who's talking, you fucking drunk."

Marco was standing up now and pulling on a pair of Greg's old jeans. The iguana was back in the aquarium sitting on top of Greg's nightstand. Greg stood up and started pacing.

"I think I should go for a run on the beach, or something. Clear out the cobwebs."

"Wish I could join, but I'd probably die."

"In that case you should *definitely* join."

There was a light tapping on the door just as Marco pulled a T-shirt on. They both froze in place. Greg hoped it was Mrs. McMillan and not a bunch of guys that arrived in a green Impala. He could hear the sound of shuffling feet. Whoever was out there was walking along the edge of the garage trying to peek in the windows. Greg got up to answer when the tapping started again.

"Greg? It's me, Quincy."

He pulled the door open and tried to force a smile. Marco took one look at her and grabbed his shoes. He wound his way between them on the way out the door. Greg tried to stop him, but Marco slid from his grip.

"Where are you going?"

"Heading out for smokes. I won't be back for a while. Have a good run."

The gate slammed shut. Greg moved aside and motioned for her to come inside. She took a few tentative steps and he eased the door closed behind her.

"Were you going somewhere?"

"It's an inside joke."

"I didn't mean to scare your friend away."

"He's actually my roommate at this point."

"Really? Hm...that puts a serious cramp in my plans."

Greg sprung into action to keep himself from over thinking the situation. If a run could help him clear the confusing thoughts that cluttered his mind, Quincy could obliterate them. He took a step forward and grabbed her by the hips. She pushed herself up on her tippy toes and met his mouth with hers. He managed to pull his T-shirt off between desperate, groping kisses. She led him backwards toward the bed, running her fingers across his chest. They fell together in a tangle as clothes flew into the air.

CHAPTER TWENTY-ONE

It was still dark outside. Greg was drifting in out of sleep. His mind was in the midst of a running conversation that flickered like a weak radio signal. Little snippets of dialogue wormed their way into his thoughts just as he was dozing, manifesting themselves as monsters while he slept. A blurry carousel of death masks whispering inaudible secrets in his ear before taking a giant bite from his throat. He dove deep down into his own lungs to release the screams forgotten there. Again and again he jerked awake, gasping for air and desperate for sleep.

He tossed and turned, shifting his feet and twisting the pillow until it was just right. Precious calm moments before the thoughts started coming back together again, rising up to form a peak. Tim becomes Ricky becomes Junior becomes Eddie becomes Mikey becomes Chris becomes the kid with the blue hat. The kid with the bullet holes in his white T-shirt. 'Where is the gun?' Still no sound, but he knew he had been heard. "Where is the gun?"

The kid in the blue hat pointed to a metal door that was flush with the wall of the alley. The hinges were covered in rust, and crude welding fused the edges of the door to the frame. It's a forgotten door that nobody has entered or exited for many years. His eyes follow the kid's arm to where his finger and thumb are outstretched. There is a gusher of blood coming from under the three remaining fingers that are folded back over his palm. Beyond the bloody hand is the rusted metal door that is the only thing between him and the gun. And then the door is turning to glass and he can make out the shape of Junior in the background cutting hair, her scissors moving fast. He starts to run at the door. The kid steps in front of him. His face is a mask that begins to morph again, faster and faster, until Ricky is leaning in to taste his flesh.

Greg screamed himself awake. Quincy pushed herself away in a sleepy panic. She scooted back to comfort him once her heart started beating again.

"Greg. Wake up!"

He brought his knees up and rested his elbows on them. He was folded up tight like a sea anemone that had been poked. She was gently rubbing his back and neck. His breathing was returning to normal when Marco came flying through the door wielding a gardening shovel.

"I'm fucking psycho!"

Greg jumped backwards and nearly knocked Quincy off the other side of the bed.

"Jesus Christ, Marco! You scared the shit out of us."

Marco let the shovel drop to the floor and ran his fingers through his hair. His crazy eyes were almost glowing in the predawn darkness.

"Dude, I thought somebody was murdering you in here. All I heard was screaming."

"He was having a nightmare." She pulled the sheet up to make sure she was covered up for their unexpected guest. "What time is it?"

"No idea. I couldn't sleep so I've just been chilling in the back of the El Camino and smoking cigarettes all night. I must have gone through two packs already."

Greg let his head fall back into the pillow.

"I can smell you all the way over here. Great line, by the way. Very threatening."

"What did I say?"

Marco stumbled into the bathroom. Quincy rolled onto her side and rested her cheek on Greg's arm.

"That must have been some terrifying nightmare."

"It was weird more than anything else."

"Well, whatever was going on it scared the crap out of you. And me too, for that matter."

"Sorry I woke you up like that."

"It's okay, I just wish we had a little more privacy."

She traced the shape of the tattoo on his arm with soft kisses. Greg gave a laugh before shutting his eyes to enjoy the attention.

"Why don't you and I get away next weekend?"

"Sounds great. Maybe somewhere with a good surf break?"

"I was thinking about something with a big bed and great room service."

"Sometimes I think our age difference is going to be the death of me."

"Don't worry, Greg. I'll take care of you when you're old. But until then…"

She slowly slid her hand under the covers.

"How old are you, anyway?"

"Really? Right now?"

"Had to ask sometime."

"Twenty-eight. Okay? Now stop wasting time. Your friend will be getting out of the shower soon."

"I don't actually hear the water running."

Marco opened the bathroom door and stumbled back into the room. Greg pulled away from Quincy and pushed himself up. Marco turned the tap on in the sink to fill the coffee pot.

"You mind if I make some coffee?"

"Might as well. I doubt anybody's getting back to sleep."

Greg reached out from under the covers and grabbed his boxer shorts off the floor. He slid them on, making sure not to expose Quincy in the process. He would have to get Marco outside for a few minutes so that she could get dressed, but coffee first. He caught a glimpse of the alarm clock through the aquarium as he stood up. It was 5:45 a.m.

The coffee finished brewing and Greg poured two mugs to the top. He told Marco to grab the stack of folders they had gotten from Ricky's apartment and head out to the garden table. He pushed Marco ahead of him and gave Quincy a glance as he was closing the door. She pulled the covers back and raised her eyebrows playfully. *Maybe Marco needs more cigarettes* crossed his mind as he stepped into the brisk morning air.

They both started whispering once they were seated. Greg could see that Marco's mind was whirring from the lack of sleep and booze. He also knew that the nicotine gave his detoxing friend just enough of a buzz to take the edge off. The coffee helped, too.

Greg pulled a sheet of paper from the top folder and spun it around for Marco to read.

"You worked with Ricky for a while. Do you recognize any of these addresses?"

The handwriting was small and scratchy. Each line had a street name and number along with a date range. A few had check marks next to them. It seemed like Ricky had been trying to figure something out.

"All of these addresses are in South Bay. We didn't do much work over there."

"Could they have been jobs that you didn't work on?"

"Maybe. I was definitely working with him a lot during that time. I would have at least been on a few of the jobs if they were his. Like I said, we mostly did smaller jobs in North Bay."

"So what are these addresses?"

"Maybe those are Barrett's job sites."

"How can we figure that out? I mean, without asking Barrett."

"We could go check them out one by one."

Quincy came outside wearing one of Greg's hoodie sweatshirts. It fit loosely, but covered her up to the middle of her thighs. Greg tried to not think about whether or not she was wearing anything underneath. She was sipping carefully on a mug of coffee as she shuffled over to where they were sitting, teasing him over the rim.

"What are you guys talking about?"

"Nothing much. Trying to figure out what this list of addresses means."

"Can I see?"

There was no connection between Quincy and Ricky so he didn't see any harm in sharing. He pushed the paper across the table to her. She considered the info on the page and puckered her lips to take sips of her coffee while she read.

"I know most of these addresses. They're in South Bay."

"How do you know that?"

"I work in parking enforcement." They both looked at her with blank stares. "It's part of my job to post those 'Temporary No Parking' signs whenever there is a street fair or 10k, or whatever."

"Or a construction site?"

"Yep. The big ones, at least. That's how I met Barrett. Outside of one of his jobs."

Greg felt a strange combination of feelings rise up inside of him. On the one hand he was almost certain that Ricky had been stealing from Barrett, and that it might have gotten him killed. On the other hand, he felt an unexpected pang of jealousy at hearing Quincy mention Barrett's name. He drained his cup and went back inside to make another pot of coffee.

His phone was buzzing when he got inside. He picked it up without looking at the screen.

"Good morning. What time are you picking Chris up?"

"Oh, hey. Right. 'Dawn patrol.'"

"He's sitting out front with his board. Please tell me you didn't forget."

"I'll be there in like twenty minutes. Got a late start."

"I could drive him over."

"Nope. On my way. Make it fifteen minutes."

He put the phone down and started moving quickly to collect his gear. He didn't know exactly what he would say to Quincy about leaving without any warning, but he didn't have much choice. She was on her way back in when he went to open the door.

"Are you going surfing right now?"

"Yeah. I promised a friend I would take their kid out for some lessons. I totally spaced on it until a minute ago."

"Uncle Greg? How cute."

"You can hang out here with Marco until I get back, if you want to."

"We'll see..."

She shut the door and unzipped the hoodie. It fell to the ground as she stepped out of it and strutted into the bathroom naked, a confident smile spreading across her face. Greg enjoyed the view for a moment before stepping out into the morning light. Marco noticed the smile on his face and asked him what was up.

"Nothing, bro. Just stoked to go surfing."

"Yeah, right."

THERE WEREN'T MANY PEOPLE in the water with Greg and Chris. It was like they had the whole ocean to themselves. Consistent sets were rolling in. Greg had never officially given lessons before, but he managed to provide Chris with a few helpful pointers on paddling to catch waves, and how to center his weight when she stood up. The boy already had a firm grasp of the basic techniques and, more importantly, enough enthusiasm to put in the necessary hours of practice. In other words, he was still young. Greg was feeling pretty young at that moment, too.

They kept at it for the better part of an hour before Greg finally pushed himself into a sitting position. His legs were dangling in the water on either side of his board and Chris soon followed suit. Greg had been surfing for most of his life but he still found himself a little worried about sharks when he was bobbing in the ocean on quiet mornings. The thought of it made him recall his nightmares and he was gripped by a wave of sickening panic.

He looked at the shore to get his bearings. The sun was up above the cityscape now, the million dollar homes crowding the hill that sloped gently to the sand. It was like a tidal wave of money pushing back against the vast expanse of the ocean.

"You ready to catch some more waves?"

Greg saw the smile on Chris's face and really noticed the pronounced gaps between his teeth. He wondered if Junior was putting money aside for braces. It probably wouldn't matter once Eddie sold out to Mikey, since they would all be set for life. Only a matter of time.

"Give me a second to catch my breath. How's your mom holding up, you know with the funeral and everything?"

"I don't know." The boy seemed to swallow his words. "Okay, I guess. She doesn't talk about it much. I hear her crying sometimes, when she's in her bedroom."

"How about you? You said he was giving you lessons, right?"

"He was giving me guitar lessons at first. Then he started taking me surfing, too. Before he, you know, died. Or whatever."

"I was wondering about that guitar. Did Ricky give that to you?"

"Yeah. I'm not very good at it. Mom said I need to practice more."

"I think it's really great you got a chance to know him so well."

"He was actually around all the time for the last couple of months."

Ten years old. Greg was trying to remember how much he knew about sex when he was ten. Probably a lot less than he thought he did. Greg got the feeling that it was okay to press for more details without doing any serious emotional damage.

"Sounds fun. Was he staying late? Like after you went to bed at night?"

"I don't know. A couple of times a week."

A chill ran under Greg's wetsuit. He thought his teeth might shatter from the way they ground together. It looked like Chris wasn't the only one spending quality time with Ricky.

"Usually on the weekends when mom would have her shows at grandpa's bar."

"We should probably catch a few more waves before I have to take you home."

Greg dropped down onto his board and started paddling hard. He didn't have to look back to know that Chris was right behind him. They managed to make the most of a few more sets and each rode a last wave all the way to shore. They were at the El Camino fifteen minutes later with Chris's surfboard loaded safely into the back.

Greg took the boy inside his apartment for a bathroom break before the drive home. Marco was out like a light on the bed when they walked in, the iguana stiff as a statue on the pillow next to his head. Greg saw his hoodie folded neatly on the chair with a piece of paper perched on top. He didn't dare read it before heading over to Junior's house.

The final notes of Agent Orange's "Everything Turns Grey" were decaying from the speakers as they pulled up. Junior was out front sitting on a patio chair when Greg parked in the driveway. He could see her flipping through a magazine and drinking a cup of coffee. He grabbed her son's surfboard from the back and told him to take it inside. A shower and video games would give the adults time to chat.

Greg took a deep breath and strolled toward Junior.

"How'd he do?"

"He's getting pretty good. Probably because of all those lessons Ricky was giving him."

She closed the magazine and tossed it onto the lawn at his feet. Her eyes were searching his over the top of her coffee mug. He could see she was weighing her options, but he made it clear that she had none left.

"You should probably sit down."

She motioned to the chair next to hers. Greg chose one a few feet away.

"How long were you sleeping with him?"

"What do you want me to say? We just were, okay?"

She rolled her eyes to stop the tears that were forming. It didn't have much of an effect. He could feel the anger welling up, like muck in a clogged sink, full of the little bits of everything he had been trying to shove deep down inside all week.

"Not okay. Definitely not okay. Why did it have to be my best friend?"

"What does that have to do with it? It was just casual. Just like you and the meter maid."

That stopped him in his tracks. He shifted to defense for a moment.

"How do you even know about that?"

"Jesus, Greg. I work at a salon. Nothing happens around here that I don't hear about."

"What's going on between me and her is different than you and Ricky."

"Why? Because she didn't go to our high school? The only reason it's different is because I'm not asking you to explain yourself."

He could hear the rage building inside of her. They both knew it was no match for his.

"Why Ricky?"

"We've known each other forever. It was easy."

Greg watched the tears rolling down her face and it made him feel good. Strong. Like she was getting what she deserved.

"I just don't understand how you could do it. You're fucking my best friend behind my back and then you hop in bed with me right after he—"

He couldn't even bring himself to say the word.

"Nothing happened behind your back. It happened—*we happened*—after Ricky died. There, I said it. He died. But none of this is about him, Greg. It's about us."

Any victory he'd felt got sucked right out of him. Like he had been on a perfect wave that crashed and now the white wash was holding him down. And then there was his anger, lifting him back up towards the surface so he could get right back on his board.

"Well, there isn't going to be any 'us' ever again."

"That's just perfect."

He watched her dissolve into the chair as he stood up to leave. He could hear her sobbing uncontrollably in the background. His skin was bristling with righteous indignation as he strode across the lawn knowing that his work was done.

He wasn't even all the way to the El Camino when he was overtaken with the urge to go back and comfort her. The shame left him paralyzed as he stood with his fingers under the door handle. The only answer was to get in the car and drive.

CHAPTER TWENTY-TWO

The yellow police tape was ruffling in the breeze at the edge of the motel parking lot as Greg drove past. He could see big black and white signs posted on all the doors. Trespass warnings.

It wouldn't be long before the bulldozers arrived to make way for another mini mall. Maybe a month, two at the most. In the meantime all the cockroaches that previously inhabited the motel were forbidden from coming back. He knew where Marco had gone, but he couldn't speak for all the others.

Greg had seen those signs on plenty of factory doors in Virgil Heights over the years. Businesses seemed to come and go, but there was always another one right behind the last one. All it took was an idea, a little cash, a license and a new sign—the American dream in a box. The image got him thinking about his nightmares again. Was it possible that there was a door that nobody knew about? He knew it was crazy, but it was also better than nothing.

The preliminary hearing was already scheduled for Tuesday. A little extracurricular police work couldn't do any harm. Besides, it might take his mind off of Junior. He stepped on the gas and merged onto the freeway, heading north. The Circle Jerks were singing "Wild in the Streets" as he changed lanes.

He tried to call the Police Chief while he was driving. It went straight to voicemail. It was Sunday morning so that meant he was either in church or on the golf course. Greg decided not to leave a message. Tuesday would be here soon enough.

Freeway traffic near The Bay Cities was always congested on weekends, but it opened up as Greg passed the airport and headed east. Then he caught another little snarl as he made his way through downtown. The skyscrapers danced around the crack in his windshield. He cursed under his breath as he listened to the El Camino creak and groan. All four lanes started to flow again fifteen minutes later and he soon found himself taking the first off ramp for Virgil Heights.

The streets were empty as he wheeled the car to the area where the shooting occurred. He parked the El Camino on the main street about a half a block from the entrance to the alley. His impromptu plan was to retrace his footsteps along the sidewalk in hopes that it would pry loose a memory. Everything looked different without the trucks and the workers milling around. He thought he did a pretty good job of getting back into the headspace from that day.

Picturing the look of terror on that woman's face was a good place to start. His heart started pumping as he chased the imaginary suspect in the blue hat.

He rounded the corner of the alley and took a few steps away from the empty street. On the day of the shooting it was like he had stepped from a concert into a sound proofed room. He tried to imagine the kid with the blue hat trying to climb the wall behind the dumpsters. His memory was playing with the speed at which these events occurred, but he knew that they ended in a standoff either way. Him and the kid alone in an alley.

His memory was only playing the final scenes from his nightmare now. Greg followed the kid's arm to where the finger and thumb were outstretched, pointing at the forgotten door in the wall. He blinked a few times and still only saw bricks. He let his head drop and started to laugh out loud.

It took him several minutes to recover. He eventually managed to search the entire alley for good measure. Still no gun. There might never have been a gun. The thought of taking over Eddie's L Bar didn't seem so absurd all of a sudden.

He turned and walked back out to the main road. The streets were still deserted when he turned the key and shifted into drive. He had the urge to swing by the station, but knew that word would get back to the Police Chief before he even got to the on-ramp. His best bet was to head back home and finish moving Ricky's things into the rehearsal space.

He flipped a U-turn midblock and almost hit a big American sedan that was headed his way. He swerved to avoid clipping the bumper and saw Manny sitting in the back seat waving a semi-automatic pistol out the window.

Greg jammed his foot into the accelerator and swung wide to make the turn. He checked the rearview mirror and saw the other car was gone. The terrifying thought crossed his mind that there had never been another car, that his nightmares were starting to seep into reality. But he wasn't having that kind of luck these days.

He slowed down a little going through the next intersection. There was half a second to brace himself before the very real second car clipped the tail end of the El Camino. It sent him into a sideways skid that he managed to correct by turning into it. He heard wheels squealing in the distance and listened as the other car rumbled down the block parallel to the one he was on.

If he went left he might risk a head on collision. If he went right he would be heading further away from the freeway ramp. He slammed on the brakes and sat idling in the middle of the block. He knew they had heard him stop but he wanted to see how they would respond. No matter what happened, getting out of his car would be suicide.

He listened as the car on the next block slowed down, probably to listen for him. They were crawling forward at only a few miles per hour. At that rate he might have enough time to place a call to the VHPD. He reached for his phone and started punching in his password on the locked home screen. The rumbling engine in the distance was getting louder as he tapped the phone icon and started to dial.

His finger was on the Call icon when the second car rolled into view, perpendicular to the El Camino up ahead. Greg froze as the windows came down to reveal two pistols pointed directly at his car. The phone flew from his hand as he dropped down across the bench seat and covered his head.

The next sound should have been gunshots. He heard laughter instead. They were either trying to coax him into sitting up, or making their way up the block on foot to finish the job up close. He eased the car into reverse and started slowly backing up without looking. He felt like a U-boat captain navigating his way through a minefield blind.

The other car squealed away in a cloud of white smoke that poured from its spinning rear tires. The scent of burning rubber filled the air as he lifted his head to peek across the dashboard. He had never been so thankful to be looking down an empty street.

Greg threw the car into park and climbed up onto the seat. He turned to survey the damage to the back of the car. A full quarter of the bed was crumpled in on itself over the rear wheel well on the passenger side. He wasn't even sure that he would be able to drive it home. His phone started ringing just as he was getting out of the car to take a closer look.

"Greg, I saw I missed a call from you. Is everything all right?"

The Police Chief was waiting for a response. The only sound coming out of Greg's mouth was uncontrollable laughter.

"Just tell me where you are and I'll come get you. Wherever it is."

"You know exactly where I am."

"Jesus Christ, Greg."

"There was no gun, Chief. I shot him and he never had a gun. That's what I'm gonna tell them on Tuesday. I just want this all to be over."

"Sit tight. I'll send the boys out to look for you."

He hung up and waited for the sirens.

"It's just a car, dude."

"It's barely even a car at this point."

"What do you mean? You just drove all the way back here from Virgil Heights."

"Look at it. It's like a half crushed beer can that's been stepped all over."

"The engine runs and the wheels spin. I'm no mechanic, but I'm pretty sure that makes it a car."

"Have you ever even owned a car?"

"Technically, no. But I've driven a bunch of them. Whatever. All I'm saying is it doesn't look any worse than when you first got it."

Greg could still picture the El Camino sitting on blocks in his father's driveway. The engine was shot and the body needed work. He and Tim had dedicated long weekends and late nights under the hood trying to get it running again.

His chest swelled with pride as he pictured the day they finally drove it down the boulevard for the first time. His brother was in the passenger seat beside him and his father was waving proudly in the rearview mirror.

"That was a long time ago, Marco. I don't have that free time any more. Or the energy."

"Shit dude, all you've got is free time. Let me help you with it."

"You just said you weren't a mechanic."

"So?"

They took another slow lap around the El Camino. The street lamp shining down on it seemed like a crime scene black light to Greg. The back half of the car and the windshield were obvious. He found another scrape, ding or dent every couple of inches.

"This car was almost perfect ten days ago."

"We've got bigger problems to worry about."

Marco had been through Ricky's files again while Greg was out.

"It was mostly invoices and stuff like that. But it got me thinking about what your girlfriend said this morning. How did you meet her anyway?"

"On the beach, and she's not my girlfriend. What's your point?"

"She's smoking hot. And about half your age, old man."

"Not about Quincy. What were you saying about Ricky's files?"

"Oh, right. What kind of name is Quincy?" Greg punched him in the arm to get him back on track. "She said that she met Barrett putting up 'No Parking' signs outside one of his job sites in South Bay. And we were already pretty sure that the addresses on Ricky's list were some of Barrett's sites that he was raiding. So I went and checked."

"You walked around South Bay checking out these addresses on your own? Pretty impressive."

"I grabbed your skateboard. Much quicker that way. Plus I had a crazy amount of energy all day. I could barely sit still."

"That happens when you sober up. What did you find?"

"A lot of the jobs are long over, but a few of them still had those lawn signs up. You know, the ones that say 'Another beautiful renovation by your friend in the construction business' blah blah blah. All of those signs were Barrett's. But that's not the weird thing."

Marco paused for dramatic effect. Greg crossed his arms and scowled in response.

"Okay, okay. Six of the houses were for sale. And the for sale signs all listed the same real estate company as we found in Barrett's office."

"Sand Castle Estates?"

"Right. So I called the number. A receptionist answered, so I started asking a lot of really specific questions about one of their properties. It didn't seem like she had anybody to hand me off to. Then I started dropping names of other real estate companies I've worked with…"

"Wait. When have you worked with any real estate companies?"

"Never, but she didn't need to know that." Marco smiled and tapped the side of his temple with his index finger. "Point is she finally let it slip that this real estate company was a subsidiary of Bay City Developers."

"Mikey's company? Not that surprising that he and Barrett do business together. Why does it matter that the houses were for sale?"

"Dude, do you have any idea how hard it is to buy real estate in South Bay? You're either waiting for some old timer to kick the bucket, or you're paying two or three times the market value in cash."

"More real estate expertise from *The Bay Cities News*?"

“You know it. So what do you think the chances are of Mikey and Barrett getting hold of so many primo properties in a short amount of time?”

Greg didn’t have an answer because his phone started buzzing.

“Greg, it’s Eddie. Get over to Edie’s house right now. Something is terribly wrong.”

CHAPTER TWENTY-THREE

Strobing police lights lit up the exterior of Junior's house. The windows on her car had been repaired but "Locals Only" was still scratched into the paint. He cut across the front lawn and walked to the gaping doorframe. Officer Bob was standing just inside. Eddie and Mikey were screaming at each other in the living room.

"Mr. Salem. I was hoping you would arrive before I left. I'm sure I don't need to remind you that this is a potential crime scene."

"What the hell happened?"

"Eddie says he made plans pick up his daughter and grandson for dinner. When he arrived the front door looked like this." He motioned behind himself and into the living room. "House was empty when he came inside."

"Any signs of a struggle?" He swallowed and braced himself for the answer.

"The living room and master bedroom are a little torn up. Whoever did this was looking for something specific. You can see for yourself when you go in. I know Eddie was anxious for you to get here."

Officer Bob stepped aside and motioned for Greg to enter the house.

"Wait. Are you putting out any bulletins? Do you have patrol cars searching for them? Helicopter support?"

"We're not even sure this is a crime scene. Things have been a little hectic around here lately, maybe she took the kid on an impromptu vacation and just got a little carried away with packing. It happens. I'll call you if I have any questions."

"Why would she leave her car in the driveway?"

Officer Bob gave no response as he strolled out onto the lawn. Greg exchanged nods with a couple of police officers that came out of the bedroom wearing rubber gloves. One of them was carrying a fingerprint kit, which Greg knew was a good sign. He stepped aside to let them pass, taking a few tentative steps toward Eddie and Mikey. Eddie gave his former son-in-law a reassuring pat on the shoulder.

"We're gonna find them, Mikey. Whatever it takes."

"I know. I know. It's just…"

Mikey staggered back to the couch, collapsing into the cushions. Eddie turned to Greg.

"I'm glad you're here. It's the damnedest thing."

"What were you two yelling about just now?"

"Me and Mikey? He was in hysterics so I tried to calm him down. I honestly thought I was going to have to slap him."

"I got the run down from Officer Bob. Any idea at all what happened here?"

"Not a clue. Edie and I spoke on the phone around seven and made plans to have a late dinner. I got here at eight thirty and found all of this."

Greg reached for a leather bound notepad that wasn't there. Right next to his invisible badge.

"Was Mikey supposed to be joining you three for dinner?"

"What? No. I called him right after I called you. He was right down the street, so he got here in a couple of minutes. He's pretty broken up about it. See for yourself."

The look on Greg's face did not betray his conflicted feelings about Junior's ex husband.

"For God's sake, Greg. Whatever you think about him, Chris is still his son."

"I know, you're right. Sorry. What did the police ask you?"

"I don't know. Same old bullshit. Where was I before I got here? Where were we going to dinner? Was anybody else here when I arrived? Nothing useful, if you ask me."

"They have to ask, even if it seems pointless. A lot of times people are in shock when they're being questioned at a potential crime scene. We have to start from square one."

They both turned to look at Mikey. His head was tilted back and he was staring up at the ceiling. His lips were moving, but no sound was coming out. Eddie went over to sit with him and motioned for Greg to follow. Eddie took a seat beside Mikey. Greg lowered himself down on the edge of the coffee table so that they were face to face.

"I can't believe this is happening." He kept his eyes on the ceiling while he spoke, breathing heavily through his nose. "I should have been here to protect them. Should have been here."

"That's not what's important right now." Greg slapped Mikey on the knee to get his attention. Mikey brought his chin down and quickly lowered his eyes to avoid meeting Greg's stare. "Right now we need to figure out what we can do to find Junior and Chris. Do you understand? That's all that matters right now."

Mikey started sobbing at the mention of his son's name. Eddie wrapped his arm around Mikey's shoulder and tried to console him.

"Greg's right Mikey. You have to pull yourself together. For them."

Mikey wiped his eyes and took a deep breath. Greg's tone was sharp and direct.

"Listen. The police won't take this situation seriously until Junior and Chris have been missing for forty-eight hours. We need to do a little police work of our own until then."

"Like what?"

"Mikey, when's the last time you spoke with Junior and Chris?"

"I haven't spoken to Edie since that night you and I spoke out in the driveway. Chris and I usually talk on the phone a few times a week."

"Did Chris mention anything out of the ordinary? Anything he was scared about?"

"He was talking about your friend Ricky a little more than usual."

"Yeah. That makes sense." Greg felt the anger rising again, but managed to keep it under control. "I guess the two of them got pretty close before he… you know. Before he…"

"Died?"

"What about Jeff Barrett? Can you think of any reason why he would want to hurt them?"

"What makes you think he's involved?"

"Just a feeling. I know you guys have done business together. Is there any bad blood there? Anything that might have set him off?"

Mikey tensed his lips and rubbed the back of his neck. It looked as though thinking caused him physical pain. Greg and Eddie exchanged impatient looks, giving him time to respond.

"No. Nothing I can think of. What about your old drummer friend, Marco? He seems like trouble."

"He wouldn't have any reason to harm Junior and Chris."

"How do you know?" Greg could see that Mikey was slowly coming out of his shock-induced stupor. "If I had to pick one person who was capable of something like this—"

"Because he's been staying with me. He's at my apartment right now, detoxing."

"About time." Eddie seemed more annoyed than supportive. "That kid's a mess."

Greg stood up and wandered over to the front door.

"Who else then?"

The front yard was dark now that the police cars had left. He could see the misshapen outline of the El Camino where it was parked on the street.

"I need to go make a few phone calls. Are either of you staying here tonight? In case they come back."

"I'll stay. You and Mikey should go home and get some rest." There was steel in Eddie's voice "Whoever did this won't be coming back for me. They got what they wanted."

Greg gave him a concerned look.

"No. You're probably right."

"I'll call if there's any news, and you do the same. Let's meet at the bar tomorrow morning and regroup if they don't turn up in the meantime."

Mikey stood up and helped Eddie double check that all of the doors and windows in the house were locked. The three men said their goodbyes. Greg triple checked that the front door was secure once Eddie closed it. Mikey was already down the steps and on the lawn, waiting.

"I bet you're a really good cop, Greg."

"What makes you say that?"

"I just never got a chance to see you take charge like that. It's pretty impressive."

"Thanks, Mikey. Listen. We'll find them. Just go home and get some rest if you can. Tomorrow might be a long day and we'll need everybody to be ready for absolutely anything."

"Thanks."

They split up at the sidewalk, but Mikey stopped.

"What makes you think I've done business with Barrett?"

"Excuse me?"

"Barrett. You mentioned inside that he and I had done business together. What makes you think that?"

Greg knew that he had said too much, but hoped it had gone unnoticed.

"I just assumed. He's the biggest contractor in town and you're the biggest developer."

"Huh. Makes sense. I'll see you in the morning."

He waited for Mikey to drive away and then pulled his phone out. He punched in a number and waited while it rang.

"Hello? Chief? It's Greg. I have a favor to ask."

MARCO JUMPED TO HIS feet the minute Greg walked through the door.

"Everything cool?"

"Junior and Chris are missing. Eddie went over to pick them up for dinner and the door was wide open. There was no sign of them."

"Sounds like you and I need to go find Barrett, like right fucking now."

"I don't know. Mikey was there and he thought I was crazy for even suspecting Barrett."

"I don't trust either of those dudes. Who else could it be?"

"I know a few other people who are capable of something like this. I'm having that checked out right now. In the meantime..."

Greg tossed his phone across the room. It landed on the bed with a soft thud. Marco picked it up and saw a thread of texts between Greg and Quincy. The last one was a telephone number.

"What do you want me to do with this?"

"Call that number and tell Barrett you have his documents. Tell him you want him to meet us at his job yard in thirty minutes."

"What if he doesn't answer?"

"Leave a message. My guess is he'll call us back."

Marco gave Greg a searching look and then tapped the screen. He kept his eyes on his roommate as the phone rang on the other end. Marco raised his eyebrows when Barrett actually picked up.

"Who's this?"

"Barrett. Sup, bro? It's Marco."

"How'd you get this number you little shit?"

"I have something of yours. Meet me at your office in half an hour. And come alone."

Greg could hear Barrett screaming as Marco lifted the phone and tapped 'End Call'.

"Come alone? Nice touch."

They climbed into the car and sped across town. He killed the lights a half block before Barrett's yard and quietly rolled up outside the gates. They immediately heard two men yelling.

"Sounds like it's coming from inside his office."

"I recognize Barrett's voice. Who's he fighting with?"

"I don't know. He definitely didn't come alone."

"Maybe they were already here when you called. Come on."

Greg slipped out of the car and shut the door quietly. Marco joined him out in the dark street. They trotted over to the fence that ran around the reservoir. Greg webbed his hands together to help Marco climb. Marco shunned Greg's offer of help and scaled it on his own. He was noisier than Greg would have liked, but luckily the screaming had just flared back up. Greg was coming over the wobbly chain link just as his partner dropped down on the other side. The suburban lights were shimmering on the water as they moved up the path to the back of Barrett's yard.

"What exactly is the plan here?"

"We go take a look around to see if there's any sign of Junior and Chris. Then we figure out who Barrett's yelling at in there."

Soon they were both skulking across the yard, hiding behind cement mixers and backhoes as they went. They were about fifty feet from Barrett's office building. Greg told Marco to go around the side of the building to investigate. He waited for his partner to disappear into the shadows before heading for the yellow light that spilled from the office window.

Greg reached the wall and pressed his back against the cool bricks. He was a few feet from the window and could see a little movement inside. He inched along the wall until he was under the sill. The screaming had stopped and it smelled like somebody was smoking a cigarette. He popped his head up to take a quick peek inside and saw the back of Barrett's leather chair. A pair of sneakers was propped up on the desk and a thin line of white smoke drifted up into the air. A second man was sitting on the other side of the desk typing on his phone, his face obscured by the back of Barrett's chair.

Greg slid under the window and tried to get a better view through the dusty screen. Somebody slid a hand around his mouth and he went stiff. He turned and drove his forearm into his attacker's throat only to discover Marco smiling back at him. One of the men inside the office slid the window open. Greg and Marco ducked to avoid being seen, but listened carefully to the conversation overhead.

"I don't know how you can still smoke. Quitting was the

best thing I ever did."

The first voice was familiar, but the man was still seated on the far side of the desk. Greg found it hard to place.

"I only smoke when I'm stressed out. Where the hell is he?"

"He called the meeting. My guess is he'll be here any minute."

"I hope so. This has gone on long enough."

"Keep your cool, Jeff. You got yourself into this situation in the first place."

"He knows way too much!"

"Calm down. We have no idea what he knows. He's half brain dead anyway."

"What if he gets his boyfriend involved?"

"Who, Greg? We'll cross that particular bridge when we come to it."

They didn't know Greg was there. So far, so good. Greg found the thought reassuring as he inched up the wall to get a better look. He leaned to the right and took a peek inside of the room. Barrett was still in the same position, but now the other man was in plain view. It was Officer Bob. His service revolver was on the desk in front of him, right next to his badge.

Greg leaned back against the wall and tried to collect his thoughts. The pieces still weren't coming together when his phone buzzed in his pocket. Barrett heard it too, and rushed to the window.

"Did you hear that?"

There was a shuffling of feet inside the office. Greg pushed the mute button on his phone from the outside of his pants. He could see a face pressed up against the screen from inside the office. The featureless profile looked like something from a horror movie. Greg and Marco both held their breath and tried to fade into the bricks.

Officer Bob's voice was clear as a bell.

"You're getting paranoid."

"Go to hell."

The bulge in the screen eventually receded. Greg put his arm across Marco's chest to hold him in place. He wanted to be sure that they weren't walking into a trap. A minute passed before the conversation in the office started up again. Greg gave Marco a little shove toward the far end of the building. He followed close on his heels.

"Who's in there?"

Marco was whispering so quietly that Greg had to lean in to hear him.

"Officer Bob."

"No way. That doesn't make any sense."

"It makes sense to me. I've never trusted that guy."

"Do you still want me to go in there?"

"I think that would be a suicide mission. I saw a gun on the desk."

"I always thought I'd get offed by a cop, but not like this."

Greg ignored the dramatic bravado.

"I don't think Barrett has Junior and Chris. At least not in his office. We should just get out of here."

"Back home?"

"Back to Ricky's rehearsal space."

THE PHONE RANG SEVERAL times on the drive over. Greg ignored the buzzing and beeping, wondering why he thought it was a good idea to have Marco call Barrett from his phone. He was thankful that his outgoing message was just an impersonal robot voice that recited his phone number. He grabbed the rehearsal space key that Ricky's mom had given him from the glove compartment and handed it to Marco.

"Go unlock the door. I need to text somebody."

Marco got out without saying a word. Greg knew the lack of sleep was catching up with his partner. He grabbed the phone from the dashboard and tapped out a response to one of Barrett's many messages.

"Change of plans. Meet me at Eddie's tomorrow at 11." He was about to hit send, but decided to add another line. He really needed a laugh. *"Come alone."*

The parking lot and building were mostly empty. Muffled thumps and distorted strumming were coming from a couple of the other studios upstairs. Greg could hear the metal door creaking and grinding as Marco pushed it up. Ricky's boxes were stacked up inside of the room on both sides, just as Marco had left them. The rest of the rehearsal space was pitch black beyond that. Marco stepped into the void with his hand groping blindly along the wall in search of a light switch.

"What's the problem? We were just here."

"It was still day time, dude. I never had to turn the lights on."

"It's probably an overhead bulb. Look for a chain dangling in the middle of the room."

Marco exhaled a stream of expletives as he banged his shin into the edge of an amplifier. The low watt bulb came on a few seconds later, casting a pale orange glow across the clutter. The room looked just like every other low rent rehearsal space the world over. Thick layers of mismatched carpet were tacked to the walls and the ceiling, leaving the room devoid of both echoes and breathable air. A basic drum set was tucked tight into the back corner, directly opposite a coffin-sized bass amplifier. Smaller guitar amps of varying sizes lined the interior walls on both sides. Guitars stood at attention nearby. Microphone stands tilted at angles through the center of the room on top of a stained and tattered Indian rug. Greg spotted a small desk and headed for it.

"I haven't been in a rehearsal room for a really long time. It smells even worse than the motel did."

"Four sweaty guys and no air conditioning. Recipe for disaster."

Greg slid the chair out from under the desk and took a seat. A small mixing board occupied most of the flat surface on top, cables springing from the back. He pulled drawers open to inspect what was inside, quickly discovering Ricky's simple system—band paperwork on the left, contractor paperwork on the right.

He thumbed through several file folders and got a glimpse of how hard Ricky's job had been. There were twelve thick folders labeled "Bids," and only one thin folder labeled "Invoices." The band drawers had even less to offer. Just a couple of half empty tour diaries and rubber-banded receipt bundles.

Greg was reaching to pull open the top drawer when Marco laid into a cacophonous drum roll. It sounded like pots and pans clattering down a concrete stairwell. The sudden shock sent Greg out of his chair and under the desk. He brought his hands up to cover his ears just as Marco ended with a series of staccato cymbal crashes. The tip of a broken drumstick nicked Greg's neck as it spun through the air like a bullet.

"Dude! What the fuck?"

"Sorry. It's been a few years. I didn't realize how much I missed playing."

Greg shook his head dismissively and turned his attention back to the desk, a pronounced ringing in his ears. The penholder at the lip of the drawer was filled with guitar picks of various shapes and sizes. Deeper inside he discovered a couple of skateboarding magazines and a legal pad covered with handwritten song lyrics. He lifted the yellow pad up and flipped through some of the pages. It was difficult to read his friend's half finished thoughts.

Greg saw the folded sheets of white paper when he put the lyrics back down. He opened the one on top and immediately recognized the ridiculous layout and Sex Pistols font. It wasn't long ago that he discovered a note like this on his own windshield.

Hope you had fun last night. I got the whole thing on video.

xoxo,

Your Biggest Fan

There were nine notes in all, each one of them a little more aggressive than the last.

Have a great show with Freddie D. tomorrow night. It's gonna be your last one ever.

xoxo,

Your Biggest Fan

Marco came up behind him and started reading over his shoulder.

"Dude, are you all right?"

"Ricky knew he was going to die."

CHAPTER TWENTY-FOUR

Monday mornings weren't normally busy at Eddie's L Bar. They might get a couple of regulars looking for a quiet place to watch the news, but not much more than that. Eddie would use the down time to do inventory and place orders for the rest of the week. He only really kept the doors open so that he might have some company.

But this Monday was different. All the stools at the bar were occupied when Greg and Marco walked in. The scene reminded Greg of his Monday morning "all hands" meetings at VHPD. They recognized a few of the regulars, including Roger and Bill, but they were permanent fixtures. Several of the other people in the crowd had taken off of work to offer their help in searching for Junior and Chris. Marco stopped to speak with one of the small groups that were huddled along the bar hatching plans for their search parties. Another team was creating missing persons fliers on their laptop computers and devising a distribution plan. Greg could see from the look on Eddie's face that he was deeply moved by the show of support.

"Quite a turn out, Eddie. Any word?"

They had already spoken several times that morning, so Greg thought he knew the answer. Eddie just shook his head in response. Greg gave him a pat on the back and they made their way through the crowd together.

"I'm hoping to get an update from Officer Bob in the next few minutes."

Greg decided to bite his tongue. He wasn't sure that Officer Bob was involved in the kidnapping, so Eddie didn't need to hear his half-baked theories. Not yet. Greg needed to hear from the Police Chief in Virgil Heights first before he could plan his next move.

"What has he had to report so far?"

"Just the usual bureaucratic double talk. 'I have my best men on it,' 'Most missing persons cases end up just being a misunderstanding,' blah blah blah."

They reached the end of the bar just as Mikey walked in the side door. It looked like he hadn't slept much the night before either. Greg was surprised to find Marco at his side when Mikey greeted them.

"Wow. I wasn't expecting this."

"Word got out pretty quick. I started getting calls with offers of help first thing this morning. Of course, offering free drinks didn't hurt. You thirsty?"

"Maybe a Bloody Mary."

Eddie ducked behind the bar as Mikey climbed onto the last remaining stool. Greg and Marco took an elbow on either side of him. They had to stand close in order to hear each other over the noise in the bar that morning. Mikey kept giving nervous glances around the room, drumming an uneven rhythm on the bar as he waited for his drink.

"Any word from Barrett?"

"I think you have the wrong impression about Jeff and me. We've done a little work together, but we aren't close."

Marco was standing behind Mikey. He gave Greg a nod and pulled a face. Greg kept his eyes on Mikey.

"I just thought that maybe—"

"Whatever you're thinking about me and Barrett, it's wrong. The truth is I don't really trust the guy."

Eddie dropped a pint glass full of ice down in front of Mikey and emptied the contents of his shaker into it. The red liquid poured out thick, little black flecks of pepper clinging to the inside of the glass. He topped it off with an olive and wedge of lime impaled on a small plastic sword. Greg could see Marco eyeballing the tempting concoction and coughed to get his attention.

"Why don't you go see how the fliers are coming along?"

Marco lingered for a moment, staring Mikey down, before sliding past them. Mikey seemed oblivious as he sat nursing his cocktail. Greg was relieved that he wasn't going to have to break up a fight.

"I didn't mean any offense."

"I know. I'm just a little on edge. I'm sure you understand."

"Yes, I definitely do."

"But if you think Barrett had anything to do with Junior and Chris, just know that I will do whatever it takes to get them back."

The glass was half empty when Mikey put it back down on the bar again. The vodka was already having a calming effect on him.

"Has there been any word since I last spoke with Eddie?"

"He's expecting to hear from Officer Bob any minute now."

Greg felt a phantom buzz in his pocket and reached for his phone. There were no missed calls or messages. He thought about calling the Police Chief again. He decided it was best to hold off. Marco wandered back over just as Mikey was draining his glass and signaling to Eddie for a refill.

"Greg, can I see your phone?"

"For what?"

"I feel useless as tits on a bulldog. I want to get a few of my motel crew together and start a search party of my own."

"What good will that do?"

"They'll look in the places that none of these other guys will want to go."

Greg handed the phone over, but pulled it back just before it reached Marco's shaky hand.

"The expression is 'bull,' not 'bulldog.' And you better not be placing any orders with your friends."

"You've got my word, bro."

Marco slipped out the side door, dialing as he walked. Eddie set another cocktail down and headed down the bar, topping off coffee mugs as he walked. Mikey took a giant gulp and wiped his lips with the back of his hand.

"You think this many people would turn up if you disappeared?"

"Probably not."

"This place would be empty if I was the one missing."

"You never know, Mikey." But Greg knew. He wasn't even sure if he would turn up to help look for Mikey. Until a couple of days ago he probably would have been one of the main suspects.

Greg spotted Quincy across the room. He gave Mikey a slap on the back as he headed her way. Mikey gave a little toast and pulled the glass up to his lips.

Quincy led a team that was going to be distributing some of the missing person fliers around South Bay. Her hair was pulled back in the same messy ponytail as before and she wasn't wearing any make up. All business. Greg didn't have to be a cop to notice that the rest of her team was all guys. She gave each team member specific marching orders and then excused herself. Greg was surprised she had a BCC T-shirt on. The band was among the many things they had never talked about.

"I didn't know you were into hardcore."

"I'm not, but I have a crush on the singer."

Greg smiled.

"It's nice of you to be here, Quincy."

"I've been worried about you. How're you holding up?"

"Good, I guess. All things considered. Hoping to get some more info pretty soon."

"I heard from Barrett last night."

"Really? What did he have to say?"

"It was a couple of texts. He was actually the one that told me about Junior and Chris."

"What time was that?"

The question came out much quicker than he intended. Quincy was caught off guard by the increased intensity.

"Some time after ten."

Right around the time that Marco was supposed to be meeting with him at the job yard. Greg wondered if Barrett knew about his relationship with Quincy. If so, he might have been trying to keep tabs on him through her—or to see if she already knew about Junior and Chris.

"God, Greg. This whole thing is just creepy. What if somebody we know did this?"

Greg tried not to read too deeply into her words. He got the feeling that she knew he suspected Barrett. Marco came through the front door and slapped the phone down into Greg's palm just as the silence was starting to get uncomfortable.

"Phone call. It's your boss."

Greg gave Quincy a searching look and stepped out into the parking lot.

"Greg, are you there?"

"What's the word?"

"Who just answered your phone?"

"He's an old friend. I'm kind of helping him out right now."

"Sounds like he can use it. I wanted to let you know that we found the warehouse where Manny's gang set up shop. I'm guessing it's the same place they took you. It's a couple of blocks from the police station, if you can believe that."

"And?"

"We took the whole gang down, or most of them anyway. There was no sign of your friend and her son, or any indication that they had been there. A couple of the boys have been grilling Manny pretty hard for the last hour or so."

"Anything worth sharing yet?"

"He swears up and down that he didn't have anything to do with kidnapping, or the shooting. It didn't take too much coaxing for him to admit they'd been threatening you. For now, he claims that's where it ends."

"Do you believe him?"

"It's hard to say. He admitted to having you kidnapped, so we can hold him here if you want to come down and ask for yourself. My gut says that he wasn't involved in anything else."

"That's enough for me, Chief. Thanks for the update."

"We're nowhere close to done with him. I'll give you an update in a couple of hours, or sooner if we get any new info. And Greg, please stay safe—that's an order."

"I'll do my best. Thanks."

"Oh, Greg. One more thing—I got a message from the Police Chief down in The Bay Cities. Any idea what that's about?"

"I'm sure he's just checking up on me again. What's your take on him?"

"Seems like a by-the-book cop, as far as I can tell. It's obvious that he's got a hard on for you, though. You must have been a real piece of work when you were a kid."

"I'll tell you some stories over coffee sometime. Talk to you later."

Greg walked around the building to sneak in the side. He wanted to avoid any further discussions about Barrett with Quincy. He had almost reached the door when Mikey came flying through it, headed for the sidewalk at the wrong angle. Greg managed to grab his arm and keep him upright. Marco and Eddie were right behind him.

"What the hell is going on here?"

"This idiot's drunk and getting in Eddie's face about selling the bar again."

Eddie nodded in agreement. Mikey tried to straighten out his clothes, stumbling on the sidewalk in a widening circle. There was a large red mark on the side of his face where Marco had already landed a punch. Greg could see that his partner wasn't planning to stop there.

"Seriously, Mikey?"

"I'm sorry, okay? Everything's all fucked up right now. I'm just not thinking straight."

Greg gave Marco a little shove to push him back. he was surprisingly solid considering how thin he was. Greg did his best to take control of the situation.

"I'm not sure the vodka's helping, Mikey."

"It doesn't matter. None of it matters now."

Mikey was slurring his words and spinning like a top.

"You can't just give up. We'll find them, but it's going to take some time."

"I know you will Greg, even if it kills you. But that won't solve my problems tomorrow, or the next day, or the day after that."

"Then leave those problems for tomorrow. Nothing is more important than Junior and Chris right now. Nothing."

Eddie took a step forward. He seemed torn between comforting his former son-in-law and ripping his head off. Greg sidestepped Eddie to insert himself between them just in case the situation went south. Again.

"I want you to understand something, once and for all. I will never sell to you. Not today, not tomorrow, not ever. You are disgusting, coming here and getting drunk when my daughter and your son are missing. I think you should leave before I really lose my temper."

"Think about what you're saying, Eddie. I'm desperate. If you don't sell I will lose everything. We will all lose everything."

"That's not my problem. You made your own bed. It's time that you lay in it."

Mikey seemed to go momentarily limp. His right foot slipped off of the curb and his knees gave out. Greg managed to hold him up long enough to keep him from falling into the street, but eventually dropped him down to sit on the asphalt. Mikey was muttering under his breath as he strained to stand up. Eddie gave him a swift kick in the ribs.

"I don't have any more time to waste with this scumbag. Do whatever you want to him."

Eddie was huffing and puffing as he walked back into the bar. Marco took a step forward and Greg thought he was about to give Mikey another kick. He stopped short, helping Greg lift him up instead. Marco stayed a couple steps back while Greg led him up the sidewalk toward the boulevard. Mikey regained his composure after a few strides and pushed Greg away.

"Get your hands off of me. I know something's been going on between you and her."

Mikey staggered across the street and fumbled with his keys before getting into his car. Greg would have tried to keep him from driving any other time, but today he was needed back in the bar. Marco joined him and they went inside without looking back.

Officer Bob was standing at the bar chatting with Quincy. He spotted Greg and Marco immediately and started pushing his way through the crowd. They turned to escape the way they had come and ran straight into two uniformed BCPD officers. Marco lunged at one of the two men and ended up face down on the sidewalk with his hands behind his back. Greg put his hands in the air and turned to face Officer Bob just as he arrived at the back door.

The officer with his knee in Marco's back stood up, yanking his prisoner up in a fluid motion. Officer Bob grabbed Greg by the wrist and led him outside. Blink and you missed it. Only a couple of the people in the bar even saw the momentary altercation. Officer Bob didn't seem to notice or care.

"You two are hard to track down."

"Well, here we are. What do you want from us?"

"I'm actually here to give you some information that might clear up a few misconceptions you seem to have."

"About?"

"Mr. Barrett, for starters."

"We're all ears."

"Just you, Mr. Salem."

The officers led Marco away toward a waiting patrol car and guided him into the back seat. Experience taught Marco when to duck his head.

"Why don't you and I take a little stroll around the block?"

Officer Bob turned and started walking quickly away from Eddie's. It took Greg a moment to catch up. Neither of them spoke until they were certain they were alone.

"What I'm going to tell you needs to be kept in the strictest of confidence."

"Whatever you say."

"We have reason to believe that Robert Fitzgerald Jr. is the person who abducted his ex-wife and their son."

The husband was always the prime suspect. Greg's legs felt like they were made of jelly.

"Jesus. He was just here a minute ago."

"I know. We have a couple detectives trailing him as we speak. We've been watching him for several months now."

"For what?"

"He's been running an elaborate real estate scam focused on the elderly."

"Reverse mortgages?"

They rounded a corner and Greg saw two patrol cars parked on the street. The officers were milling around on a nearby lawn, waiting for Officer Bob to arrive. He could see somebody seated in the backseat of one of the two cars. Greg was overcome with relief at the thought that they already had Mikey in custody.

"He's been targeting single occupancy homes in South Bay, long-time residents in their golden years. Men and women in their seventies with no family nearby. He gave them a substantial amount of money against the equity in their homes..."

"...and then took possession once they defaulted or passed away."

"Exactly. But it seems that he got impatient and started helping the grim reaper along."

"Murder?"

"We don't have definitive proof yet, but that's what we suspect."

"How involved was Barrett?"

"Why don't you ask him yourself?"

They approached the patrol cars and one of the officers opened the rear door. Barrett stepped out onto the grass median and nodded toward Greg. It was good to see they had the idiot in custody, but Greg wasn't falling for it. Not after what he had seen last night at Barrett's office.

"What the hell's going on here?"

"Mr. Barrett's been working for us. Collecting evidence against Mr. Fitzgerald."

"In exchange for immunity, I'm guessing."

Greg found it hard to hide his disgust as Barrett tried to speak.

"I had no idea what he was doing. I went to Officer Bob the minute I figured it out."

Greg turned to Officer Bob for confirmation. The older man nodded in agreement.

"That's how he was getting all that cash to buy up the property around the reservoir. He must have been planning this for years. But why the sudden urgency?"

"According to what Mr. Barrett has been able to find out for us, he leveraged everything to build a massive housing development on this side of the reservoir. Time was running out."

"Without Eddie's properties, he was cornered."

"And broke. The perfect motive."

"Okay. So what does that have to do with Junior and Chris?"

"The best we can figure is that, at some point, he snapped."

CHAPTER TWENTY-FIVE

Greg pulled the El Camino to a stop about a block away from the address. He had no idea what to expect once he knocked on the door. A big part of him wished that Marco was there to help. Instead his partner was being detained by the BCPD on suspicion of drug trafficking. Greg, on the other hand, had been temporarily deputized by Officer Bob and handed a badge. Every part of him wanted to walk away, but he only cared about finding Junior and Chris. If that meant working for Officer Bob, and with Jeff Barrett, that is what he would do.

"For whatever reason, Mr. Fitzgerald has been cozying up to you." Officer Bob said after he explained the situation. "Besides, you've already been operating like a Bay Cities cop. You might as well be one—for a little while, at least."

Greg tried to make Marco's release a condition of the deal, but Officer Bob wouldn't budge.

"We've had him in our sights for too long to let him slide. You might even say we're doing him a favor, considering all his enemies."

"He's gotten by just fine without your protection."

"Finish what you started here and we'll talk about your friend later on."

Greg got out of the car and shoved the badge into the pocket of his new windbreaker. He scuttled up the block feeling the small wireless radio unit tugging at the back of his belt. Mikey's house was set back from the street on top of a rise across the reservoir from Eddie's.

Greg skipped up the steep concrete steps and headed for the front door. He rang the doorbell and waited, rocking back and forth on the balls of his feet. The plan was for Greg to claim he wanted to check on Mikey after what had happened at the bar earlier. Once he gained entry into the house, he was supposed to use their history together to coax a confession out of him. Anything he said would be captured on the wire that was taped to Greg's chest.

If Mikey didn't answer, Greg was supposed to call for back up before entering the house. Several cars were standing by less than a half a mile away, ready to respond in either case.

Greg rang the doorbell a second time. Still no response. He counted to twenty before ringing the bell a third time. It was a small comfort to him that no dogs were barking inside the house. He sent Officer Bob a text message to send in the troops after the fifth ring.

The patrol cars rolled up seconds later without fanfare. Two officers in bulletproof vests brought a battering ram up the front steps and made short work of the door. Officer Bob and Greg were among the first officers to enter Mikey's house, their revolvers raised before them. More officers came rushing in and fanned out to secure every room. The two men listened from just inside the front door while the 'all clear' was shouted from room after room. A second team gave the "all clear" from the backyard and garage.

Greg awaited further instructions from Officer Bob.

"What now?"

"Could be some useful information here that we can use to find them. I'll take the bedroom, you check his office."

"What are we looking for exactly?"

"Find out whatever you can in five minutes and then we move on to his office across the reservoir. We'll leave some of my team behind to do a more thorough search."

The interior of the house was much larger than it appeared from the street. Greg got turned around trying to locate the bedroom that Mikey had turned into a home office. The room was on the small side and well appointed with soft leather chairs and an antique mahogany desk. There were four large framed photos of Mikey and Chris on the wall opposite the desk. The same professional photographer took all of the pictures. There was one for every year since Mikey and Junior had split up. Greg never thought that Chris looked like his father until he saw them posed side by side.

He sat down behind the desk and brought the computer to life with a shake of the mouse. To his surprise the home screen was not password protected. He clicked on the email icon and scrolled through a few pages full of work-related subject lines. There was nothing to indicate that Junior and Chris were, so he checked Mikey's browser history instead. It had recently been cleared. He was starting to get up from the chair when he noticed the framed photos on the wall again. He slid the mouse over to the "Photos" folder and sorted by "Most Recent."

The first few shots were of Chris surfing, obviously taken from the safety of the beach. He was two or three photos into the series when something in one of the frames caught his attention. He zoomed in and saw himself paddling to catch a wave in the background. The next series of pictures was from Ricky's funeral, starting with several shots of Junior running from the church. The rest of the pictures from that day mostly focused on Greg and Junior at the reception afterwards. The final shots were of Greg leaving Junior's house sometime after midnight. He was still going backwards in time through the photo files when Officer Bob walked in.

"Find anything interesting?"

"Come look at this."

Greg started at the beginning, quickly skipping ahead. There were a hundred shots of Junior cutting hair in her salon. Greg was caught off guard when he clicked further back in time and discovered a series showing Junior and Ricky holding hands on the beach. Officer Bob could sense Greg's anger and urged him to step away from the computer all together.

"Mikey's a stalker on top of everything else."

"Or he was paying somebody to follow his ex wife around. Wouldn't be the first time somebody came up with that brilliant idea."

Officer Bob moved toward the office door. Greg immediately went back to the photos.

"Take a couple more minutes, but then we have to move on."

Greg's phone started buzzing in his pocket the moment Officer Bob left the room. He looked at the text message on the screen. It was from another anonymous numbers, like the ones that had sent him similar pictures earlier that week.

"Smile, you're on video."

Greg looked up and tried to locate the video camera. The phone buzzed again in his hand and he jumped.

"Fire alarm."

This time Greg brought the phone up and typed a response.

"Where are they?"

The response came immediately.

"You'll find out soon enough"

"What do you want?"

"Tonight. Will send details"

Officer Bob was waiting for Greg out on the sidewalk when he emerged from the house. There was a look of concern on his face as Greg approached.

"You don't look so good. Sure you're still up for this?"

"I'm fine."

Greg knew that raiding Mikey's office would be a bust, but he had to go through the motions. He didn't know what Mikey's state of mind was and he wasn't willing to jeopardize Junior and Chris any further just to follow police protocol.

The receptionist was the only person in the lobby when Greg arrived. She was surprised to see him, but managed a big smile as he approached.

"I didn't know we were expecting you today. I just got back from lunch, so I'm not even sure if he's here."

Her tone was friendly. She tried to pull up her boss's schedule on the computer.

"It looks like he should be here. I'll just go up and check."

He flashed his BCPD badge and informed her he would be coming along. She led him upstairs and toward Mikey's office. Greg noticed the plants in the boxes that lined the staircase were brown and dying. A couple of the ceiling lights up above were burned out.

"Does anybody work here besides you and Mikey?"

"Do I have to answer your questions?"

"Might be a good idea."

"This place used to be full of real estate agents. Mr. Fitzgerald was forced to lay them off over the last few months, because of the economy."

"Does he hold many business meetings here these days?"

She hesitated for a moment, considering his question. Deciding what to share.

"Not too often anymore. He does have weekly meetings with one of his investors, but schedules those himself. I'm not even sure what her name is, but she is all business. I can assure you of that."

"In what way?"

"She is very well put together. Stylish in a sort of severe way. And she has extremely specific needs whenever she is in the office. I can't tell you the number of times I have had to drive half way across town just to find the right latte for her. I hate being away from my desk for all that time, but Mr. Fitzgerald insists that I cater to her every whim. She has South Bay tastes, if you know what I mean."

What Greg did know is that Mikey had a new girlfriend. And from the sounds of it, the two of them were into kinky office sex. If this mystery business partner with the expensive taste was half as controlling as the receptionist made her out to be, then she was definitely his accomplice in the real estate scam. Maybe the kidnapping, too.

The receptionist knocked on the office door, waiting a moment before calling out her boss's name. She turned the knob when she got no response. Unlocked. The office was empty, just like Greg knew it would be. She let him in and went back down to her post in the lobby.

He was looking out the window at the reservoir and thinking about what the receptionist just told him. He pulled his wallet out and searched through the receipts and dollar bills looking for a specific business card. It was a long shot, but he knew he didn't have anything to lose. He pulled out his phone and dialed the number. It rang four times before her outgoing voice message kicked in.

"You've reached Margaret Keane from Bay Cities Venture Capital. Please leave a detailed message and I will get back to you at my earliest convenience."

He killed the call when the detectives flooded into the office and started going through Mikey's things. Greg ducked out at the first opportunity to find somewhere private that he could check his phone, just in case.

He slipped down the hall for the bathroom. Something was blocking the door. He pushed again with his fingers and then with his palms. Then he put his shoulder into it. The door gave a few inches. He recognized the designer shoes first and then quickly followed the line of perfectly creased pants. Mikey was lying motionless on the tiles. A mush of bone, blood and pulp where his head should have been. He was clenching a pistol in his left hand. Greg stumbled backwards, slamming into the wall and sliding to the floor.

"Man down! Help!"

The officers rushed down the hall and crashed through the bathroom door. None of them noticed Greg sitting on the ground behind, staring at his phone.

"This doesn't change anything. We're still on for tonight."

THE SCENE AT THE bar was less chaotic when Greg returned that afternoon. Eddie was still pouring free drinks for the volunteers, but there weren't many takers. Most of them were still out on the streets distributing missing persons fliers. Greg wanted to let them all know that their time was being wasted, but knew it was too much of a risk. The lull in activity gave him and Eddie a chance to talk. They took a table in the darkest part of the bar, so they could have some privacy.

"Where the hell did you and Marco disappear to?"

"There have been some developments, but I'm not really sure how much I can share."

Eddie frowned. Greg patted the table to emphasize his point.

"We're getting closer to finding them. You just have to trust me."

"Okay..."

"Right now I can tell you this much—they're alive."

A flush of red boiled up on Eddie's face until it looked like he might explode. That didn't change a thing about how much information Greg was willing to share.

"Stop it with all this cloak and dagger bullshit and tell me what the hell is going on. Do you know where they are or not?"

"I'll know for sure in a couple of hours. Then I'm going to get them back."

"So I'm supposed to just sit here twiddling my thumbs while you play the hero. That it?"

The conversation was over, whether Eddie knew it or not. There was nothing else Greg could say to comfort him. He didn't have all of the answers yet himself.

"I know it doesn't seem fair, but it's all I have to give you right now. Promise me you won't tell anybody."

"Christ. What about all these people who volunteered? Should I send them home?"

"Keep your voice down, Eddie. Let them keep doing what they're doing. We can't let anybody think that we might have a lead. You have to understand what's at risk here."

Eddie took a deep breath and stood up. He couldn't look Greg in the eye any longer.

"This is my family. Not yours."

"I know."

"I think I need a drink."

"Me too...but I'll have to settle for a little chill out time."

Greg trailed Eddie back to the bar, grabbing the spare key to the salon on the way. The sickening exhaustion he'd been trying to ignore all day took hold when he let himself in. The air inside was hot and filled with the sickly sweet scent of hair care products baking. He went straight to the back of the salon and turned on the air conditioner.

He wondered why barbershops didn't have big, fluffy sofas like salons did. It was a fleeting thought. A sense of dread was already creeping in all around him as he kicked off his shoes to lie down. His tired mind was whirring, but his body felt heavy. He checked his phone one more time before setting it down on his chest.

Greg was dead to the world in minutes.

A familiar scene.

The kid in the blue hat was standing on top of a dumpster trying to climb into a second story window. Greg leveled his revolver and shouted 'Stop! Police!' The kid turned to look and then jumped down off of the dumpster. The floor of the alley became a giant splash as the kid disappeared under the surface of the water.

Greg tossed his gun aside and dove in after him. His clothes absorbed the water and started dragging him down. He unbuttoned his shirt and wriggled out of his shoes and pants. He couldn't see the kid anywhere through the murky, churning salt water. His lungs were starting to burn so he headed for the surface to catch a breath. He emerged with a gasp and found himself treading water in the middle of the ocean.

Something was tugging at his ankle. He started paddling to get away. It had a firm grip on him. He dove down to see if it was the kid with the blue hat, but got tangled up in his surfboard leash. Chris was calling his name when he surfaced again.

Greg climbed onto his board and started paddling. The sky went from sunny to stormy in the blink of an eye. Greg found himself rolling over massive ocean swells, chasing the boy's voice. The wind was kicking up and a light rain began to fall.

Chris was beside him now, waiting to catch a towering wave. Greg turned and started paddling with all of his might. The next moment Chris was standing up and carving across the face of an impossibly tall wave. Greg pushed himself up into a standing position as the wall of water curled overhead. They were in a glassy green cathedral now, their boards slicing across the endless glassy surface beneath them...

The phone was buzzing. Greg gasped for air as he broke the surface from a deep sleep. He could still feel the tacky ocean water surrounding him as he forced his eyes open. The salon was dark and the air conditioner was blasting cold air at him. He grabbed his phone and found three text messages waiting. They had all come in over the last couple of minutes.

"It's time"

"Locals Only"

"Come alone"

Greg stood up and stretched before heading for the bathroom. He splashed cold water on his face and rubbed some onto the back of his neck. There was no way to know what lay ahead, but at least he knew where he was going. He walked across the salon and brought the door shut behind him. Dusk was settling in, wispy orange clouds streaking the sky along the coast. He climbed into the El Camino and drove into the darkness.

CHAPTER TWENTY-SIX

The moon was overhead now, leaving a trail of shimmering lights that danced across the ocean far below. Greg brought the car to a stop. The badge was on the passenger seat beside him. Useless. His gun was in the glove compartment, loaded and ready.

Greg could hear the waves crashing, the rocks grinding out a chorus as they forever chased the tide. There were no streetlights this high up along the cliffs, so the kidnapper must have seen him arrive. He flashed the high beams a for dramatic effect and let the car idle.

He knew what the BCPD wanted from him, but not the kidnapper. Whatever it was, Greg doubted that he could deliver. That wouldn't stop him from trying to save his friends. He just had to wait. Greg turned up the volume on the stereo and listened to Rancid doing "Time Bomb," one of Ricky's all time favorites. He hit the repeat button and tapped along on his steering wheel, waiting for some kind of signal. The volume was too loud for him to hear the buzzing, but the screen on his phone lit up.

"Get out of the car and go to the trailhead..."

Greg felt like he was stepping on stage. He twisted the key out of the ignition. He shoved the Glock into the back of his pants and stood up in plain view. There was a strong off shore breeze kicking up. He zipped up his windbreaker and walked toward the cliffs. He knew the kidnapper would search him, but he wanted it understood that he had come to fight.

He reached the trailhead and stopped to look around. The entire area seemed to be deserted. He couldn't remember if he had been to the tidal pools at night.

"That's far enough!"

A woman. The wind and background noise from the waves made it hard to identify where the voice was coming from, or who it was. Greg wondered if he had guessed correctly about Margaret Keane.

He stopped and gave a little spin in place to show that he had heard her.

"Take your jacket off!"

Greg obliged, exposing the gun as planned.

"Drop your weapon!"

Greg pulled the gun out and tossed it a few feet away. He put both arms over his head, assuming that would be her next command.

"Down on your knees or we'll kill your friends!"

Greg hadn't even considered the possibility that there was more than one kidnapper. Not until that moment. It could also be a trick. He laced his fingers behind his head and waited.

"Forehead to the ground."

He started to bend forward, lost his balance and had to steady himself with one hand.

"Hands behind your head! Now!"

Greg fell forward and banged his face on the rocky ground. He could feel a thin trickle of blood starting to form on his forehead. The sound of footsteps came thudding toward him from the direction of the trail. The kidnapper was soon patting him down. Greg could smell the strong scent of sweat mixed with a familiar aroma, something sweet and flowery. Was she wearing Junior's perfume?

"Was that your only gun?"

Greg kept his forehead down. He answered quietly in an attempt to draw her closer. She didn't fall for it. Greg knew that he wasn't dealing with an amateur. The cold barrel of her gun was pressed against his temple. He repeated his answer, with more volume this time.

"Yes."

"Get up, slowly."

Greg waited a beat and then carefully pushed himself up onto all fours. He could hear her taking cautious steps in response to his every move. There was no way to know how many others might be lurking around them in the dark, outside of his field of vision. The blood from his forehead was starting to deposit tiny droplets into the eyebrow over his left eye. His vision was getting cloudy as he rolled onto the balls of his feet and into a standing position. A blurry figure was standing a few feet away with both hands wrapped around the handle of the gun. It was pointed right at Greg's face.

"Are you alone?"

"Just like you told me. You?"

"Don't think I can handle you on my own?"

The shape in front of him slowly began to come into focus as he blinked the blood away. Her hair was still pulled back in a messy ponytail, just as it had been that morning at Eddie's.

"Quincy. What is this all about?"

"I hate to see you bleeding. It won't matter much longer."

"Who put you up to this?" Greg tried to control the fury that was building up inside of him. He was speaking loudly to be heard over the wind. "Whoever is making you do this, you can just stop right now. I can help you. Nobody has to die tonight."

"Oh, somebody is definitely going to die tonight. Maybe a few people. It all depends."

"What do you want me to do? Just tell me so we can get past this."

"Don't try any police negotiation bullshit on me. I'm the one who made this all happen."

"You're Mikey's business partner?"

Quincy snorted like a teenage girl.

"I like to think I was more of a muse."

"Look, why don't you put the gun down—"

"SHUT UP!"

Greg flinched as she tightened her trigger finger. She responded with another laugh, shaking her head in disbelief.

"We have a lot more in common than you know. My brother was your biggest fan when we were growing up. He used to play your music all the time. It was still on repeat when I found him in his room, hanging from the ceiling fan."

"Quincy, I'm really sorry about your brother..."

"Don't be sorry. That's the thing that brought us together. After he died I kept on listening to your music and digging up whatever I could about you. Once I found out that your brother died the same way as my brother did I knew that we had a special connection. That's when I decided to find you. So we could be together."

"What do you know about my brother's death?"

"Oh, sweetie. I was still in pigtails when he died."

Greg knew for sure that he had brought something evil back to The Bay Cities. It happened years before he ever shot the kid with the blue hat. She was there all along, lurking in the background. Hiding in plain sight. A time bomb with a twenty-year fuse.

"And now you're going to kill me."

"Don't be silly. I'm doing all of this *for* you. For us."

"All of what?"

She tilted her eyes upward for a moment, getting frustrated with all of his silly questions. The barrel of the gun bounced up and down. Greg shifted his weight forward, ready to rush. Her eyes came down to meet his and he eased back onto his heels.

"I wanted you to kill Barrett so he could take the blame for all the murders. You got so close when you came up here that day. But then you chickened out. Don't worry, I'll forgive you one of these days."

"Tell me what to do."

"We just have to wait. It won't be long now. Go ahead, take a look."

She nodded toward the cliff's edge. Greg walked over and peered down at the jagged outcropping several hundred feet below. He could see the tide beginning to swallow the rocks in a churning spray of icy water. It all became perfectly clear. Junior and Chris would soon drown to death in the underwater cave.

He knew they had less than fifteen minutes left. Quincy was still standing in the same spot when he stepped back toward her.

"Why?"

"Because that whore isn't good enough for you. She's got you wrapped around her finger so tight that you can't even see it. All these leeches that you call your friends are sucking the life out of you, Greg. Little by little, day by day. I couldn't let them get away with it any more."

"Mikey too?"

"Mikey was a no-brainer, after what he did to your career. Once I moved out here and finally found you, when I saw what all of these bloodsuckers were doing to you…Well, it became pretty obvious what I had to do."

"You killed him. It wasn't a suicide."

"He was a bad citizen. One of the worst, and he was only going to get more powerful. So I did what I had to do. It wasn't hard once I figured out how lonely he was. He just wanted a woman who could dominate him. You men are all the same."

"Except Mikey was a murderer."

She squinted her eyes. Tried to make sense of what he'd just said.

"I'm disappointed, Officer Salem. I thought you would have figured out by now that I did all the killing."

"But he must have helped you with the kidnapping."

"Wrong again. Junior and Chris were my insurance policy. There he was, sitting on all of that property, going broke while he waited for those geezers to die. Crying himself to sleep at night over his failed marriage. That's when I knew how weak he was. So I gave him an option—get me the money or his family dies."

Greg could see she was enjoying herself. Showing him how she had manipulated everybody in his life. Normally, he would want to keep a kidnapper like her talking, but time was running out fast.

"I don't understand. Who helped you bring Junior and Chris up here?"

"Same crew that took care of Ricky. Flew them in special just for those jobs. It was kind of perfect, though, the way it worked out."

"He was my best friend, you crazy bitch."

"Careful, Greg...you know the dirty talk turns me on. He wasn't worthy of sharing the stage with you, so he got what he deserved. I know you don't understand right now, but you will one day. When we're far away from here and spending Mikey's money."

"Are the men who killed Ricky down there with Junior and Chris?"

"No, they're long gone. It's just you and me. Alone at last."

Quincy was getting cocky as she watched her plans play out. That meant she was probably telling the truth about her accomplices. Greg knew he still had a chance to save his friends if it was just the two of them. At east he hoped so. He had to act fast.

"I can't let them die."

"That's really sweet, but it's probably too late."

"If you truly want us to be together, you won't shoot me."

"Why aren't you listening? I love you so much that I would rather kill you than let you keep hurting yourself. After that I would only be one bullet away from being with you forever."

Forever never sounded so creepy.

"You know that's a chance I'll have to take."

"I've already given you so many chances to figure it. Even today at Eddie's, they were right outside in the trunk of my car the whole time. All you had to do was tell me that I was the only one for you. Run if you have to. I'll be with you soon."

"I love you too, Quincy. "

Greg took off at a sprint before he finished his sentence. He hoped that his final words had the stunning effect he was looking for. A strong wind was coming up from the ocean and gave him the sensation that he was running in place. He only needed a few more seconds to disappear into the darkness that swallowed the trail. There were many things he didn't know about Quincy, but he guessed she couldn't hit a moving target at night.

The first switchback in the trail was quickly approaching. A shot rang out and the dirt sprang up from the ground near his ankle. The turn was only a few feet ahead now, but he knew he couldn't make it. The next two shots came in rapid succession just as Greg reached the scrubby edge of the cliff. His right foot caught a large round stone and the momentum flung him over the edge. His back arched and his arms flailed as he flew through the air.

He crashed into a large outcropping of rocks on the cliff's face. The wind was knocked completely from his body. He couldn't breathe or move for an excruciating minute. He lay there motionless, disoriented by the brief flight and sudden landing.

The wind was whipping around his ears and he could see the ocean churning below. There were no more shots, or anything that sounded like footsteps, so he started to claw his way back to the trail. His eyes were peeking through the scrub brush just above the edge of the cliff when the final shot rang out.

Greg looked up in time to see Quincy's headless body falling to the ground. A fine mist of red was still swirling in the wind up above her. He was back up on the trail and running before her body came to a final rest on the ground.

His feet slid on the loose gravel and he almost tumbled over the edge. He stood back up and was running full tilt when he remembered the shortcuts that generations of surfers had carved out. It was dark and the paths were steep, but it could knock minutes off of his race to the bottom. He slowed down enough to look for the next entrance and took it. The strong wind coming up the cliffs offered just enough resistance to keep him from flying head first onto the rocky beach below.

The rising tide and sea spray coated the round rocks on the beach in a thin film of water. Greg tried to move quickly, but his feet kept slipping and his shins were paying the price. He was eventually reduced to crossing on all fours, scurrying like a crab across the uneven landscape. He reached the outer edge of the tidal pools just in time for a huge wave to come breaking across the outcropping of rocks. The force sent him skidding on his back for several yards, shredding his shirt and delivering several gashes to his back. He jumped up and retraced his path, keeping his eyes on the horizon to avoid being caught off guard again.

The entrance to the cave was between two vertical walls of slick rock. There was a narrow space of a couple feet that descended into a pool of rising water. It would have resembled a staircase when Quincy forced Junior and Chris down into the cave at low tide. Right at the moment it looked more like the shallow end of a brackish swimming pool. He kicked his shoes off and took a deep breath before he plunged into the freezing water.

Greg was groping with his hands along the craggy walls, trying to find his way through the elbow-shaped passage. In the end he just gave up and started swimming toward the sound of Junior and Chris screaming. He nearly hit his head on the roof of the cave when he emerged moments later.

It was inky inside with only a few inches of air space left. The sound of waves crashing on the rocks overhead was like a thunderous round of applause as he clawed along toward them.

"Junior. Chris. Say something so I know where you are."

"Greg! Over here!"

He found Chris first. The boy was flexing painfully as he grasped at the rope that connected his wrist to his mother's. In between, the rope was looped several times through a steel piton wedged into the stone. Greg had nothing to cut it with so he went to work untying the many knots. Then he and Chris both unraveled the binds digging into Junior's wrists. All three of them were practically kissing the roof of the cave, struggling to breathe, by the time she was free.

"We still have to swim out."

"Take Chris. I'll never make it."

"Don't say that. I came down here for both of you."

He could hear her forcing back tears as she tried to summon the courage.

"Chris, listen to me. It's straight across and then as far down as you can dive. You'll find the opening. The passage is shorter than you think. Whatever you do, don't stop swimming. Do you hear me?"

"Yes."

"We'll be right behind you."

Chris gave them a look that was equal parts brave young man and terrified boy.

"I love you mom."

"Go!"

They watched as he followed the curve of the roof, receding into the darkness a few inches away. Junior dug her face into Greg's shoulder. The water was churning like the inside of a washing machine, and rising quickly. They would have to start from the middle of the cave.

"We take three deep breaths and dive. I'll go first. You grab my ankle once we're under. Don't let go no matter what."

She exhaled and tried to take her first stuttering breath. Greg pressed himself up against her body so that their noses were touching.

"We can do this. Together."

He inhaled deeply three times without letting go of her. She followed his lead as he plunged under the water. She reached down, found his ankle and started kicking hard to the bottom. It was calm down under the ocean, weightless and silent.

Raging surf engulfed the tidal pools where they emerged. The sound of crashing waves gave way to the rotors of the police helicopter that circled overhead. They emerged and scurried up the jutting rocks, waving to the blinding spotlights that swirled all around them. She clung to his waist as the salty ocean spray stung their eyes, both of them gasping for precious air.

CHAPTER TWENTY-SEVEN

It was almost noon when Greg woke up on Junior's couch two days later. Chris was already sitting on the living room floor playing video games as though none of it had happened. Greg wasn't surprised when he heard the pop of a baseball bat and the roar of a crowd instead of the usual gunshots.

Greg could smell the coffee brewing in the kitchen and guessed Eddie was already awake, too. He stretched and rolled onto his side with a yawn to prolong facing what was left of the day. He was on the verge of falling back asleep when Eddie plunked a coffee mug onto the table next to his head. Greg managed a croaky 'Thanks,' but didn't open his eyes all the way.

"Least I can do for a hero."

"Does the hero get cream and sugar?"

"You name it."

Greg considered asking for a little more time to sleep, but Eddie was ready to talk. He rolled onto his back and sat up o reach for his coffee. Eddie didn't even wait for him to finish his first sip.

"How're you feeling?"

"Sore. I think the past week has finally caught up with me."

"I bet. I can't imagine what you went through on those cliffs up there."

Greg didn't even know where to begin. So much of it felt like a dream. He wasn't sure that he would ever be able to tell the whole story. Some things were better left to the wind.

"Junior awake?"

"I heard her rustling around in there a few minutes ago. I'm guessing she'll show her face any minute now."

Greg nodded his head to where Chris was sitting.

"What's the prognosis with that one?"

"Good right now. Hard to say in the long run. It isn't going to be easy."

"I can't even imagine."

The words were automatic, but Greg immediately understood that they weren't true. Losing his brother continued to cast a shadow over his own life, and probably would until the day he died himself. He didn't have to dig too deep to understand that it was the reason he became a cop in the first place.

"At least he won't have to go through it alone. Thanks to you."

Greg wanted Eddie to stop with the accolades, but he didn't know what to say. He wasn't feeling like much of a hero as he lay there thinking about how to make his escape—from Junior's house, from his job, from his life. From the kid in the blue hat.

He swung his legs from the couch and let his feet settle into the carpet. The pain didn't hit him until he was upright. By then he was committed. Electric jolts were shooting down his arms and legs, and his back was locking up in pockets all along his spine.

Eddie was watching him carefully, trying to keep his distance but poised on the edge of his chair. It was touch and go for a few long seconds but he eventually gritted his teeth and took the first few steps toward Junior's bedroom. He was rounding the corner and starting down the hall when he heard Eddie scooting Chris out the front door.

Greg knocked lightly, waiting for a response before he let himself in. Junior was propped up on a pile of pillows with a stack of photo albums on the bed beside her. She had a small square album in her lap and was leafing through the pages slowly. Greg stepped into the room but stopped several feet short of the bed.

"How'd you sleep?"

"Much better than the night before. You?"

"I was unconscious until just a few minutes ago."

"Well you don't have to stand all the way over there. I won't bite you, not after you saved my life."

There it was. Eddie would probably be referring to Greg as a hero until the day he died. His daughter would only acknowledge it once and move on for good. Her comment helped him relax enough that he decided to join her on the bed.

She pushed a few of the albums out of his way when he finally arrived, but he still tried to keep his distance. Junior went back to flipping through the pages of the album in her lap. Greg could see that it held Chris's baby pictures.

"Taking a trip down memory lane?"

"I guess so. It's funny to think that Chris is going to grow up as part of a generation that will probably never bother with photo albums. All of their memories will just be digital files stored in a cloud somewhere. You know?"

"That sounds pretty good to me. Did I tell you about the boxes of pictures we found at Ricky's apartment?"

"I know the pictures you're talking about. He was obsessed with them. He used spread them out all over his bed and kept talking about how he wanted to do something really special with them. I guess he never figured out what that was."

The mental image of Ricky and Junior in bed together with pictures completely shut Greg's brain down.

"You probably don't want to hear this right now, but I never meant to hurt you. What happened between Ricky and me, it's just...you and I were ancient history. I didn't even know there was a possibility."

"Neither of us knew. How could we?"

"Everything's really messed up right now, but it doesn't mean it will be like that forever."

A chill ran down his spine at the mention of the word "forever."

"I wish I could say that was true. I'm just not sure. Right now I feel like I am ready to crawl out of my skin. Like I need to do something really important, but I don't know if that means surfing or drinking or just getting into my car and driving away. Too much has changed and everything still feels the same."

They both retreated into their own dark thoughts. Greg stayed flat on his back and listened to her turning the pages in her album. She finally set the last one down with a soft thud and then slid her legs down until she was stretched out right beside him.

"So what's next for you then?"

"I guess I should probably head home."

"And what about after that?"

"I honestly have no idea."

"I can't promise you I'll be here when you get back."

"I'm not asking you to wait."

THE PLAN STARTED TO come together the moment he climbed into the El Camino. He became more certain of exactly what he needed to do with every passing block on Bay Cities Boulevard.

He stopped at a hardware store and picked up some moving boxes, packing tape and a couple of padlocks on his way to the apartment. Marco was still in custody, which meant the place was empty. He got straight to work.

Greg was impressed by how few possessions he actually had. Almost everything he owned fit neatly into the back of the El Camino. He decided to leave the paddleboard and the futon for whoever rented the apartment after him.

His hiking backpack was stuffed with clothes and gear, but there was still enough room to fit some freeze-dried food above the all-weather sleeping bag. He put the gear in the passenger seat and strapped it in to keep it from sliding around on his way up the mountain. Mrs. McMillan was standing in the middle of the empty apartment when he came back in to make a final sweep.

"I've been seeing you on the news again. I like the story much better this time around."

"Don't believe everything they tell you."

"I'm just glad to see you made it out in one piece. Is there something you were planning to tell me?"

She motioned to the empty apartment. He reached into his pocket and produced a check that covered three months rent. She took it from his shaking hand and considered her options.

"Does this mean you'll be back in three months?"

"I'm not sure. I'm hoping you can hold off that long before you rent the place to somebody else. If not, I will understand. You should take the money either way, since I'm leaving without giving notice."

It all sounded so strangely formal, but he couldn't see any other way to maneuver through the awkward situation. Mrs. McMillan finally broke through the tension by ripping the check into small pieces and throwing them over her shoulder.

"You can pay me when you get back."

"What if you aren't here when I get back?"

"I'll leave a forwarding address. Now give me a hug and I'll let you get on your way."

She spread her arms wide and Greg stepped into her gentle embrace. She gave him a few soft pats on the back and he planted a kiss on her papery cheek before stepping away.

"I think it will do you some good to get out of this town for a little while. Lord knows I lived a whole life before I ever discovered The Bay Cities. It's helped to give me perspective."

"Thanks Ruth. Try not to miss me too much."

"Hold on. What are you planning to do with the lizard?"

Greg looked over to where the aquarium sat on the edge of the futon. There was a small pile of clothes and couple of twenty-dollar bills stacked neatly beside it.

"Something tells me that Marco will be by to pick that stuff up later on today."

She started toward the door, turning to face him again before she stepped outside.

"At least now I can take care of those termites. This place will be in much better shape when you come back."

Greg watched her leave and then stepped through the back gate for the last time. He drove slowly with all the extra weight taxing the back shocks. It took him a little while to get to Ricky's rehearsal space. The old padlocks sprung open when he slid the key in. He walked them over to the dumpster as soon as he had the door open. His stack of boxes took up the back corner of the room and engulfed Ricky's desk.

He stood in the middle of the room catching his breath once everything was unloaded. A copy of *CoreNoMore* was sticking up from one of the boxes. Greg pulled it out, flipping it open to the last page. He still hadn't read the whole interview and guessed he never would.

CNM: *Bad Citizen Corporation called it quits after the third record came out. What made you finally walk away?*

FD: *It wasn't fun anymore. Too much had changed.*

CNM: *The band changed or you had changed?*

FD: *Both. You know, every musician starts out as a fan. They sit in their rooms and listen to their favorite records over and over. Maybe they strum along on a guitar or bang on a drum. Then one day they form a band of their own, and kids start looking up to them. By the time we broke up I couldn't even listen to my favorite records without wanting to smash them to pieces. The whole experience really screwed with my head.*

CNM: *Do you ever listen to the old BCC records?*

FD: *Once in a while. I like to hear Tim play guitar, since that's all I've got left of him. And my buddy Ricky will spin them for me, too. You know, when he's had a few. He and I still play shows together sometimes, but these days it's strictly for fun.*

CNM: *Any plans to record any new music?*

FD: *You never know what might happen.*

Greg put the magazine down. The silent musical instruments all around him seemed haunted somehow, daring him to make noise. He settled for giving Ricky's electric guitar a soft strum with his thumb and turned to leave. The notes vibrated into nothingness as the metal door came down with a clang. Greg slid the new padlocks into place and secured them with a click. He was the only one with a key now.

There were a couple more stops left on his way out of town.

IT FELT GOOD WALKING into the BCPD station with nothing to hide, probably for the first time in his life. The same old clerk was behind the desk. He greeted Greg with a big smile this time and picked up the phone without saying a word. Officer Bob and Marco emerged into the lobby a few minutes later. Greg couldn't remember a time when Marco looked so rested.

"Dude, I slept like a baby. And they let me workout in the police gym this morning. Getting ripped, bro!"

Greg looked from Marco to officer Bob to confirm what he'd just heard.

"Least we could do. Your friend here helped us figure out Fitzgerald's real estate scam."

"So does that mean he's free to go?"

"We're not going to press charges, but I think we've come to an understanding."

Marco nodded and batted his eyelashes. Officer Bob ignored him, turning to Greg.

"How are you holding up after last night?"

"Good as can be expected."

"I gave your Chief a call this morning and filled him in on all the details. I wouldn't be surprised if you were in for a commendation."

"I appreciate that, but I think my days on the force are numbered."

"Well, I'll let you discuss that with your Chief. But if you ever consider working closer to home, you should give me a call. Of course, there's no guarantee that I'll even have a job myself after what happened."

"Come on. Nobody could have guessed that a parking enforcement officer would get this mixed up in some real estate racket."

"That might be true. We still have to determine just how much she knew and how she got the information. It's like she was right there in the middle of everything the whole time. You just couldn't see her."

"Well, let me know if there's anything I can do to help."

"There's still the matter of Ricky's murder."

"It'll be almost impossible to find the guys that did it. I think I mentioned it at the hospital the other night, but Quincy said she flew them in for the job. Maybe you should start in her home town?"

"Any idea where that might be, Mr. Salem?"

"Sorry Officer B—" Greg paused mid-sentence. He swung his head to where the sun was glaring in the cloudless ocean sky. "Sorry, Chief. I guess I never really got to know that much about her."

"You aren't the only one. It looks like all of the information she gave on her application was bogus. Let me know if you remember anything else she said to you up there. I'm guessing you'll be thinking about that night a lot over the next few months."

They shook hands and went their separate ways. Greg opened the passenger door and moved his hiking pack into the bed of the El Camino. The weight of it briefly made him doubt his plan to strap it on his back.

Marco climbed in and pulled his door shut. He was already buckled in by the time Greg made it around the car and climbed behind the wheel. The opening guitar riff of Bad Religion's "Recipe For Hate" came blaring from the speakers as they pulled out of the parking lot. Neither of them spoke again until the song was over a couple of minutes later.

"Where are we going?"

"I'm taking you over to my old apartment so you can grab a few things, including Godzilla. What you two do after that is up to you."

"What do you mean, your 'old apartment'?"

"I just need to get away for a little while. Clear my head."

"I know things got a little weird the last couple of weeks, but you can't just bail on me. You're the only thing that's keeping me clean at this point."

Marco could have said anything else at that moment and Greg would have been fine just dropping him off on the side of the road.

"Come on, Marco. I don't think you want to depend on me too much right now. I'm barely hanging on myself."

"Dude, those drugs that got stolen from my hotel room were worth a couple hundred thousand. I'm a dead man if I stick around The Bay Cities. Your nightmare might be over. Mine's only beginning."

"You don't even know where I'm going."

"It doesn't matter. You're stuck with me. Get used to it."

CHAPTER TWENTY-EIGHT

It was a slow day at Eddie's. The pool tables were empty, there was nothing playing on the jukebox and no games on TV. Roger was engrossed in a lengthy newspaper article. Bill was bored out of his mind and hungry.

"Man, I'm starving."

"Go get a slice of pizza across the street."

Roger responded without even looking up.

"I'm sick of that place. Besides, my doctor told me I need to lay off the carbs."

"Uh huh."

"I wish there was somewhere else to eat around here."

"Go to Juan's. It's just a few block down the boulevard."

"No thanks. I don't like Mexican food."

Roger set the paper down on the bar and slid the reading glasses from his nose.

"You don't like Mexican food?"

"It's gross. I don't know why people around here get so excited about it."

"You're an idiot."

"Calm down, Roger. Jeez. That's the most I've heard you say all day."

"Hey Eddie, come here."

Eddie looked up from his crossword puzzle and took a few steps over to join his friends.

"You guys ready for another round? This isn't a public library, you know."

"Guess what Bill just told me? He doesn't like Mexican food."

"Bullshit."

Eddie leaned in to give Bill a piece of his mind.

IT WAS DUSK BY the time the El Camino finally broke free of the city highways and started the windy one lane ascent into the Angeles National Forest. They had stopped by the apartment to collect Godzilla and then did a quick shopping trip at a sporting goods store to outfit Marco for the trip. He was fast asleep with his head bumping against the car window as they flew past the last couple of suburban outposts on their way deep into LA's forgotten wilderness. His new wool cap was pulled down over his eyes and his fleece jacket was zipped up to his chin.

Greg's phone call with the Police Chief in Virgil Heights was short and sweet. He told Greg that his position would be waiting for him if he ever changed his mind.

The phone was still in his lap and he was looking down occasionally to watch the reception drop from four bars to one. It wouldn't be long now until they were totally lost to the world. He turned his headlights on and watched the grey road unfolding beneath his wheels. The iguana eyed him suspiciously from the dashboard.

ACKNOWLEDGMENTS

First things first, I wouldn't have made it this far if it weren't for the endless patience and tireless support of my wife, Heather, and our two beautiful daughters. From there, the list gets long, so bear with me. High fives for my trusted inner circle of readers—Scott Ross, Ken Basart, Jeff Solomon, Jeff Whalen, Heather Havrilesky, and Travis Richardson—thank you for pushing me to make the book better. To my incredible lawyer, Kim Thigpen, who is equally skilled at dissecting contracts and plots; and Marc Soulema, my law enforcement sounding board from the LAPD. Every new writer needs a strong editor, and I am very lucky to have Elaine Ash in my corner. To Colleen Dunn Bates and Patty O'Sullivan at Prospect Park Books for introducing me to my publisher. And last, but most certainly not least, a round of applause for Tyson Cornell, Julia Callahan, Alice Marsh-Elmer, and Winona Leon at Rare Bird Books.